SO IT GOES

GUY CARLISLE

First published in 2012 by
Pebble Bay Publishing

ISBN 978-1468192537

For Catherine

All moments, past, present, and future, always have existed, always will exist.... It is just an illusion we have here on earth that one moment follows another one, like beads on a string, and that once a moment is gone it is gone forever....
Now, when I myself hear that somebody is dead, I simply shrug and say what the Tralfamordorians say about dead people, which is 'So it goes'.

SLAUGHTERHOUSE-FIVE

So It Goes

How the hell did I end up on the school roof with Don Jefferies, the caretaker? It's not even eight o'clock for Christ's sake. One minute I'm sitting at my desk smearing coffee rings across the life-affirming assembly I'm writing for Years Five and Six and the next I'm following Pebble Bay Primary's *Site Manager* - to give him his official title - up a set of step-ladders. Step-ladders lifted straight from a Hollywood props department: next to useless for reaching high places; perfect for breaking over the back of some low-paid extra during the climactic scene of a 1940s B-western - '*Never mind fetching Susie-May's feather boa from that thar chandelier Mitch, we gonna have us a barroom brawl!'*

From the moment Don strolls nonchalantly into my classroom at a quarter to eight and says, 'I need a hand,' I know my goose is cooked.

What part of, 'Sorry, I'm busy,' *Now get the hell out of my classroom you neo-Nazi*, does Don not understand? Shaking my head vigorously does little to prevent the man thrusting a yard broom at me and turning off the classroom lights. Bloody hell, you'd think the school electricity bill came straight out of Don's wage packet.

I consider swinging for the bald bastard, maybe lopping that misshapen head off with the five foot of wood he's just handed me. But instead I follow him meekly out of the classroom, down the corridor, past mops and buckets of detergent, their scent rendered novel again by the two week Christmas break. Where is he taking me? 'Where are we going Don?' I ask, 'I'm busy. Supposed to be giving an assembly this morning.' Might as well be talking to myself. The broom in my hand would seem to indicate some kind of sweeping activity lies ahead but why are we stopping at these step-ladders?

Half way up the balsa rungs, Don pauses. 'Wait for me to get through the skylight,' he calls down, 'these things won't take the weight of both of us.'

I give the bottom rung an experimental kick to test the veracity of this assertion.

'Forgot my tin hat today,' Don says cryptically although in truth his thick West Country burr lends most of what he says a certain mysterious quality. 'I hope you're handy with that thing.' The broom? *Stand still long enough mate and you'll find out.*

With some difficulty, Don pushes open the skylight above us and continues upwards. I feel a certain reluctance to follow but the patch of blue that replaces Don's posterior proves surprisingly irresistible and I obediently follow him up. For primary school teacher read: political activist emerging from South American dungeon a decade after witnessing the senseless slaughter of his family at an anti-government protest rally. Let me know if I'm getting too melodramatic for you.

Passing the broom through the narrow hatch I very nearly pull the skylight closed and retrace my steps to Class Five - *You haven't seen Don today have you, Hugh? No, but that screaming and banging coming from the roof is beginning to grate somewhat* - but by this time the cerulean square above my head has assumed hypnotic powers and, with some difficulty, I pull myself up and onto the roof.

And here I am. Confused and frustrated in the bright morning sunshine.

Once upright I retrieve the broom. Don is squatting a few yards away with a couple of broken tiles in his hands. I put two and two together: last night's gale; the school roof fund about as healthy as my current account. As far as I'm aware though, a*ssisting the caretaker in the assessment of storm damage* is not specifically referred to in my job description. Why *am* I here? And what was all that crap about a tin hat? 'Don,' I say, 'why am I here? What tin hat?'

Now that he has me on the roof Don is considerably more communicative - less caretaker, more small-time crook snatching cop's proffered tenner. He appears to be on the brink of illuminating me. I'm all ears.

At first though I think I've misheard the man. His explanation makes no sense, his words twisted somehow, mangled by the blades of that bloody combined-harvester lodged deep in his throat. Don recapitulates. I experience a sense of relief: no, nothing wrong with my ears. But I look back at him just the same. 'You've got to be kidding,' I say.

Apparently not. Seems I'm *riding shotgun*. Don't even ask.

I have never been aloft at Pebble Bay before and

while Don prods at the roof I look around me. A central strip of bitumen about four feet wide separates two banks of lichen covered tiles that rise symmetrically to either side. Ahead of me the bitumen veers 90 degrees to the right and vanishes between more rows of pitched slate. Though this is my first time on the roof I quickly conclude, à la John Mills at the South Pole, that others have been here before me, several of them members of my current class if the graffiti etched onto the slates is to be believed. Most of the poorly spelt inscriptions serve merely to alert others to their relatively belated arrival at this inaccessible spot like the rigid *Stars and Stripes* we're supposed to believe Armstrong and Aldrin planted in the lunar dust. Some are of a more personal nature. The scribes' dexterity with penknife and Tippex brush casts renewed shame on their inadequacies with fountain pen and pencil. Their spelling of words unlikely to feature on the weekly spelling schedule is impressive. In some cases the font is *very* familiar.

'Disgusting some of that,' Don says looking my way.

'Libellous too.' I point at a particularly graphic account of what Mrs Warden, the Headteacher, is supposed to have done with a member of staff not long departed.

'Ah well, there's no smoke without fire,'

'You might want to read this one before you say anything else, Don.' Now *that* handwriting I know.

I follow Don along the bitumen. He is already halfway up the lichened tiles by the time I begin to clamber after him. *Is this broom really necessary?* Some of the cap tiles seem to be loose. At least they are by the time Don has finished inspecting them.

'These are going to kill somebody one of these days!' he mutters to himself. Alongside Pebble Bay's caretaker I suddenly lose interest, if such a word can be applied to my state of mind thus far, in storm-damaged roof slates and stifle a gasp. This high up it's possible to see down past the grey tarmac of the playground and onto Chesil Beach itself. The huge bank of stones stretches westwards into the distance. In the dull light of morning the pebble bank could easily go on forever. Huge waves hurl themselves on to the shingle below then beat an ill-tempered retreat, hissing through stony teeth,

We know you built that new sea wall but we have all the time in the world. To the east, steep, grey limestone cliffs rise upwards, their contours softened by the tons of spoil tipped down from the disused stone quarries above. My lips tingle under their coating of sea spray and the scent of seaweed, carried upwards by the still rampant *so'westerly* fills my nostrils. For several seconds this and the view obliterates everything else from my mind. There is only me, the smooth opalescent stones and the white capped sea flashing its disingenuous smile, denying boldfaced its complicity in the dozens of wrecks that litter its hidden depths.

It's the piercing screech directly above my head that finally drives a stick firmly between the free-wheeling spokes of my reverie. I am neglecting my duties. *The mail, goddamn it, is under attack.* I hoist the broom above my head and shout, 'Bandits at twelve o'clock!' an octave or two higher than planned. I watch with mild alarm as Don instinctively checks his watch, almost losing his balance in the process, and immediately return my attention to the sky above, its blue now obscured by dozens of beating white wings.

Having steadied himself, Don is in time to see an excessively territorial herring gull attach itself to the head of Pebble Bay Primary School's Year Five teacher. Frantically waving the broom above his head, his purchase on the forty-five degree slope severely impaired, the teacher is sliding downwards and appears to be seriously considering the nearest skylight as a viable means of escape.

A couple of pecks to the head and the gull detaches itself from my scalp. Thoughts of having legitimately fought the brute off evaporate when I realise that my feathered assailant is merely being equitable, retreating only so that one of its brethren might have a turn.

Don is somewhere nearby.

Forgot my tin hat today.

'Come on!' he says waving his arms at herring gulls that look a lot smaller than the monsters currently queuing up to pluck nest-building materials from my cranium. I improvise a controlled slide down the slates and follow Don back along the bitumen screaming the kind of obscenities my class have spent the Christmas holiday daubing on the tiles. My eyes flit between my attackers and the skylights / accidents waiting to happen that line our route to safety. A quick succession of pecks to the head confuses my sense of balance sufficiently to send me toppling sideways towards one of the transparent pyramids. My right foot comes to rest on the skylight's apex, its strongest point, and I'm able to push off the glass and force my body weight back towards the sloping slate bank to my left. Over-compensating, I stagger against the tiles jarring my knee and simultaneously dislodging a moustachioed gull which wheels away, a clump of hair protruding from its beak. No sooner has it gone than I feel something else land on my head. I yelp in pain. Don grabs the broom from me and dislodges what feels like a fucking pterodactyl from my scalp.

'Down you go,' he shouts.

I'm like *way* ahead of him. I pray to God the balsa holds though in truth my feet do not come into contact with much wood during my descent. At the bottom I dodge the broom hurled from above and hold the steps steady for Don. He slams the skylight shut, recoiling as beaks continue to peck ineffectually at the glass above us and slowly climbs down the splayed ladders.

Half an hour later, I've almost stopped shaking. My hair, what's left of it at any rate, no longer acknowledges Newton's law of universal gravity. Stylistically speaking it resembles a bird's nest. Ironic considering the likely fate of my missing locks. My head hurts terribly. But what, I console myself, is pain? A cheap neurological party trick? The brain's melodramatic unscrambling of electro-chemical signals? Scientists have proved this to be the case. Maybe so. But it's a convincing trick nonetheless. My head bloody hurts.

Dishevelled but basically still in one piece I have sixty-four children for company. Besides the thirty-two members of my own class strategically positioned around eight square tables, a similar number sit, cross-legged - in some cases cross-eyed - in the spaces and gaps between and indeed *under* the classroom's furniture. Every Friday at 9 o'clock Years Five and Six amalgamate for the purposes of a *collective act of worship,* an assembly to you and me. This is the first such gathering of the new term. As such a precedent needs to be set, a benchmark laid. Opportunities like this are few and far between. Whole-school assemblies are necessarily dumbed down in order to cater to all seven of the school's year groups. Fridays provide a chance to challenge the thinking of the school's upper echelon. The opportunity is not always taken.

Twelve months ago my Year Six counterpart, Keith Aston, began the new term with a slide show detailing his Christmas ski-ing holiday in Switzerland. The assembly proved to be one of the more successful of its genre for although the forty-three images of Keith and his wife, Penny *on the piste* were short on life-affirming messages his slide show had at least been edited for its intended audience. It's three years since Keith treated Years 5 and 6 to a slide show of his summer holiday that included a topless shot of his wife relaxing on a sun-kissed Catalonian beach.

I prefer to start the term in more meaningful fashion viewing such assemblies as an opportunity to hone my life-coaching skills. The kids at Pebble Bay could certainly use them. Described by some as *challenging* and by others, okay Don, as *thieving shysters*, the pupils at the most infamous of the Royal Manor of Portland's primary schools are not so dissimilar to those at any other educational establishment in that irrespective of their socio-economic status they obey the maxim, *Give us an inch and we'll take a yard.* In this respect at least, our headteacher is a magnanimous human being. Outside of the classroom, in the school's corridors, toilets and playgrounds discipline is conspicuous by its absence as indeed are some of the children. The kids get away with murder. One of these days the phrase is going to lose its figurative quality.

Negativity is rife within the school, the 'I can't' culture permeating all sections of its community. *I can't* do that sum. *I can't* finish that story. *I can't* remember why I shoved David's head down the toilet and pulled the chain.'

With this in mind I have chosen to begin the new term with an assembly on the power of positive thought. Don may have robbed me of half an hour's precious preparation time but every cloud has a silver lining. This morning I have had the opportunity to put my theories to the test: *I can* outrun this flock of razor-sharp-beaked seagulls. *I can* stem the flow of blood from my head with this piece of tissue. *After all, the subconscious mind is highly susceptible to suggestion.*

'If you say *I can't*, then chances are you won't be able to do something,' I explain and pause long enough for the thought to sink in and for Gregory Jackson in year Six to heckle.

'In that case *I can't* come to detention at lunch-time Mr Bradley!'

Hilarious Gregory. Now shut the fuck up.

'The thoughts you have are seeds. There's an old saying: *As you sow, you reap*. Be careful what thoughts you plant in your mind. If you sow *I can't* seeds you'll grow fear and failure. *I can* seeds bring success!'

What kind of an idiot uses overtly agricultural metaphors when addressing the youngsters of a fishing community? Am I a fucking moron? *Be careful what bait .... Check the holes in your net.... Oh forget it*. I console myself that I too am sowing seeds. Not bad for a bloke who, as a depressed teenager, responded to the proffering of *The Power of Positive Thinking* by Norman Vincent Peale with the words, 'What good will that do Mum?'

Morning lessons follow. Let's move on shall we?

The narrow path leading down from Pebble Bay Primary School to the beach is a treacherous one. Many an unwary soul has met a foul end here. Let me correct my spelling. That should be *sole*. There is dog shit everywhere. The eight feet traversing the path's cracked tarmac today belong to hardy souls indeed. They are a small group; all that is left in fact of the *Friday Club*, an organisation that once boasted a dozen members or more. Membership these days consists of Keith Aston, Brenda (the school secretary), Lorraine Hopkins (Literacy Co-ordinator) and myself. 'Yellow and soft on the starboard bow!' Keith calls back at the three club members picking their way carefully in single file behind him.

'What the hell do they feed dogs round here?' I reply.

'Why don't you bag it and send it away for analysis, Hugh?'

'If I can't face mustard on my chips today Lorraine, I'll blame you.'

We are headed for *The Wreckers,* the eighteenth century public house constructed from local stone that squats astride Chesil Beach a hundred yards from school. Recently afforded extra protection by the new sea wall, The Wreckers is the traditional meeting place of the Friday Club. The pub takes its name from the disreputable nocturnal characters that once frequented its environs. You know the type: hang a few lanterns round the necks of some ponies borrowed from the nearby quarries, march them up and down the beach for a bit and wait for a ship or two to run aground having mistaken the shifting lights for boats bobbing safely on their moorings in not so far off Weymouth Bay. This done, a swinging club applied to the head usually prevented any of the stranded mariners from drowning and then of course it was just a matter of unloading whatever cargo the unpredictable currents had swept ashore. It was at the Wreckers that I'd spent the lunch-time break the day I'd secured employment at Pebble Bay Primary School five years before. Since then there have been occasions when I have empathised with those sailors, unsuspecting fools lured to their doom by the cleverly crafted illusion of safe harbour and their own misguided complacency.

Inside the pub we congregate about our usual table beneath a window that looks out onto the beach. There is no need for menus, Brenda having phoned through our order during the course of the morning. A reduction in membership has not been without its benefits. Besides the acquisition of the best seats in the house, the quality of the cuisine has markedly improved. There is no mystery to this. As teachers we are well aware of the benefits of smaller class sizes.

With a sizeable swell still doing its thing off shore and the wind rattling the Wrecker's less robust windows the scene is a cosy one. Wood and stone dominate the pub's interior. The walls are almost obscured by prints depicting some of the dozens of vessels to have met their end, via fair means or foul, on the rocks and steeply shelving beach outside. 'Don't go,' the images seem to say, 'you'll be much safer staying here and having another pint.' Talking of which.

The drinks order is normally a good indication of the kind of morning club members have had. Keith Aston and Lorraine Hopkins order glasses of red wine. Large ones. I order a bottle. Of mineral water that is. 'It's alright for you locals,' I say, 'some of us have got to drive home later.' Never mind teach a full afternoon's lessons without falling asleep during the Geography video again.

Our meals arrive with our drinks, the kitchen as efficient as a Japanese railway. This is just as well since we haven't got long. One of the reasons for the Friday Club's numerical decline was the lopping of fifteen full minutes from the Pebble Bay lunch hour. The thinking behind this act of barbarism was that since most problems in the playground occurred during the final quarter of the midday break much trouble could be avoided by removing the said last quarter. The school's theoreticians reminded Sue Warden that no reduction in the length of the lunch hour could ever remove its final fifteen minutes and that, like inebriated patrons at a pub panic drinking following the unexpected ringing of *Last Orders,* the unruly element of the school population would quickly adapt to the time restrictions placed upon them and start beating the bejesus out of each other a quarter of an hour earlier by way of compensation. The initial trial period, however, had been deemed a success and for more than a year now the Friday Club had been bolting its food as well as reaping the benefits of finishing school fifteen minutes earlier than they used to.

And of course there is still time for a truncated form of communication between mouthfuls. This being the first Friday of the new term there is some catching up to do. Christmas vacation anecdotes initially take precedence over the usual tales of horror from the classroom. But not for long. 'I called Joan Masters this morning to see if she'd cover Keith's class next Tuesday,' Brenda informs us. 'She says she's not doing any supply at the school anymore.'

'What, *ever*?' I ask. Brenda nods.

'Can't say I blame her.' Keith doesn't seem unduly concerned that he may have to forgo the joys of a Special

Educational Needs conference. 'Sue never gave her any support.' This is true. Obviously the incident at the end of last term had been the final straw. Linzi Oldham has verbally abused several members of staff during her time at the school but calling Joan *an old git* and following it up with 'Are you deaf as well as stupid?' when Joan had asked indignantly 'What did you say?' had evidently been too much for the now departed Mrs Masters.

'It's been a long week,' Lorraine chips in blandly.

But a short lunch-time. I take a couple of bites at my salad sandwich and cram some chips into my mouth.

Our waitress approaches the table as I'm striving heroically not to gag on this unadvisedly large quantity of food. 'Sauces anyone?' she asks, 'Tomato ketchup, HP sauce, *mustard*?'

Friday afternoon is never an easy teaching assignment. The weekend is within spitting distance – '*That's just an expression Joseph Hartnell, don't you dare do that again!*' but for pupils and teacher alike the phrase, *so close and yet so far* just about says it all. A feeling of excitement at the weekend's proximity is infused with frustration due to the seemingly never-ending properties of this final afternoon of the school week. It is a highly combustible brew. It can be unpleasant on the palette. Tracy Watkins, for instance, spends the entire afternoon slumped sullenly in her seat ripping paper into increasingly tiny pieces. I say *paper* when technically the material Tracy is shredding like a stir-crazy hamster is a worksheet. This is somewhat frustrating. However, when you've been teaching for a few years you begin to pick up certain tricks of the trade. Possessing a less than fearsome countenance means I have developed a non-confrontational style of behaviour management. Several display boards bear testament to this. The *merit chart* rewards the good work and obedience of individual pupils while the *Wall of Fame* contains the photographic images of eight children who have excelled in a variety of disciplines over the course of the preceding week. Since Year Five are currently studying the Victorians, a hand drawn map of the world adorns one board.

The coloured stickers scattered across it indicate each table group's progress in colonising newly discovered regions of the world. At the end of each week a table's success is appropriately rewarded as a battered old silver plated trophy on Table Four and a packet of chocolate biscuits in my top drawer attest.

Of course teachers may employ a variety of different teaching and behaviour management strategies but the constituent members of any given class remain constant year upon year. There are key players, there are sheep, and there are loose cannons. The key players are controlled via subtly playing to their interests. The sheep are controlled by the key players. The loose cannons are controlled via *prescribed medication.* The three groups' make up can be fluid. Key players have been known to temporarily merge with the flock. A Sheep will occasionally take up the shepherd's crook. Loose cannons *remain* loose cannons. Things will run smoothly as long as I have a currently active key player on each table and I space out the loose cannons. Sorry, inappropriate phrase. This isn't to say there aren't blips. At the end of yesterday afternoon's science lesson all Tracy Watkins had to show for her efforts was the date (not underlined) in her exercise book and the sentence *Mr Bradley is a bossy wanker.*

Weymouth Harbour 1348: the Black Death arrives in England, carried ashore by rodent mariners. By the time I park beside the selfsame quay it's nearer 15.57. The Town Bridge, traversed in the nick of time, will rise in three minutes. I leave the warmth of the car to watch the four o'clock show. Fishing trawlers and sleek cruisers bob idly in the water. A small flotilla of yachts, poised mid-channel, await access to the marina beyond the bridge, a gift, if the plaques are to be believed, from the inhabitants of the port's North American namesake. The sky is still clear but already a January murk smudges the edges of the scene before me, the tall Georgian houses, the old Devenish brewery behind them on the opposite quay and the disfiguring gasometer stubbornly blighting the skyline beyond the Town Bridge. There's a chill in the air that discourages inertia. A couple of men emerge from the Harbour

Master's building behind me and climb down a partially rotted wooden ladder onto a floating pontoon to which their craft is moored.

'Daddy!'

Turning, I catch sight of a dark-haired gangly seven year old girl skipping towards me. I feint to run away, slow-motion style, but Mary's arms are around me before I can follow the Harbour Master down the ladder. Close behind come her elder brother and sister. Freddie, a freckle faced ten year old, reaches me three strides ahead of the fair-haired Hatty. Their mother Beth, from whom Mary has inherited her dark locks, follows and, smiling, applies the palm of her hand affectionately to my rump as is her Friday afternoon wont. 'What happened to your head?' she asks, concerned.

I raise a hand to my scalp which still smarts to the touch. 'Long story,' I reply hoping the matter will be dropped.

'Why don't you *cut a long story short* then Dad.'

Let me guess Freddie. Today in Literacy: idioms? Since Mary is still clutching my leg I opt for *tall* rather than *short*. My youngest is scared of pretty much everything and there's no point adding seagulls to her burgeoning list of phobias. Besides, our current location isn't exactly devoid of avian life and birds are not unlike aeroplanes, phobia number 23.

Bournemouth Airport, two years ago. Mary is weeping in the back of the car at the prospect of flying to Corfu for a family holiday. Her father has spent the forty minute drive stressing the infinitesimal risks involved in powered flight. Since the only aircraft Mary has seen up to this point in her life are the ones painted red that streak across the skies above Weymouth trailing blue and red smoke on Carnival Day he is at pains to describe the *level* trajectory employed by the majority of commercial jetliners once take off has been effected. Mary seems to understand. Her father is confident she will be okay. This is Bournemouth Airport we're talking about not the Fleet Air Arm at Yeovilton. Which is why it's a surprise to see some kind of jet fighter plane performing cartwheels above the control tower upon arrival at the NCP long stay. Ah yes, Mary's father thinks, the Aviation Museum the other side of the main road. A member of the ground staff standing outside the terminal building tells the nice family consoling the weeping child that the silver blur streaking across the sky is a de Havilland Sea Vixen, the last of its kind still flying. Much later Mary's father finds out why. Online, the Sea Vixen is described as *a mean looking, noisy machine that filled onlookers with awe.* 145 were built. Nearly 40% crashed. In peace time. No wonder the families of the dead air crew have set up a website drawing attention to their plight. No wonder Mary's father finds himself back at square one. By the time the family check-in Mary is chewing on a restorative chocolate bar. The nice lady behind the desk bestows a smile then asks her father if that will be smoking or non-smoking. Mary's father is too late to explain to his daughter that the nice lady is not referring to the plane's engines.

Weymouth harbour. Today. Cause of head injury. I regale my family with an implausible tale involving a minor rock fall while leading my class on a beach scramble earlier in the afternoon.

'You mean there was a *landslide*?' Freddie asks excitedly.

'Not a landslide,' I say, trying to minimise the impact this remark will have on Mary's phobia of losing one or both parents to falling masonry. Fortunately before I can give details of boulder size and the names of those members of my class killed or maimed the Town Bridge starts to rise and everyone's attention is grabbed by this marvel of civil engineering, no less impressive and a whole lot less ostentatious than its Gothic Revival big brother straddling the Thames.

As the waiting yachts pass beneath its elevated span we saunter along the quay, duck down an alleyway redolent with the stale aroma of human urine and purchase tea from the Marlborough fish and chip shop where my loyalty card ensures a satisfying 10% discount. On the way back to the car we pause at Harpo's, a hole in the wall refreshment shack open year round.

'Don't say a word!' our eponymous host says before proceeding to serve up a cappuccino and double espresso.

'Have you thought about loyalty cards?' I ask.

'No gimmicks necessary at Harpo's; the coffee demands loyalty, it is its own reward.' He smiles, hands over the drinks and, grinning at Hatty, says, 'Give us a chip Beautiful.'

Still blushing, Hatty leads the way back along the rapidly darkening quay.

'I can't see the Travolta,' Beth mutters. She is referring to *my wheels* or as my *Grease* loving kids prefer, my *hunk of junk*. I prefer the label *Morris Traveller* although the compromise *Morris Travolta*, or simply, *Travolta* is more commonly used by all concerned.

'The doors are open,' I say pointing the ignition key with dramatic flamboyance towards the car parked not twenty feet away. In truth it's been nearly two years since the Travolta possessed a viable security system. Hatty, Freddie and Mary dash ahead and have already started in on their chip butties and mushy peas by the time the adults follow them inside and sink into the classic car's luxurious vinyl upholstery. While the kids smear mushy peas over themselves and the seats I exchange, *Had a good days?* with Beth who is looking tired.

'*Bad* day,' she says, taking a sip from her Styrofoam cup.

'Nigel?' I ask, referring to the Head at the school in Dorchester where Beth works.

'Who else?'

Beth is Nigel's deputy. Nigel, as he takes pleasure in pointing out, is Beth's superior. Ipso facto, Beth is Nigel's *inferior.*

'What *is* the misogynist's problem?' I ask. We've had this conversation before. The dialogue follows a well worn path.

'I don't know what I have to do for the man to take me seriously.' Beth pauses to take on more caffeine and returns the cappuccino to its resting place atop the open glove compartment.

'You could start by losing the Mr Whippy moustache,' I suggest, 'that or grow a penis.' Beth grimaces and removes the offending facial froth while I swipe a chip from Hatty who in contrast to her mother continues to add rather than remove edible substances to her visage. 'You've got pea all over your face,' I tell her, choosing my words meticulously. Freddie cracks up obligingly and while he explains my homophonic humour to his younger sister I take Beth's hand and give it a squeeze. 'It was par for the course on The Rock today too.' *Yeah, like I get attacked by frickin sea gulls every day.*

'Maybe you should look for another job.'

Very clever, I think.

'I'm no quitter,' I tell her.

'You're my hero,' she replies, feigning a swoon, 'for two and a half days a week anyway.'

A low blow. Going part-time had not been my idea. It had been borne of necessity. I have nothing to be ashamed of. All the same a change of subject wouldn't hurt. 'The light is amazing this afternoon,' I say nodding towards the water, a liquid mirror undisturbed now by water craft of any kind, a quivering replica of the illuminated quay. A cormorant breaks the smooth surface, ripples radiating from its sleek body lending the scene a surreal quality. I lean across and kiss Beth. There are groans from behind us. My children have a problem with parental displays of affection. Either that or the mushy peas have finally been upended all over the floor.

The Travolta whisks us towards the outskirts of Dorchester in a little under twenty minutes, the speedometer nudging fifty as we descend the Ridgeway, the elevated chalk spine, that separates the county town from the ravages of the Dorset coast.

'Slow down, Dad!' goads Freddie.

My son's burgeoning sense of humour was initially a source of great pride. The novelty is beginning to wear off. It won't be long before he's telling me to watch I don't run down the bloke with the red flag walking in front of the car.

I park the Morris in the grounds of *Keller House*, a Georgian edifice, now converted to offices, where, legend has it, the Tolpuddle Martyrs were interrogated over 150 years ago. The 18th century stone cottage just across the road on the corner of Kirk and Durnford Streets (the one surrounded by those pretty yellow lines) is the place we call home. Ten minutes later, Hatty, Freddie and Mary have vanished upstairs, their arms laden with sweetmeats and the latest DVDs from *Lovefilm*. Beth is sprawled on the sofa making the weekly phone call to her mother, a former college lecturer, from whom we suspect Mary inherited her susceptibility to fear. The closer the sixty-two year old, Anne Brin advances towards the grave the more obsessed she becomes with those who have beaten her to it. A typical phone call invariably includes graphic accounts of the means by which friends, acquaintances and former colleagues have met their end. That Harold Shipman practised medicine close to the Brin family home has not helped Beth's mother's condition nor has the fact that a loquacious neighbour worked for many years as a nurse at the maniac's practice. At the end of a hard week it isn't exactly uplifting fare. If she's lucky Beth's father will lure his wife to the television set with the promise of an air crash or meteorite catastrophe in a not too distant locality. I grab a few cloth carrier bags and head for the supermarket. *Groundhog Friday.*

Waitrose is less than a minute's walk away. I grab wine, beer and chocolate from the shelves before giving any thought to nutritional considerations. I suspect my subsequent purchases: peanuts, pain au chocolat, pancakes and sweet waffles won't exactly count towards my *five a day* either.

Beth is still on the phone when I return. As I enter the kitchen via the back door it is possible to see across the dining area to the living room where my wife theatrically places a fist beside her head and yanks it upwards simultaneously allowing her tongue to flop out of her mouth. I toss her a smile then start to unpack the bags. Beer cooling in the fridge, I wave on my way out the back door again. I have one more errand to run.

Walking along Kirk Street I note that our local, the Dolphin, has yet to open. The cold evening air revives my brain's interest in the patches of pain dotted about my seagull-molested head. I turn the corner into the High Street and head down the hill. The scent of curry fills the air as I approach the *Massala* and for a moment my nostrils, aided by a procession of vehicles, prevent my legs from propelling me across the street to *The Imperial Garden* Chinese restaurant.

Inside there is no sign of life, customer or staff. Over the years I have developed a paternal concern for the well-being of my favourite restaurant. I glance at my watch; it's still early. Closure may not be imminent after all. Three years ago business at The Garden was booming. Profits were ploughed back into the business. Renovation work, which included roofing over part of the back yard to increase seating capacity was undertaken. The old green carpet was ripped up and the black ash furnishings politely shown the door. With them went the Garden's cosy ambiance, replaced by cold marble and the glare of empty seats. Three months is a long time to be closed. It's not as if there aren't other Chinese restaurants in town. Some of us returned however. Never mind that the old place now had more the feel of an operating theatre than an eatery, the food was still damned good. It's not as if we ever eat in anyway.

Back at the house Beth has been busy with the tea lights. As I unpack our meal and pour myself a beer I can't help noticing that the candlelight has cranked Beth's undeniable beauty up a notch or two. Her dark hair cascades, her full, *French film star,* lips glisten, her amply equipped chest heaves. It's clear by the way she's advancing towards me that the half bottle of red my wife has consumed in my absence - god I love difficult mother/daughter relationships - seems to have lent my own less than photogenic features an irresistible quality. Before I have time to cut myself on the corner of the aluminium tray containing the fried rice, Beth is pressed against me and I know we'll be eating cold bean curd again.

This time of year it's dark when I wake. Even on a Saturday morning. I don't do lie-ins, can't seem to break the routine of early starts established between days one to five of the week. It doesn't matter what time I retire, the next morning I wake promptly at six. Seven days a week. 365 days a year. Going back to sleep is not an option. This morning the urge to rise is stronger than usual. This morning I have a mission. I shower quickly and lather my face. Unlike its owner, my razor rarely gets its act together at the weekend. Today is an exception. I've already nicked myself before I apply adequate concentration to the job in hand. A bad workman always blames his tools. My mind is elsewhere. I'm nervous. Take care of the details and the big picture will look after itself. What was it the wise sage told his pupil when asked the secret of enlightenment? *Attention, attention, attention.* I focus and complete the pruning of my face without further incident. I slip on a pair of jeans and a charcoal grey roll-neck and head downstairs. In the living room I squat in front of the gas fire. The house's sole source of heat is the size and shape of an oil drum (although considerably more pleasing to the eye) and would have you believe it burns logs. It dominates the large fireplace and indeed the room itself. Ignition is a complicated process, a test of auditory, occular and fine motor skills that invariably defeats the ill-prepared. Like a Promethean safecracker hunched before an *Ironclad* I depress, rotate and release the concealed dial, listening for the hiss of gas, watching for the tell-tale spark before, with a final twist of the wrist, flames issue forth. One false move, any deviation from prescribed protocol and disaster can strike. The shaving experience must have severely drained my powers of concentration. The smell of singed hand and wrist hair follows me into the kitchen where I set about preparing a flask of coffee with the prosaic flick of a switch. I have my jacket on and I'm tying my shoe laces when I hear a voice behind me.

'Where are you going, Daddy?' It's Mary. I rack my brains trying to recall the last time the girl was up and about before eight on a Saturday morning. I treat her question as rhetorical. So does Mary. 'Can I come?' she asks.

I could say 'no'. I would say 'no', after all I'm ready to hit the road and my daughter has yet to wipe the sleep from her eyes let alone discard her pyjamas. However, I know already that I won't be leaving the house alone. The choice is a simple one: leave the house with one child or leave it with three. And now probably isn't the time to wheel out the 'When I say *no* I mean *no* and there's no point in you screaming the house down' lecture. So while Mary goes in search of socks and a cardigan with which to adorn her pyjamas I grab some pain au chocolat from the bread bin and slip the letter I have to deliver inside my jacket pocket.

Having parked the Travolta in the shelter of Keller House there is no ice to scrape from its windscreen and, risking frost bite, I grasp the steering wheel with my left hand and insert the key into the ignition. In spite of Mary's feeble 'Hunk of junk' routine – *Do you want to come with me or not?* - the car starts first time which I take to be a good omen. The gods are smiling on this early morning excursion. The traffic lights on Kirk Street flash green obligingly at the junction with the High Street and turning left I point the Morris up the hill and put my foot down.

On the outskirts of town we pick up the A35. Mary bombards me with questions none of which seem to have any immediate relevance. At Winterbourne Abbas we turn left towards Portesham and as the sun begins to rise to our left we navigate the narrow road without encountering other traffic. At Portesham we bear right and minutes later we're passing through downtown Abbotsbury (population 505). It's touch and go whether the Travolta will make it up the similarly named hill on the far side of the village but having adopted the vehicular equivalent of a crawl for the last fifty yards we eventually trundle over the summit and begin our descent towards West Bexington. As we approach the village I check instinctively for the letter in my pocket. 'Look out for the pub,' I tell the, by this time, chocolate smeared Mary.

Although it's starting to get light I'm still far from convinced that I'm going to be able to locate my intended destination. After all it's not as though I have a postal address to go on. But then that's not something famous authors tend to reveal to all and sundry. I'm still a little sceptical that the man behind the historical bestseller *Death of a Prime Minister* actually shared the whereabouts of his Dorset bolt-hole with the thirty or forty people who'd gathered at Dorchester library two months ago to hear him talk about his latest novel. Why would the great Thomas Chandler do that? Beth, a member of the audience that night, had been adamant however. 'The *Old School House* across from the village pub,' she'd told me, little suspecting that her husband would pen a presumptuous note requesting an interview and deliver it by hand very, very early on a Saturday morning.

But unlike her husband Beth has no literary aspirations. I have a hunch Dorset Scene magazine will jump at the chance of an interview with the great man, particularly as his soon to be published eighth novel is set predominantly in the county.

I spot the pub as we turn the ninety degree corner into the village's main street. Directly ahead I can make out the English Channel. Since the pub is on our left, my attention now alternates between the road ahead and the houses to our right. The *Old School House* is not difficult to find. I park the Travolta opposite and kill the engine.

'Why have we stopped Daddy?'

'We've something to deliver ,' I explain attempting to take the letter from my jacket pocket but abandoning the procedure amidst a flurry of mumbled obscenities aimed specifically at my seat belt which I belatedly unfasten. Letter finally in hand I pull back the as yet unsealed flap of the envelope and remove its contents. I read:

Dear Mr Chandler,

My name is Hugh Bradley. I am a primary school teacher and aspiring freelance writer. My wife attended a talk you gave at Dorchester library a couple of months ago (which she thoroughly enjoyed) and told me about your forthcoming novel set in 18th century Dorset.

Local history is a passion of mine (I'm always up at the County Research Centre) and I was wondering if I might interview you about your book? If you are agreeable I will contact Peter Swinton, the editor of Dorset Scene magazine, about the possibility of his publishing the interview.

I look forward to hearing from you.

Best wishes,

Hugh Bradley.

Would Peter Swinton be interested? I'd put money on it, some of it my own. It's not as if I'm completely unknown to the man. He'd published that article I wrote about the old tunnel at Charmouth hadn't he?

'What are we delivering, Daddy?' Beside me Mary is becoming impatient.

I replace the letter and seal the envelope. 'This,' I say glancing across at the house and noticing for the first time a car parked outside. Thomas Chandler spends most of his time in London - at least that's what it says on his book jackets - but he retreats to Dorset whenever the opportunity arises. Although I had half expected there to be someone home I am anxious to deliver my note without detection. When exactly does: *TEACHER REQUESTS INTERVIEW WITH FAMOUS AUTHOR* become *STALKER APPREHENDED OUTSIDE RECLUSIVE WRITER'S HOME IN SMALL HOURS OF THE MORNING?* I begin to lose my nerve. 'Mary? Daddy's got a little job for you, sweetheart.' I look at the chocolate coated oik in the passenger seat beside me, the one that would trust me with her life.

'What is it Daddy?' she says innocently.

Her voice brings me to my senses. Have I no shame? This is man's work, not an errand to be entrusted to a small child. I would never do anything to put my daughter at risk. Besides, she'd only get chocolate all over the bloody envelope. I tell Mary to stay put and ease open the driver's door. Closing it with a soft click I cross the street. The upper most section of the front door to the *Old School House* is partially glazed. I can see directly across a small lobby into a kitchen illuminated by several spot lights set into a beam-crossed ceiling. It's barely 7 o'clock and coming face to face with someone on the other side of the glass is not part of the plan. I feel like a member of the Paparazzi merely delivering this letter to Thomas Chandler's weekend retreat, never mind scaring the bejesus out of the man by leering through a window at him. Did I read somewhere that he had a heart condition? *PROWLER INDUCES MASSIVE CORONARY AT RECUPERATING AUTHOR'S SECRET HIDEAWAY.*

A coffee pot stands beside a kettle apparently awaiting hot water. A few wisps of smoke hover above an adjacent toaster. I really should be going. Someone, not necessarily Chandler, is going to come into the room any minute and I'd rather he wasn't alerted to the arrival of my letter by the screams of his wife. The letter. God I'd almost forgotten *that.* I look for a letter box, an aperture of some sort through which to post my missive. There isn't one, vertical or horizontal. Nothing. What, the man communicates by frickin' e-mail alone? I hear a series of high pitched beeps coming from within and look up in time to see a couple of pieces of charcoal spring from the toaster. As the beeping continues I ponder the best course of action vis-à-vis the envelope in my hand. A figure dashes into the room and I duck below the transparent portion of the door intent on sitting this thing out at least until things quieten down inside. I hear a woman's voice calling, 'Open the door and let the smoke out!'

Well, duh!

Whoa!

Fuck.

I'm about to flee when I spot the letter box a few inches above ground level set into the foot of the door. Fatally, I pause. The door starts to rattle as though someone were trying to yank it off its hinges. What now? I can't post the letter without drawing attention to myself. A hunched figure legging it towards the nearest car is similarly likely to catch the rattler's eye. Crouching in a foetal position on the man's doorstep isn't going to look particularly good either. A rabbit hypnotised by headlights, I wait for the door to swing open.

'I can't find the blasted key, love!' A man's voice. A reprieve!

'It's next to the kettle where you left it last night, Tom!'

The rattling stops. Cue *Indiana Jones* theme music. Or is it *Stars Wars*? Or the *Superman* theme? Shit, when will someone tell John Williams they all sound the bloody same. I shove the letter through the flap and improvise a stooped run back towards the car stifling the urge to shout, *'Start the engine!'* to the watching Mary. As the Travolta coughs and splutters to life the door of the Old School House opens and a tall man in a dressing gown emerges clutching something in his hand. As we roll towards the sea I check my mirrors and spot Thomas Chandler, one hand partially covering his nose, mouth and greying beard, wafting smoke through his front door using something white, rectangular and decidedly crumpled.

Sunday lunch at my mother and father's house is something of a routine. The journey across town to Zennor Road takes five minutes. Getting from one end of the tree-lined avenue to another can take considerably longer. This is learner driver territory. Throughout the week Zennor Road and its tributaries teem with life, an infestation of wannabe motorists queuing to perform emergency stops and nine point turns in an attempt to drag themselves from the quagmire of pedestrianism. Like the first creatures to crawl tentatively from the primordial swamp millions of years ago they lurch dangerously about their new environment without so much as a cursory glance in their evolutionary rear-view mirrors. Sundays are different though. On the Sabbath they rest.

We gain entry to the house via its side entrance. My mother is alone in the kitchen. Saucepans bubble on the stove before which she waves a wooden spoon as though conducting a symphony orchestra and not simmering frozen peas and broccoli. She smiles, then reinforces the greeting with a 'Hello, Love.' I respond appropriately. 'You're just in time to make the gravy,' my mother tells me, stepping away from the Aga in order to receive unbidden, but not unwelcome, hugs from her grandchildren. There is no sign of my father who my mother assures me will be along in a minute. I am relieved to hear her refer to her husband, James as 'Jim-Bob', a term of endearment adopted by Hatty, Freddie and Mary to the total exclusion of 'Granddad'. My mother's use of the term implies the presence of calm at Zennor Road. Alternative, less affectionate, nomenclature includes *Popeye* , a less than sympathetic reference to my father's thyroid condition, and *Pinhead*, a name coined several years earlier when my mother claimed, more through spite than conviction, that her husband's head was noticeably shrinking. The name and its ramifications were taken up enthusiastically by other members of the family, one going so far as to suggest a point of critical mass would be reached in the shrinking process whereupon Jim-Bob's head would separate from his neck, hurtle about the room like a rapidly deflating balloon and disappear down the back of a radiator never to be seen again.

The kitchen at Zennor Road is large enough to render the rest of the ground floor superfluous to requirements. The children have already commandeered the sofa at the far end of the room and switched on the TV by the time the French doors swing open and my father strides in. 'Morning!' he says, apparently unaware that the sun began its slide towards the western horizon almost an hour ago. No one bothers to correct this slip in my father's temporal vocabulary. Such errors are far from uncommon. Christmas Day, three years previous, the man stepped from the master bathroom following his Yuletide ablutions, smiled at those assembled on the landing and promptly wished them all a hearty 'Happy Birthday'. Jet-lagged phraseology aside, my father has, physically speaking at least, weathered well. Still in possession of his own teeth and hair (the latter now considerably whiter than the former) he could pass for a man seven or eight years his junior. Holding his six foot two inch frame erect and directing his not inconsiderable nose skywards one could be forgiven for thinking the man aloof, as though he were aware that by accentuating his own height he might elevate himself as far as possible above the low life with which he frequently comes into contact. Similarly, my father's facial features do little to betray his age, a slight slackening around the jowls being unlikely to illuminate the pound signs in a plastic surgeon's eyes. His bladder is a different matter. His head may not actually be shrinking but his bladder certainly is. The man could urinate for his country. His, 'Back in a minute,' suggests he's about to put in a spot of training prior to lunch.

My mother too can still boast a relatively youthful mien. Arthritis may have sent her fingers off at crazy angles but there is still the same glint in her blue eyes that exasperated teachers first observed during a largely misspent stint in the Northern Irish education system. Little evidence remains of her decadent Irish upbringing however, save a quick temper, a mischievous sense of humour and a maternal warmth inherited from her Gaelic brethren. 'Where's your shit of a father gone?' Oh yes, and a filthy mouth. Popular opinion has it that when my father married my mother he bit off more than he could chew.

Lunch is good. It always is. No one cooks roast dinners like my mother. For years I tried to replicate the phenomenon. It was only recently that I discovered the secret to my mother's culinary success: salt. A mountain of the stuff. It took worries over Jim-Bob's blood pressure to alert me to the fact. Meals following his diagnosis seemed to lack something. Flavour mostly. Ladling on the white stuff at the point of consumption didn't seem to help. Besides, empty the salt cellar over your meal and you might as well tell the chef she can't cook. When Jim-Bob's blood pressure stabilised the roast dinners rallied. I'm polishing off my fifth roast potato when my mother asks after my ankle. I tell her it's fine. It's been nearly two weeks since I gashed it badly dismounting in less than nonchalant style from my bicycle.

'Let me have a look,' she says.

I protest on the grounds of hunger and age.

'Don't make me come round there,' she says. I'm not going to win. Time is on my mother's side. She likes to build pauses into her meals on account of the difficulty she has always had swallowing food. Copious amounts of water and distractions such as this aid the digestive process.

I push myself away from the dinner table. 'Tell your grandma she's being silly, Hatty,' I say. My eldest child demurs. Once around the other side of the table, my mother instructs me to lift my trouser leg, to pull down my sock. It is clear for all to see that the wound has healed.

'Ah, look at his little ankle! I've always loved Hugh's ankles,' she says and proceeds to highlight the perennial heart melting properties indigenous to my lower leg joint. I have always considered my ankles to be robust and hairy but my mother is having none of it. 'Bless,' she concludes returning to a meal that Freddie, who has found the whole discussion hilarious, seems incapable of now finishing. Several minutes and three mashed up potatoes later my mother levels an arthritic finger at me and says, 'Tomorrow I need you to feed Sparky for me.' Sparky: the vastly overweight tabby cat that shares my parent's living quarters and daily calorific intake. Since my mouth is full of *Maris Pipers* I raise an inquisitive eyebrow by way of response. 'We're going to visit Louisa for a couple of days. I'll leave some fish in the fridge.'

'And for dessert?'

Beth kicks me. I'm about to inquire as to the purpose of this rare jaunt to my sister's home when Mum, Gaelic warmth suddenly gone, growls at me, '*Don't* forget to feed

Sparky.'

I know better than that. Cats and my mother go *way back.*

The brakes on my bike are shot. In the wet I'm a bona fide menace to myself and other road users - gashed ankles are not the only souvenirs I've collected on my travels around the local road system. A properly maintained bicycle could drastically reduce my consumption of sticking plaster. I really should earmark some time and/or cash towards a restoration project. Both commodities are in short supply however. The term *part-time* applies purely to my professional duties on Portland.

By 8 a.m. Monday morning I've usually already been up two hours. There are packed lunches to be prepared, uniforms to be pressed and shoes to be polished. Breakfast doesn't just make itself either. Beth generally vacates the family residence by 7.30 wearing an outfit chosen half an hour before departure and offered up with the words, 'Iron this for me, Babe.' I obey uxoriously in the guise of a husband who knows which side his bread is buttered. Hatty and Freddie are the next to leave the house. They make their own way to St Olaf's Middle School and are usually gone by 8.20 roughly five minutes behind my patience. Despite a series of increasingly demonstrative reminders, Freddie invariably leaves it until his sister is ready to depart before attempting to locate shoes, PE kit, pens, pencils and coat. At any given time at least half the aforementioned items are technically missing. Today it is Freddie's school shoes. He suspects he may have left them at St Olaf's the previous Friday. I suspect he hasn't a clue where they are and categorically refuse to pen a note to his teacher setting out spurious mitigating circumstances regarding my son's oversight. I tell Freddie to get his act together, get his trainers on and to delay coming home until *after* he has tracked down his errant footwear. Only when this drama is played out do I discover Hatty's toothbrush is as dry as the Atacama and her teeth a similar hue. She stomps upstairs while Freddie exacts revenge, tutting volubly prior to an impressive impersonation of the speaking clock.

Mary and her father tend to leave the premises in more sedate fashion. Pushing my bicycle en route to St Paul's First School, we pause at the recycling skips to off-load the weekend's *empties* before merging with the general stream of school children and parents, a slow moving current that gradually broadens as it approaches our destination. At St Paul's I watch Mary skip towards class before wheeling my bike onto the glistening tarmac in preparation for the expedited journey home. I try the brakes in turn during the first few yards of forward motion. An ear-piercing screech, not unlike the death throes of some exotic bird ensnared by a foraging olive baboon, confirms the rear wheel's readiness to halt when required to do so. The front brake, however, mimes its indifference. My bicycle's velocity remains unchanged.

Chronos, back up there a little if you will. Last spring. Hugh Bradley, having just purchased a hanging basket from the town market, and as usual running a little behind schedule, decides that riding his bike, rather than walking beside it, will hasten the process of transporting his purchase home. It will of course mean holding the handle bars of his bicycle in one hand and the chain attached to the surprisingly cumbersome basket in the other. He notes that the basket has a tendency to swing from side to side. He will adjust his speed accordingly. *Or at least he will try.* Approaching the traffic lights near home Hugh wishes he'd chosen to hold the basket in his left hand. This would have enabled the digits located on the right side of his body to apply pressure to the bike's only viable brake. There is a choice to make: use the back of the fast approaching pick-up truck to reduce speed or ditch the pretty flower basket. Hugh does not have to think for long. There's another tenner down the toilet.

And now. At the traffic lights on the railway bridge the olive baboon bags another bird. In the wet its appetite is voracious. Feathers continue to fly during the short journey back towards the town centre. When I hit South Street I slow down. The non pedestrianised portion is one-way. This time of day though a contra-flow system can be unilaterally adopted without undue danger of injury or chastisement. Pedestrians are both alerted to my approach and given time to take evasive action by the timely application of my rear brake. A mere five minutes after bidding Mary goodbye I'm propping my bike outside the newsagent's where I purchase a paper before rescuing my wheels and continuing homewards.

It is usually when I reach the top of Durnford Street that the vigour I've experienced since waking begins to ebb. Optimism, enthusiasm, confidence one by one raise the white flag to fear, dread and anxiety. I try to reason with myself. A blank computer screen awaits me back at the house, not an armed intruder. Right now it's difficult to say which is more daunting: using my head to fend off a baseball bat or attempting to create meaningful patterns on a page. The situation isn't helped by the potentially finite nature of my fledging writing career. My going part-time had had nothing to do with my literary aspirations. It had been a prudent financial move at the time. Besides shifting the bulk of parental responsibilities to my shoulders it had also just happened to provide me with the opportunity to write during daylight hours for the first time in my adult life. The continuance of the arrangement in the long term, however, is by no means certain. Beth is having a tough time of it. Her struggles as Deputy Head at Dorchester First School would be more bearable if they had a raison d'être. My conscience could do with one too. The writing *has to pay.* Consequently a probationary period had been agreed upon. Success criteria are in place. Targets must be met. Namely, that I publish or *have accepted for publication* six financially remunerated articles by the occasion of my 40th birthday at the beginning of April. A twelve month period to prove my writing is capable of contributing significantly to the family finances. To bring you up to speed: *three* months remaining to shift another *five* articles. Succeed and I continue in my current role. Fail and the process of role reversal begins. Beth would exercise her newly bestowed statutory rights as a mother to force Nigel to grant her a job-share and I would apply for full-time teaching positions undertaking supply work for the first two and a half days of the working week until successful. The prospect appals me. And time is not the only issue. There's the small matter of talent too. Its existence or otherwise. The jury is still out on that one. Financially at least, progress has been slow. Last year I'd enrolled on a writing correspondence course. I'd diligently completed each of the non-fiction assignments, submitting some for publication. My article on the pre-Victorian road tunnel at Charmouth had been my very last assignment. By the time it was accepted by *Dorset Scene* magazine two thirds of the trial period had already elapsed. By the time it was published this figure was closer to three quarters. The article had earned me £150, a sum negotiated with the editor who had initially surprised me by inquiring as to my own ideas on the article's monetary value. Since I'd hoped to receive £120 for the piece I wrote back suggesting a figure that would allow room for manoeuvre. Peter Swinton professed reluctance at paying such a sum to a first-time contributor. Nonetheless he agreed to my suggestion in the same letter inviting me to invoice the magazine at the earliest opportunity. Not a fortune, I know. However, not only was I to be paid more than I'd anticipated I was also to be paid *on acceptance* and not *on publication*. Initial elation at this first success proved short lived. Following it up had proved no easy thing. National newspapers and magazines declined to comment on my output. Article outlines, finished pieces, follow-up letters had all been ignored. My tutor suggested concentrating purely on the county's glossy monthly. Build up a portfolio of published work that could be used to woo the nationals later.

So *Dorset Scene* alone provided hope. Peter Swinton is currently in possession of a 1200 word article on Dorset's post-boxes. The idea had been sparked by the chance discovery that the oldest operational post box in the country is located in Dorset. No, really. Further inquiries had led me to Ken Bagwell, a retired postman. By the end of a three hour interview (ill-advisedly held in my own home) I was familiar with every unusual post box in the county: the 'anonymous' box at Sherborne with no royal cipher, the pair of Edward VIIIs in Poole, the Puddletown box with inverted base not to mention the 150 year old octagonal pillar-box at Holwell complete with hinged vertical aperture. By the time Ken had left I'd gleaned enough information to write the post-box article as well as an in-depth psychological piece on the plight of lonely old men. Einstein's theories on the subjective nature of the passage of time were making a lot more sense to me too. Two weeks following my submission of the finished article I am still waiting to hear. It is make or break. If the article is rejected I really don't know what I will do.

At home, I resist the urge to check the sports pages and turn on the computer which takes an age to boot up. I do not waste the time. I slap in a CD and brew some coffee. There are ways of countering the creative strait jacket donned each time I near home. Namely, rousing music and caffeine. The main theme to *True Romance* could prompt a convention of pacifists to enlist and by the time Hans Zimmer is through strutting his stuff there's a large espresso steaming on my desk.

Besides attempting to publish six articles I have also begun working on some ideas for short stories, themselves the precursors, I hope, to an attempt at writing a novel. I have grand ideas of publishing a book that will alter the way people view their world. Since I'm still waiting to hear whether Dorset's post-boxes will be published or passed to the police and filed under 'dangerously deranged' and since it's also unclear whether Tom Chandler ever read my letter - *LOCAL AUTHOR PERISHES IN UNEXPLAINED COTTAGE INFERNO* - fiction would appear to be the best use of my time this morning. It is strange then that, having logged on, I *Google* Tom Chandler. Researching background material for the interview I tell myself.

Chandler's entry in Wikipedia is not particularly illuminating:

Born in 1960, Thomas Godfrey Chandler was raised and educated in north London where he learnt his 'trade' (as he likes to call it) while penning obituaries for a well-known national daily newspaper. He wrote his first novel in his spare time. *The Man Who Banned Christmas* was a well-received historical drama set during the English Civil War. It portrayed Oliver Cromwell as an insensitive bully and was roundly ignored by the general public. It was Chandler's second novel dealing with the assassination of Spencer Percival - the only British prime minister to be murdered whilst in office - that caught the public's attention and elevated him to the bestseller lists. *Death of a Prime Minister*, if unimaginatively entitled, weaves an enthralling fictitious tale of love and betrayal into the real events leading up to the shooting of Perceval in the lobby of the House of Commons on May 11th 1812 by the mentally unstable bankrupt, John Bellingham. Subsequent novels, of which there have been five, have secured Chandler's place in the literary firmament even if they have not quite matched the success of his second book. Tom Chandler lives in London and Devon.

Aside from erroneously moving Chandler's weekend retreat fifteen miles to the west the piece tells me nothing I didn't already know and, more to the point, nothing of particular interest to the editor of a magazine solely concerned with Dorset. But the county's most famous literary resident is not the only string to my bow.

I rattle off an e-mail to Peter Swinton at *Dorset Scene* pitching him my latest idea: an article on Dorset's breweries, past and present. During preliminary investigations I have unearthed several microbreweries in addition to *Hall and Woodhouse* in Blandford and *Palmer's* of Bridport. *Eldridge Pope* in Dorchester may have gone but there's still plenty of beer being brewed in the county. My outline does not do the subject matter justice but I click send all the same. Swinton is no fool, he'll know instinctively whether there's any mileage in the idea or not.

I'm in danger of opening the folder *short stories* when I decide to *Google* Spencer Perceval. It turns out the man warrants my interest for reasons other than his untimely demise. Perceval was, apparently, an expert on Biblical prophecy and for a time worked as a commissioner of bankrupts -interesting considering the financial predicament of his eventual assassin. If there was a link Perceval, for all his knowledge of prophesy, failed to spot it. It seems the man was prime minister in all but name whilst serving in the physically ailing Duke of Portland's Tory administration - he even lived at 10 Downing Street. Perceval came out against Catholic emancipation but his stance on Wilberforce's bill to abolish the slave trade is not made clear. In 1809 a stroke curtailed Portland's political career and Perceval officially became Prime Minister. King George III was mad. Not cross, mad. The new PM feared the Prince Regent would seek to appoint a

Whig replacement. He didn't. During the three remaining years of his life Perceval oversaw Wellington's Peninsular campaign in Iberia and the government response to rioting Luddites at home. He was on his way to the House of Commons in May 1812 when Bellingham shot him through the heart. Perceval's powers of prophecy did not desert him in his hour of need. 'I'm murdered!' he gasped before crumpling to the floor, dead. Bellingham was hanged within the week but not before he had defended himself extremely lucidly for a man described by some historians as mentally unstable. He asked that his actions be a warning to future leaders of the dangers inherent in failing to do *the right thing*, a sentiment enthusiastically endorsed by those attending his public execution and the subscribers to a fund which saw his widow pocket £50,000! *Old money*.

Time for a coffee break. The stove top espresso maker is a pain to clean. I have promised myself something more substantial on the publication of *article six*. Something Italian and impossible to pronounce. I search the kitchen cupboards for food. Hazelnuts. They'll have to do. I'm careful not to chew on the left side of my mouth though. I lost a chunk of tooth last summer eating chocolate - the last time I refrigerated the stuff - and Bombay Mix recently accounted for another piece of my disfigured molar.

Suitably refreshed and buoyed this time by Buddy Rich I feel ready to open *Short Stories.* I have already completed 600 words of 'Love is Not a One-Way Street', the tale of an insensitive couch potato who whisks his girlfriend off to Paris not, as she supposes, to propose marriage but to watch a football match in place of, Dave, his sick best mate. Tight fisted in the extreme, Todd parks his pride and joy, a 1978 TR7, in the Parisian suburbs in order to avoid extortionate city centre parking charges then breaks Susie's heart when he whips out two tickets to a Champions League match during what she thought was a pre-theatre dinner. The climax, which I have yet to write, comes the following day when Todd, accompanied by an irate Susie, recites the name of the street where he parked his car to a taxi driver. Todd is as au fait with the French language as he is with the lore of courtship. The cabbie tells him the address he noted down the day before actually means *one-way street*. Their ferry sails in three hours. Todd has no idea where he left his car. Susie's broken heart isn't exactly bleeding for him. She tosses Todd his ferry ticket and takes the taxi to the Gare Du Nord where the Euro Star, complete with tall, dark, love of her life stranger, is waiting to whisk her home. Just the sort of heart-warming tale that the women's weeklies will snap up. Module four of my writing course: *Research your intended market.*

However, during the next hour my attempts at completing the story are hindered by its inherent flaws, chief amongst them being the cost of a taxi to and from Todd's car as opposed to the parking tariff at the hotel. When I'd run my concerns regarding the respective costs past Beth recently she'd accused me of possessing autistic tendencies. 'Definitely on the *spectrum,*' she'd said. Special Needs co-ordinator she may be but she clearly hasn't read module 5(c) *making your writing believable.*

Before lunch I check my inbox. Peter Swinton makes no mention of my article on post-boxes but does express an interest in my breweries idea. However, he wants me to concentrate on *one* brewery, preferably a 'micro' (*Hall and Woodhouse*, and *Palmer's* have been *done to death*). After the tribulations of the Paris road system this cheers me greatly. I feel extremely good. Confidence swells within me. I *am* a writer. I *can* do this. Consulting my notes, I decide I rather like the sound of the brewery in Beaminster, a tiny operation run by two brothers who, if their website is to be believed, relocated from Wales five years ago. I phone the pub to which the brewery is affiliated and speak to Peter Williams. He seems delighted at the prospect of some free publicity. I, on the other hand, am delighted at the prospect of some free beer. We agree a mutually convenient time a week hence and I hang up.

It is expected that whereas I spend my mornings at home pursuing my writing career the afternoons should be set aside for domestic duties. These include, in ascending order of popularity: dusting, toilet cleaning, vacuuming and ironing. The practice of transfering microscopic particles of desiccated household matter from one surface in a room to another with a yellow rag is to be avoided at all costs whereas the removal of creases from the family's laundry is a chore which I embrace with enthusiasm. Ironing is not a task that requires my undivided attention (even if the odd scorch mark on some of Beth's more delicate tops might suggest otherwise). The smoothing takes place on the second floor in the master bedroom. On a small table by the dormer window sits a combi TV/DVD. Beside it is a box of Discs removed from their bulky plastic packaging and slipped into paper wallets for easy storage. The films date mostly from the 1940s, 50s and 60s when directors like Douglas Sirk were churning out movies for leading men such as Rock Hudson, Glenn Ford, Montgomery Clift, Gregory Peck and my personal favourite, William Holden. While the Bosch X80 works up a head of steam I eject *Sunset Boulevard* from the combi (a machine that lends added weight to Gloria Swanson's claim, 'I *am* big, it's the picture that got small') and replace William Holden with the thoroughly wicked Errol Flynn starring today in the Warner Brothers classic, *Gentleman Jim*. I gather coat hangers and, with wetted finger, check the Bosch is good to go. Ouch. I'm all set. Lights... camera... action!

There is no sign of Sparky when I call in at Zennor Road. In the fridge I find a plate of coley. I remove its cling film covering and place the plate on the floor next to a bowl of water which I immediately lift to replenish. An assortment of dry *Kitty Treats* and a saucer of milk complete my feeding duties although not the evening's work. TLC must now be administered and in Sparky's continued absence I return to the fridge for a beer and sit down to await the big fella's arrival. On the sofa I find one of my newsletters. Published weekly, *Life in Dorset* is a diary of sorts. It is not a personal journal; nor is it great literature. It is living proof that you can't always believe what you read. Despite containing the kernel of truth, a faithful chronicling of the exploits of the Bradley family and their entourage it is not. Some members of the family emerge from its sometimes libellous pages with more credit than others. The narrator for one seems to be a very likeable and mild-mannered chap. His wife and family are a more unpredictable bunch. The hole-punched double sided sheet of A4 I find on the sofa is illustrated by three contemporaneous scanned images. It was written several years ago. It is a prime example of its writer's susceptibility to exaggeration. I begin to read:

Extract from *Life in Dorset* 23rd May 2002.
Mother and son arrive at the Pavilion Theatre, Bournemouth in plenty of time for the evening performance of the highly acclaimed' Straight from the West End' *production of* Grease *twenty-six years after seeing the cinematic version of the world's greatest musical at the Palace Cinema in Crewkerne. Beth took Hatty and Freddie to see the previous incarnation of the theatrical show last year and came back raving about it. When Rose Bradley found out her daughter-in-law had gone without her she was raving about it too. Grease without John Travolta though is like a war without people ready, willing and able to kill other human beings for spurious reasons: Nigh on impossible to stage. Not a viable proposition. This production boasts a former presenter of* You've been Framed *in the leading role and both mother and son are a little perplexed as to how hosting squalid Saturday evening Television qualifies a man for the rigours of playing Danny Zuko. Who's playing Kenicky for Christ's sake? Jeremy Beadle?*

The theatre is packed. At least half the audience can't have been alive when Travolta first strutted his stuff back in '78. The show starts. By the end of the first song I know that something is terribly, terribly wrong. The choreography? No. The orchestration? No. The direction? No. The tub of lard in the leather jacket that can't act or dance? Now we're getting somewhere! Mum's body language leaves me in no doubt that she shares my misgivings. When her rolled up programme narrowly misses Danny Zuko's head I seriously consider escorting her from the auditorium. Zuko has no natural rhythm and appears to be on stilts. He gives the impression that if he tries anything too nifty he'll be delivering his next line from the orchestra pit. Even the Grease groupies two rows in front of us have stopped dancing by the end of the first act. If Danny Zuko isn't jiving why the hell should they?

The interval sees groups of stiff-legged people wandering about the theatre in stunned silence. For a minute I think the second half of the show has started. Mum spent the ten minutes leading up to the interval trying to purloin her neighbour's programme for another crack at Zuko. 'I want to see if I can make the bastard move!' she'd hissed. She is in no mood to behave. I offer to buy her a cup of coffee. On this of all nights though the coffee machine has broken down in the bar and the silent shrugs of the chap behind the counter don't improve Mum's mood even if it's nice to see someone dressed in black actually moving. The doors leading to the car park are locked. We decide to stay for the rest of the show but by the time Zuko has sat out the Rydell High dance-off *(who the hell cast this bloke?!) and failed to do that thing with his hands in his pockets at the end of* You're the One That I Want *Mum is ready to torch the place. Belated attempts by some of the audience to get things swinging by standing up to dance only draw attention to the fact that no one on stage is doing likewise. We leave before Zuko has sashayed off the stage following a decidedly* un*rousing sing-a-long-a-finale, Mum proving unequivocally, as we vacate our seats, that there is more rhythm in her extended middle finger than there is in Danny Zuko's entire body.*

The County Research Centre opens its doors promptly at nine o'clock *Tuesday to Saturday*. By the time I arrive it's nearer 9.30, Mary and her father having earlier conspired to leave the house without book bag and PE kit, necessitating on my part a return trip to St Paul's and a conversation with the decidedly creepy school secretary who had looked at me as if she'd never seen a heavily perspiring man hammering desperately on the school doors before.

The 1950s two storey, red brick building has been my first port of call on a Tuesday morning for some weeks now. At reception I am 'greeted' by Janice, if the badge on this grey haired lady's copious chest can be trusted. She peers at my membership card as though she has never seen it or me before. Beside her is a new face or at least one I have not encountered before: Dark, wavy hair, blue eyes and a warm smile; a definite improvement on Janice. The Centre's policy of stationing unsightly females at the front desk is clearly under review. Janice snatches my membership card and shows it to her companion. 'Make sure you check the membership number *and* the expiry date, Alex,' she says solemnly before returning the dog-eared card. Thus dismissed, I walk to my right, past the coat hooks and lockers and the sign saying 'no bags beyond this point'. No cheap jibes at Janice's expense Hugh, they're beneath you. I scribble my name in the signing-in book and run my eyes up and down the list of those who have arrived ahead of me. James Martin from Massachucetts for instance, currently researching his family history somewhere within one of the Centre's five rooms accessible to the public. Two of these rooms contain the Research Centre's collection of books and periodicals on local subjects. The reading matter is 'organised' using a system that I have yet to make any sense of. Each title bears a letter, usually a 'D', and a number emblazoned on its spine. Volumes bearing identical letter and number combinations tend to crop up in various locations however and it is clear that subject matter and size are only two of several criteria used to decide a title's ultimate location. I am convinced someone is employed specifically to file books in a random manner so as to reduce wear and tear on the centre's stock - if a volume cannot be found it can't be damaged. Volumes that have, despite the staff's best efforts, fallen into the hands of the general public so often that they have become especially delicate can only be viewed in the Archive Reading room which is also where stock of particular value can be perused and this only upon the successful completion of the relevant forms. There is usually a wait and a trip to the Common Room for a coffee is one way of passing the time, although to get there you have to walk back past Janice at reception who has on occasion subjected my membership card to fresh scrutiny. The woman has the memory of a goldfish but none of the charisma.

Today I head straight for the Microfilm Room. Grabbing a blunt pencil from the pot on the Enquiries Desk - '*Yes, could you tell me why there are no fucking pencil sharpeners in the building?*' - I walk across to a row of filing cabinets. The *Dorset County Chronicle* occupies three drawers. Inside, spools of microfilm packaged in card boxes contain consecutive editions of the newspaper covering the period 1824 -1957. I need ideas for articles and I hope to find them here. After all this was where, during the researching of my article on the road tunnel at Charmouth, my thus far disappointing investigations sprang to life. The January 1832 edition had contained a detailed and typically verbose account of the tunnel's opening that had sent a shiver down my spine. I'd only re-discovered the tunnel myself a month or two before. The structure, a memory from my childhood spent in the far west of the county, had literally vanished during my time away from the area accumulating debt and dubious academic qualifications. For several years following my return to the county I would implore family members to keep their eyes peeled whenever we made the thirty minute journey to or through the area. There were those that doubted the tunnel had ever existed. I couldn't understand why it remained so elusive. A report in the local paper regarding the dilemma facing the County Council as to the fate of the old tunnel finally provided the impetus for a more thorough search of the area in question. My mind had played tricks on me. The tunnel was a good three quarters of a mile from where I had supposed it to be. Under a different hill. Beside a different road. A by-pass had been cut through Thistle Hill relegating the tunnel and the stretch of road that ran through it to little more than man-made oxbow lake. Its discovery whetted my appetite for more information. The tunnel became my personal intellectual property. The traveller's vehicles that blocked its western end lent the structure an air of faded grandeur. People needed to be alerted to its plight. The Research Centre seemed as good a place as any to start delving. It was only when I discovered the piece on the tunnel's opening that I began to consider writing an article about it. I still needed more information though. Documentation from the Transportation sub-committee filled in the gaps concerning the events leading up to the tunnel's closure although it was not information that anyone but myself seemed to appreciate hearing. Beth, for the first time, had alluded to the autistic spectrum. Hours spent poring over the notebooks of a local historian (brought to me in the Archive

Reading room together with special latex gloves and laid on protective pillows for my perusal) provided me with anecdotes relating to the tunnel including the mugging of an old lady during the Edwardian era, an attack that led to the tunnel's illumination. Phone calls to the County Council and a meeting with a local farmer who owned the land above the tunnel and part of the way through it completed my researches. I wrote up the article and posted it, together with my own photos and an image from the 1920s I'd procured from the local history society, to Dorset Scene magazine. Peter Swinton promptly accepted it for publication. That, of course, had been almost three months ago. Since then, nothing.

I select microfilm boxes dating back 100 and 150 years respectively in the hope that impending anniversaries may breathe new life into otherwise dull subjects. Attaching the film to one of the antiquated machines used to magnify and illuminate their contents is tricky but in no time I'm rattling through film, looking out for anything of interest. An hour's research yields scant reward. An article on the origins of the name 'Dorset' from 1907 is interesting and could be worth a closer look. The Chronicle is full of advertisements for cold cures and other miraculous remedies. There doesn't appear to be anything for writer's block however.

Replacing the spools I head to one of the reading rooms and check the *periodical articles and book extracts* index contained within a series of narrow drawers that are frustratingly difficult to manoeuvre in and out. The article on Beaminster Brewery will need a preamble of sorts. I could do with some background information on the history of brewing in the county. However, there appear to be no relevant articles. The index for books on the subject is housed in a more easily accessible set of drawers. It cites a couple of useful sounding titles. Finding them is another matter. For that I'll need assistance. The help desk is unoccupied but there's an open door behind it through which I can hear voices. As I reach the desk help arrives. It's Janice's accomplice from reception. I explain my predicament. Alex seems eager to help although upon rounding the desk warns me, 'I'm still getting to grips with the system here myself.' I hand over the index cards. 'What is it with blokes and beer?'

I fall into step. 'I'm doing some research on the county's breweries,' I say.

'Just,' Alex says turning to point a finger at me, 'what an alcoholic would say.'

'I prefer the term dipsomaniac. More classy.'

'Tell that to their friends and family.'

Ouch. I want help locating books not a moral dressing down. But just to set the record straight I say, 'I don't *really* have a drink problem.'

Alex stops abruptly and, ignoring my protestation, takes a prolonged look at the two index cards, running a well manicured finger along each volume's handwritten reference number before bending down and returning to the vertical with a couple of books. 'Here we are: *The Dipso's Guide to Dorset,* and *Places to Get Wasted in Wessex, Volume 2.* Remember, always read responsibly.' With this Alex hands me the books and, squeezing past me, heads back towards the Enquiries Desk. Pleased though I am at this turn of events I'm a little concerned that I may have upset the first person to have been of use to me at the Centre since I began frequenting it. What's more it had only taken seven carelessly phrased words to accomplish. God only knew what damage I could wreak in the finished 1200 word article. This thought dogs me during the half an hour's note-taking and photo-copying that follow. I decide to make amends. A *Thank you for the help,* perhaps on my way past the Enquiries Desk, something like that. I do not get the chance however. Of Alex there is no sign. Coffee break? Sent out to buy pencil sharpeners? Quit in protest at the Centre's unthinking clientele? I leave the building somewhat frustrated at being denied the opportunity to put things right.

Wednesday, 11.30 a.m.: The Travolta starts third time. Not bad. This isn't Le Mans for Christ's sake. It's a damp, cold day but by the time it starts to climb the Ridgeway the Morris Traveller Deluxe is warmed up and approaching top speed. Having rolled off the production line in 1968 it is no spring chicken. Though susceptible to folly, even I hadn't been taken in by the *one lady owner* boast in the free ads. Nor had I trusted the bearded chancer reeking of nicotine with whom I'd haggled over the asking price (or believed his repeated references to a frail old mother and her rising winter fuel bills). The car's rear external ash frame was partially rotted and I'd suspected, with just cause as it turned out, that the bodywork's impressive rust free rigidity owed as much to filler and fibre glass as it did to the magnetic material from which it was originally constructed. Still, the asking price wasn't *that* unreasonable and I knew from a fortnight's acquaintance with Glass's used car price guide that Morris Travellers tended to hold their value. It hadn't broken down when I took it for a test drive and the interior appeared to be as well cared for as the exterior even if several cigarette butts had sprung at me from the ashtray when I'd finally managed to prise it open. 'Mum's been trying to give 'em up for years,' the vendor had remarked sheepishly.

Geographically Pebble Bay Primary School is thirteen miles from home. Culturally the distance would be better measured in parsecs. Portland is famous for two things: its quarries and its prisons. Crossing the causeway and driving past the old naval base, its former barracks still awaiting re-development, what first catches the eye are the road signs directing visitors to the various penal establishments situated on, beneath or beside the isle. A prison ship is moored in the harbour bobbing in the shadow of the Manor's highest point, itself re-modelled to accommodate the subterranean gaol beneath. On a windswept plateau to the south a Victorian facility houses some of the country's finest young offenders. All sign-posted for easy access. Getting out of course is a different matter. The route to Pebble Bay Primary School is not demarcated. An oversight in the view of some.

The school car park is full when I arrive so I leave the Travolta on the road outside and descend the steps to the front door noting for the first time how easy it would be to gain access to the roof from this relatively elevated position. Brenda buzzes me in, the new entry code having temporarily eluded me. Having exchanged pleasantries – 'Joan Masters is emigrating!' - Brenda rings the lunch bell and I head for Class Five where I encounter pupils spilling into the corridor with the same sense of decorum as rabid beasts fleeing a forest fire.

My partner in crime, Luke Johnstone, sits in a

meditative state behind our desk. 'My work here is done,' he says, catching sight of me.

I notice half a dozen reprobates hunched over dictionaries scribbling feverishly in far flung corners of the room. Luke follows my gaze. 'Observe, Grasshopper,' he says, 'the path to nirvana: '*de*tention, *de*tention, *de*tention.'

I ignore this swipe at past, ill-advised, attempts at discussing matters of the spirit and plonk my bag on the desk. Luke stands. He motions to the chair he has just vacated, and in a strong West Yorkshire accent says, 'All yours mate.' Although only three inches taller than myself Luke is a different physical specimen entirely. Good looking and solidly built the man once played Loose Forward for the Leeds Polytechnic rugby league team. There was apparently talk of his turning out for the city's professional side whose ground was less than half a mile from the polytechnic's Headingley campus. The idea of being paid good money to throw his weight about on a rugby pitch sporting the blue and amber of the team he had supported as a boy had appealed to Luke; the training regime that would ensure he didn't leave the pitch on a stretcher hadn't. 'You've got to graft,' he told me, 'you've got to be bloody fit.' *Bludeh fit.* 'It's not like your game, *kick and clap*. Biggest danger to a winger in Union is getting frostbite while hoping to God the fly-half decides against hoofing the bloody ball into touch again.' *Your game* Luke had called it. I'd sat 'A' levels more recently than the last time I turned out for my house fifteen.

It had quickly become clear to me that Luke conducted his personal and sporting lives in a similar vein. In short, he put himself about. *What you see is what you get* is the man's motto. It could just as easily be, *What I see is what I get.* His handsome features attract the interest of the opposite sex in much the same way that a rampaging run from the back of the scrum once drew the attention of tacklers from the opposing team. Bodily fluids tended to be spilt either way. The similarities ended there. A hand shake and a pint and the travails of a rugby match were as easily cast off as Luke's muddied shirt: number thirteen. Unlucky for some. His personal life was not so easily mended. A series of affairs had put paid to his marriage and although Luke's private life had recently encountered calmer waters it had rounded an emotional Cape Horn getting there. That the voyage had begun under my roof meant for some I was complicit.

The same attitude applied *in* school as well as *out*. We lived and died by each other's successes and failures. It helped that we'd always got on. That we'd ever share a classroom had never entered my head though. At least not until talk of redundancy lent the school the air of a Saturday night talent show moments after the phone lines have closed. The school had, in Local Authority parlance, been *haemorrhaging children* for some time. A falling roll attracts the wrong kind of attention from the suits at county hall. For a time there were rumours that Sue might go. She stood her ground however. It was a good school, she'd argued and what was more she was the person to lead it out of trying times. Prospective parents seemed not to agree. Class sizes continued to shrink. The school's budget followed suit and the suits began to circle. There would have to be a redundancy. At a tense staff meeting Sue outlined the complicated procedures involved including the option of voluntary redundancy. One or two members of staff had expressed an interest in falling on their swords but their enthusiasm waned somewhat when they heard details of the packages on offer. If no one was prepared to walk then someone would have to be pushed. Sue assured us the decision would not be compromised by emotion. It would be discussed by the governors who would consider the qualities and responsibilities of individual members of the teaching staff before deciding who the school would miss least. The Literacy, Maths, Science and ICT co-ordinators appeared to be safe. As RE co-ordinator my place in the school hierarchy fell somewhere between Margaret, the grumpy dinner lady and Mrs Chapman, the foul-mouthed old girl who came in voluntarily every Friday to hear children read. In short I did not rate my chances of making the cut. As PE co-ordinator, Luke felt the same about his own prospects. During an evening spent mulling things over at the Dolphin we'd come to the conclusion that one of us was for the chop. Hungover the next day, Luke claimed to have a plan.

'Neither of us can risk losing our jobs,' he said, nursing both his head and a black coffee in the staff room before registration.

'But someone, and probably one of us, has to,' I reminded him unnecessarily.

'That, my friend, is the beauty of my plan,' he replied.

Which in essence was this: Instead of a redundancy the school would create a job-share. No one would lose their jobs. Instead Luke and I would go part-time. Any short fall in salary could be partially alleviated by supply work undertaken during the portion of the week we were no longer needed at the school. Even if supply work proved difficult to come by a part-time wage was still better than no wage at all. The idea made sense. The prospect of a curtailed working week particularly appealed to me. Its success though depended on the consent of others. Beth for one. At the time my wife was herself part-time but Dorchester First School was experiencing difficulties of a different kind. The post of Deputy Head was proving a problematic one to fill. Two rounds of interviews had failed to yield a suitable candidate. The situation at Pebble Bay prompted Beth to admit that Nigel, the Head, had recently all but begged her to take on the role. From such synchronicities are our lives nourished. I think that's how I put it to my wife anyway. With Beth on a deputy's salary and me part-time our joint income would actually rise if the job-share got the go ahead. There were still some people to convince however. But the governors did not keep us waiting long. Directed by Sue, they jumped at the idea primarily, I suspect, because setting up a job-share was a hell of a lot easier than negotiating a path through the minefield of redundancy. In addition, the humiliation of having to lay off teaching staff could be avoided.

The rest as they say is history (a subject I subsequently volunteered to co-ordinate in addition to RE in order to boost my professional cachet in the event of further staffing culls).

Today. Progress through the note book we use to communicate important information to one another is slow. Screams from the playground do not help nor does the staggered arrival at the desk of penitent miscreants bearing etymological jottings. I can tell there's something on Luke's mind as he absentmindedly leads me through the burgeoning *things to do* list. The last of the wrong-doers is gone before he says, 'Jen's in Year Two today.'

'I thought I saw her car outside,' I reply.

'Why the hell does she have to do supply *here*?' he asks me.

'She did used to work here,' I remind him.

'She quit!'

'Only because she couldn't face seeing you anymore.'

'Thought we'd both moved on that's all.'

'Maybe that's why she's doing so much supply. What's the matter? You're not developing a conscience are you?'

By 12.45 Luke is gone leaving behind him Olympian coffee rings on our desk and black rubber scars across the staff car park. My attempts to prepare for the afternoon's lessons are hampered by a burning desire to be somewhere else as well as interruptions from other members of staff suffering from what Sue Warden drolly calls *midweek myopia,* a seriously debilitating condition capable of inducing in a teacher thoughts of self-harm. The beginning of the week, approached if not with energy and enthusiasm then at least with an untarnished mind, is a fading memory while the weekend to come is too remote to contemplate. Like a ship adrift mid-ocean neither departure point nor destination is discernible. Unable to recall the previous weekend's revelries or to give credence to crazy prophesy suggesting another weekend will eventually follow a crew can lose perspective, start to behave irrationally.

'Hugh, I need those reading test scores today!' Lorraine Hopkins enters the classroom more like Stanley Kowalski than a placid fifty-two year old mother of three. She has a clip board in her hands but it may as well be a length of lead pipe. 'Sue's on my back. I need your reading test results today!' *Better still, yesterday ass hole.*

'Was *Goodfellas* on the TV last night?' I ask. I keep my eyes on the clip board. Tracey's knuckles are white. I want to retract the Goodfellas quip. *Mrs Hopkins, with the clip board, in Class Five: Cluedo!*

'I'm coming back at four,' she calls over her shoulder once it becomes apparent I haven't got what she needs. Plenty of time, I think. It'll be a bit of a push but I'm sure I can be packed up and gone by then.

Midweek myopia is particularly virulent the first couple of weeks of a new term. Before the lunch break is over I catch the end of a conversation between Keith Aston and Katherine Jones, Head of Key Stage One, as they hurry from the staff room to their respective classes. 'No, Katherine,' Keith says, 'the stationery order never went off.' Something in the timbre of Keith's voice saves him the effort of appending the word *bitch* to this statement.

'Well, Keith the oversight was certainly *not* mine!' Likewise Katherine's intonation spares her the hassle of being so impolite as to conclude her reply with *bastard.*

'We'll speak later, Katherine.' *Bitch.*

'I want to get to the bottom of this, Keith.' *Bastard.*

Teaching on a Wednesday afternoon is not so dissimilar to the Friday afternoon experience. The children suffer from their own midweek contagion. It can be unpleasant to minister to. This term in science we are learning about sound.

'How does sound travel?' I ask the class.

'In waves, sir!'

'Waves like the ones outside?'

'No, Mr Bradley, like the ones on a slinky.'

'You mean all tangled up, sir?'

'My slinky doesn't go down stairs properly!'

'George Barnes *stole* my slinky.'

'No I didn't!'

'Yes you bloody did!'

'Does anyone know how we hear sound?' I ask when the case of the stolen slinky has been less than satisfactorily settled .

Silence. *Hello? Can anyone hear me?*

'It goes in our ear sir.'

'And?'

Continues unmolested straight out the other side?

I distribute diagrams of the inner ear and talk through what can be seen. 'The outer ear collects sounds,' I say, 'which travel down the ear canal where, incidentally, ear wax is produced.'

'Ear wax tastes disgusting, sir!'

'That's because it wasn't designed as a source of sustenance Caleb.'

'You're not supposed to eat it you moron!'

'The middle ear's job,' I say, raising my voice, 'is to turn the sound waves into vibrations. The eardrum does this, causing three tiny bones – the hammer, anvil and stirrup - to move. The vibrations enter the cochlea which is filled with liquid and covered in microscopic hairs. It's these hair cells that create nerve signals that our brains 'hear' as sound. Copy the diagram into your books and label it neatly.'

I begin to move around the room checking for early signs of poor work. 'Yes, Jenny?'

'Did you say the brain turns the vibrations into sound, sir?'

'That's right,' I say, seizing the chance to go beyond the Key Stage 2 curriculum, 'It's the brain that hears, not our ears. It's the brain that creates *sound* rather than the source of the *sound* waves. Until our brain interprets the vibrations in our ears there is no sound.'

So, as you can see Jenny the seventeenth century Irish philosopher, George Berkeley was right, 'The objects of sense exist only when they are perceived'. Though subjected to much derision at the time, Berkeley's insight was eventually endorsed by scientists. The magazine, Scientific American posed this question Jenny, If a tree were to fall to the ground on an uninhabited island, would there be any sound? And the answer? 'Sound is vibration, transmitted to our senses through the mechanism of the ear, and recognised as sound only at our nerve centers. The falling of the tree or any other disturbance will produce vibration of the air. If there be no ears to hear, there will be no sound.' Two hundred years before this, Berkeley had stated, 'The trees... are in the garden...no longer than while there is somebody to perceive them.' In America, Jenny they ended up naming a university after Berkeley although they've been pronouncing his name wrong ever since.

Thursday morning. Don is fixing the fence in the car park when I roll up in the Travolta. 'More graffiti on the roof,' he tells me in lieu of a greeting.

I couldn't give a shit Don. 'Really?' I reply, scanning the vicinity for Don's tin hat.

'Yeah and someone's been playing silly buggers with this fence.'

'Well it's not one of the teachers,' I tell him, beginning my walk towards the school building, 'we're digging a tunnel.'

Thursday morning means whole school assembly. Sue Warden presides; the rest of us are there for crowd control. The assembly is mind numbingly tedious. I consider taking my own life. A length of rope slung over one of the beams above my head. Don's step-ladders spread beneath. A couple of kids to hold it steady. 3,2,1…

I snap back to the here and now and glance along one of the rows of children that I'm supposed to be policing. Jamie Goddard, the maddest, baddest boy in the school, is pointing two fingers at me, his thumb cocked. Smiling, he jerks the fingers upwards releasing an imaginary bullet. Several more rounds follow.

My maths lesson is interrupted by the fire bell. I'm not aware there's a drill scheduled but then we're not always told. I've never seen my maths group leave the class room in so orderly a fashion. Do they know something I don't? Lined up in the playground we wait for Sue Warden to appear. When she does her demeanour suggests if it is a drill no one told her. She doesn't let on to the children however, congratulating them on their quick and relatively peaceful exit from the building. Out here in the playground it's very pleasant. Blue sky, no breeze, the scene unadulterated by the school's wearisome jetsam: the screams of children and the barked instructions of their masters. Just the sound of the relentless surf below and the soaring gulls overhead. Bastards. No one seems in too much of a hurry to go back inside. At length Keith appears. I hadn't even registered his absence. He shakes his head as he approaches Sue. A brief mumbled conversation follows. Frowns all round. Drill or no drill the interlude is much appreciated by pupils and staff alike. There are only fifteen minutes of the first period remaining when we file solemnly back into class.

Break time in the staff room: a chance to recount anecdotes, to seek advice from empathetic colleagues and to listen to the teaching assistants quote Sue's response to their latest request for a dishwasher.

'Fuck off!' The words emanate not from Pebble Bay's headteacher but from the playground where there seems to be a dispute of sorts raging between two pupils.

'Who's on duty?' Lorraine Hopkins asks.

Keith has his head out the window. 'Sue. She's taking notes,' he says, referring to our leader's habit of recording bad behaviour as opposed to dealing with it. I join Keith at the window in time to see George Brownton (messed up and violent - Year Six) sneer at his headteacher before making an aggressive gesture with his arm and stalking off.

Keith looks at me and snorts. 'Stop the world I want to get off.'

I'm about to sit down when I notice steam billowing from the kettle. 'Never mind a dishwasher,' I say to those assembled, 'we need a kettle than can turn itself off first!'

'So what's the deal with the fire alarm, Keith?' Lorraine asks, her tone in marked contrast to the one employed in my classroom yesterday. For a man who has revealed his wife's more distinguishing physical features to the entire upper school Keith seems surprisingly reticent. He glances out of the window. 'Sue doesn't want this broadcasting,' he says. 'But Chloe Barton set the alarm off.'

'Why would she do that?' Lorraine asks. *Have you taught the girl for Christ's sake?*

'Oh, it wasn't on purpose,' Keith replies. For a moment I feel guilt. Shame at having judged the ten-year-old so harshly. 'No,' Keith continues, 'her cigarette triggered the smoke detectors in the toilets.'

I am a selective blephoraspastic. At least Beth says I am. And no, I'd never heard of the word either. It turns out my wife has a point - as well as a larger vocabulary than I'd previously given her credit for. The condition, *blephoraspasm* hinders a person's ability to open their eyelids. Hence Beth's refrain, 'You only see what you bloody well want to!' I've heard the phrase on numerous occasions. It's not as if I suffer from *presbycusis* - look that one up, Beth. I am most susceptible to the condition on a Monday or Tuesday when, having returned from an exhausting day at school, my wife discovers cobwebs festooning lampshades in rooms I swear I've dusted. The fact that I have, despite my best efforts, failed to see what was staring me in the face is a worry. How, for instance, did I fail to see this latest *domestic responsibilities* bollocking coming?

Mild short-sightedness aside, my optical equipment is in reasonably good order. Pupils, lenses, retinas have all been endorsed at regular intervals by the town's opticians. Messages *are* being relayed to my brain. But on a *need to know* basis. Raised flag stones, oncoming vehicles, my wife's empty wine glass? No problem. Cobwebs and other signs of household neglect? Not so much. Why is this so? The passage of time plays its part. Live with something or someone long enough and their luminous properties diminish. Invisibility aside, their cries for attention go unheard and their scent undetected. When does a husband start to associate his wife with the pattern on the living-room wall paper? When does a wife no longer notice that her husband's breath smells uncannily like canine excrement? When does the familiar simply cease to exist or at best is banished to the blurred edges of our consciousness? And what kind of external stimuli are required to resuscitate it? A bollocking from a loved one? Certainly. A chance remark in a conversation – '*Have you trodden in something Darling?'* An unexpected departure from routine?

The cataracts afflicting the inattentive mind can be removed, blephoraspasm permitting, in the blink of an eye. Provided we know they're there. Their acquisition can be so gradual that their presence goes undetected. How many times have I driven to Pebble Bay Primary School and wondered how the hell I got there? Or for that matter, why. How many times have I headed west along the A35 with my eyes to all intents and purposes closed? Today they are wide open. The external stimulus? A letter from Peter Swinton at Dorset Scene magazine. My article on the post-boxes is to be published! A couple of articles on subjects of an historical nature under my belt, and relics of the past are practically throwing themselves under the wheels of the Travolta, itself a relic of sorts. Heading towards Bridport on a wet Monday morning, eighteenth century toll-houses, World War II pill boxes, dilapidated tithe barns and a host of other paraphernalia of the past jostle for my attention. I lose count of the number of milestones I pass. Articles crying out to be written.

Turning right on the outskirts of Bridport I realise that the road I'm on, constructed in the 1980s, is actually laid on the former track bed of the old branch line from Maiden Newton, closed now these past thirty years. A cobweb at three paces? No chance. But show me a weathered piece of stone or a gate post fashioned from a railway sleeper and I'm suddenly 20:20. Fighter pilot material. The human equivalent of a great horned owl reared on carotenoids.

I arrive in Beaminster half an hour early for my interview with Peter Williams and, having ascertained the location of the microbrewery, hole up in a café on the main square. Sipping an americano I absentmindedly slip a few sachets of sugar into my jacket pocket and let my eyes adjust to their surroundings. I check the ceiling and light fittings for cobwebs. I notice with some satisfaction a few silken creepers dangling above a floral display on top of a piano. A piano! Jesus, where did that come from? I turn my attention to the main square outside. Surrounded on four sides by decorative buildings that include shops, houses and pubs, the square is an attractive if sparsely populated sight. I recall that Beaminster and in particular this very plaza featured briefly in John Wyndham's book, *The Day of the Triffids*. The square is as *void of life* today as it was when visited by the characters in the novel - it's amazing how similar are a wet Monday in February and the day after a cataclysmic meteor shower.

Gradually the sense of well-being inspired by the morning's post is amplified by the caffeine's clandestine infiltration of my arteries where its up-beat manifesto inspires localised euphoria. Researching an article is terrific fun. The words, 'My name is Hugh Bradley and I'm writing an article for Dorset Scene magazine,' open doors. At least in this part of the world. Compared to the humdrum nature of the other half of my working week, stuck on a rock jutting out into the English Channel, my researches are akin to the exploration of an exotic paradise. The realm of tunnels, post boxes and microbreweries is one populated by diverse folk. Who knew where they might lead me?

At 10.15 precisely I walk across the main square and bang on the door of Quinnell's Bar which is situated next to a tired looking fish and chip shop. Peter Williams is a big man. He practically fills the doorway once he has belatedly acknowledged my knocking. 'Hugh?' he says. *Yew?* 'Peter, pleased to meet you.' *Chew.* He leads me down a corridor and through a door that opens not into a cosy bar room but into a brightly lit fish and chip shop. It takes me a moment to orientate myself. 'This is Michael,' Peter says pointing at another large man, quite clearly his brother, employed not in the preparation of real ales but in the dipping of fish fillets into batter mixture.

'Excuse me if I don't shake hands,' the brother says, smiling warmly, 'but someone's got to do the work around here.' *Round yer.* With this he flicks batter at Peter who ushers me quickly on.

'You're probably wondering where the brewery is,' he says as we pass buckets of peeled and chipped potatoes.

Fucking right I am.

'Not at all,' I assure him.

'Follow me.' We walk into a back-room containing a stainless steel sink, several more buckets of chips as well as trays of soft drinks stacked from the slippery floor to the stained, strip-lit ceiling. 'Nearly there,' he says as we pass through an open door into a large back yard. A narrow gangway leads between piles of debris to a flight of steps and up to a tract of waste-ground upon which stands a garden shed.

You've got to be kidding.

'We used to do the brewing in the old yarn mill down the road,' Peter explains after I've narrowly avoided breaking my neck on the litter strewn steps. 'But spores kept getting into the beer. This is much better.'

Than a listed building with a vaulted brick ceiling? The beer had better taste really good.

Inside the shed/brewery Peter begins to identify the equipment he and Michael employ in the production of their beer. This does not require a great deal of effort on my host's part since, from where the two of us stand on an unidentified length of hose in the middle of the room, we can touch almost everything else (although in the interests of self-preservation I make a point of resisting the urge). To our left and just inside the entrance is a *mash tun* 'where we add malt to the Burtonised water.' Peter gives the cylindrical metallic tank an affectionate pat. *Now wash your hands.*

'Burtonised water?'

'Water,' Peter tells me, 'that has been artificially enhanced to bring it up to the standard of the water at Burton-on-Trent.' I look around for the text book he's reading from. 'Water that is considered to be of an exemplary quality.' The Welsh accent lends Peter's pronunciation of *exemplary* a poetic quality. A hose leads from the mash tun to a *copper* which, my guide explains, is where the wort is heated.

'Wort? I say sounding like a retired colonel requesting elucidation.

'When the water is mixed with the malt it becomes the wort.'

I'm with you.

'Just before the wort boils we add hops.'

Ops boyo isn't it now. Peter's accent is at times almost indecipherable.

'The hops are boiled for exactly an hour. Then we check the original gravity.'

Now that I've heard of.

'If the gravity is too high we dilute the wort. Then we let it cool a little and add more hops. For aroma, see?'

The next piece of equipment is hidden behind the copper and I don't get a clear view of it which is a shame because anything bearing the name *plate heat exchanger* sounds worthy of attention. It seems that rather than being some machine used by nuclear physicists to alter the space/time continuum, the plate heat exchanger is actually used to both cool the brew and heat the next batch of *Burtonised* water.

'Am I going too fast?' Peter asks me when my pencil

lead snaps and I pause, fumbling about in my pocket for a replacement.

'What's this?' I ask, nodding towards another metallic tank at the very back of the shed in order to demonstrate that I have everything under control.

'The fermenting vessel. When the liquid is about 16 degrees Celsius we pour it into that and add yeast. We call it *pitching* the yeast.'

And at what point do you add the potato peelings and batter scraps?

'Wort?' I say before correcting myself, 'what?'

'Why don't we finish this in Quinnell's Bar?'

You mean it really exists?

Before we go I snap a few pictures of the interior of the brewery and then, outside, ask Peter to stand behind a couple of firkins bearing the *Beaminster Brewery* logo. *There is no way Peter Swinton is going to put these in his magazine.*

Quinnell's Bar turns out to be located above the fish and chip shop which Michael appears to be on the brink of opening when we again pass his way. We ascend a flight of stairs that doubles back on itself. After the disappointment of discovering that my *master brewers* peddle fast food and ply their trade in a ramshackle wendy house I'm not expecting much. As it is Quinnell's Bar exceeds expectations. 'Wow!' I gush as we enter. About forty feet in length there is no single feature that prompts this reaction. Rather it is the amalgam of real fire (already stoked and glowing), low, stripped-beamed ceiling, distressed floorboards (with furniture to match) and antique wall mounted enamelled advertisements. The bar itself is situated to the left of the door through which we enter and is little more than a hatch fronted by a couple of high stools.

'Take a seat,' Peter commands.

By the time I've clambered onto one of the stools my host has appeared behind the bar and is pulling on a pump. He places a half pint glass filled with a golden coloured liquid before me.

'What have we here?' I say lifting the glass for closer inspection and, determined to employ my burgeoning brewing vocabulary (even if only for humorous purposes) add, 'wort? Fermented brew?' *Golden Ambrosial nectar?*

Peter looks at me. 'It's beer,' he says, 'try some.'

If the name on the pump is anything to go by the beer I'm about to taste is called *56. What, Proof?*

'*56*?' I say taking a sip.

'Named after the number on the front door,' Peter says.

The beer is decidedly pleasant. I'm relieved that I don't have to lie when I inform him that I'm impressed. I tease from Peter a description of the beer that might impress the more discerning of Dorset Scene's readers.

'It's a light citrus beer that gets its distinctive taste from the Styrian Golding hops.'

That'll do nicely. I make a note of the alcohol content printed on the pump label. Before I can finish *56* another glass is placed in front of me.

'This is drier and stronger,' Peter says without prompting. 'It's called *Tunnel Ale* on account of the old tunnel up the road and its dark colour.'

Peter is not referring to the Charmouth tunnel but another that passes beneath Horn Hill a mile or so to the north that I intend visiting after I've left the brewery. Assuming that is I'm not too pissed to drive. Tunnel Ale is even more palatable than *56*. 'Nice,' I say. *That's the best adjective you can come up with?* I make a note of the beer's name. *Tunnel Ale, 56.* The christening of the ales on a local theme appeals.
'How many beers do you brew?' I ask.
'Just the two,' Peter says, 'but we're developing a third at the moment.'

Yes, Cod and Chips Twice *will be full-bodied and exude the scent of burnt caramel.*

I question Peter about Quinnell's Bar which, it turns out, is named in honour of his grandmother, herself a relative of a former Welsh international rugby player. Peter takes down a photo from the wall behind the bar. The familial resemblance is irrefutable. There aren't many women who can hold a rugby ball in one hand. Replacing the picture he takes up from where he left off in the brewery. I make notes on the fermenting process, jotting down useful terms such as *cropping the yeast* and *remote cooler.* Half an hour later I have everything I need.

'I'll take you downstairs,' Peter says handing me a couple of spare pump labels that I suspect will illustrate the article rather better than the photos I snapped outside. Back in the chip shop the brothers are keen to know two things: when will the article be published and what do I want for my lunch?

Extract from *Life in Dorset Life,* 17th March 1999.
A shopping trip to Bournemouth with Mum begins with a nose around the shops at Westbourne. In the bookshop my mother suddenly squeals excitedly. I'm confused: the new Penny Vincenzi isn't due out for months yet. 'Bob!' Rose Bradley cries. She starts running towards the man standing behind the till. She lunges forward, discarding items of clothing in the process as a glint of recognition establishes itself in the eyes of the now smiling man. With one bound my sixty year old mother clears the counter. She and the man embrace. 'Bob' kisses her. Long and hard. Time stands still. Behind me someone is humming Lara's Theme. To my left, Hatty places the back of a hand against her forehead and passes out mumbling something along the lines of, 'Jim-Bob gonna hit the bloody roof!' Later, drinking coffee at a café in the Victorian arcade around the corner, my mother attempts to play down events while reapplying her smeared lipstick and adjusting her clothing. 'Bob's just a book rep who used to visit the shop in Sherborne,' she says. Hatty is not convinced. 'Why man use tongue when kissing Grandma?' she asks.

I call round at Zennor Road late Saturday morning. I've not heard anything from my parents all week. My knock goes unanswered. The side door is unlocked. This in itself is strange. Inside the kitchen it's very warm. I smell the delicious concoction bubbling on the stove before I see it. 'Hello?' I call and walk towards the front of the house. I hear movement above me. I repeat my greeting, louder this time. The living-room is deserted. Something catches my eye on the coffee table though, a word traced into the layer of dust that has settled on its surface. A word seldom heard in polite conversation. Its communication via the current media is, as far as I know, unprecedented. The footsteps I hear on the stairs turn out to be my mother's. We come face to face as she reaches the ground floor. She looks surprised to see me. Normally I would mark such reunions with a greeting of some sort. But not today. 'Mum,' I say, 'who wrote *cunt* on the coffee table?'

Hand on heart, my mother attempts to catch her breath. 'I didn't hear you come in!' she says. She takes a second or two to compose herself. 'Do you want some lunch. There's soup.'

My mother's potato and leek soup is a legend within its own *best before* date. Likewise her lentil-and-carrot and her tomato-and-red-pepper. We sit down to eat. A hunk of french bread appears beside me on the table. 'I can warm it up if you like.'

'Don't worry,' I reply, 'unless you want it warm.'

'No, I'm just having soup.'

My mother suffers from oesophageal achalasia. For as long as I can remember she has struggled to swallow her food. The severity of her complaint varies unpredictably but bread tends to be the first food crossed off her personal *carte du jour* whenever the problem escalates. In such circumstances my mother is forced to eat slowly, masticate meticulously, and drink excessively between mouthfuls. Hence her predilection for stage managed natural pauses during meals. Soup is a prominent constituent of her diet at such times. Over the years she has ingested barium solutions, undergone oesophageal motility studies and submitted to surgical procedures without complaint. Her reward: temporary alleviation of a condition that has recently shown signs of unparalleled deterioration. My mother's GP likes to be kept abreast of such developments. Compliance on the part of my mother tends to follow a period of persistent cajoling. Not something I wish to attempt at the moment. Today I have other fish to fry. I'm demolishing seconds before I bring up the coffee table again. 'I see you've been doing some dusting?'

'*Not* according to your father.'

'Where is he?'

'In the garage. And he'll stay there if he knows

what's good for him.' My mother's voice cracks slightly. While I polish off my soup she explains the chain of events that ultimately led to the defacing of the coffee table. It seems that in erecting a new curtain pole Jim-Bob had drilled holes in the wall above the large bay window in the lounge. His work complete, he had then cleaned up with the same attention to detail exhibited by a burglar who has just seen the landing light go on. Next morning it was Jim-Bob, not his wife, who had noticed the besmirched coffee table. Failing to connect the covering of dust with his blue collar activities of the day before he'd asked his beloved when the front room had last been dusted. A question he would come to regret. This, on top of my father's reluctance to sanction a weekend away to commemorate my parents' impending forty-fifth wedding anniversary, had restricted communication to the exchange of essential utterances and the etching of obscenities into geographically significant household surfaces. 'You should see,' Mum says proudly, 'what I wrote on the bedside table in the spare room.' Where my father no doubt currently passes the hours of darkness. 'We never *go* anywhere,' my mother says, the glint of triumph in her eye turning abruptly to one of defeat. Pity consumes me.

'Why don't we go to the cinema tonight? I say, 'there's bound to be something on at The Plaza.' My mother's face lights up. She goes in search of the local paper to check the listings.

My father has still yet to make an appearance but then he's pretty much self-sufficient in the garage which also doubles as workshop and sanctuary. Kettle, hot plate, emergency food supplies stockpiled for periods of civil unrest (like now), the garage is equipped to deal with any emergency - my father sulked for a week when fears regarding the *Millennium Bug* proved unfounded. 'I'd better say *hello* to Dad.' I shrug apologetically to my mother who has by this time donned reading glasses.

The side door into the garage is locked. The lights are out. Jim-Bob is not at home. There's no sign of him in the garden either. Back inside, Mum reels off a short list of films currently showing. I suggest the film with the latest starting time to give me the opportunity to fulfil my domestic obligations and explain to Beth why I'm deserting her on a Saturday night. 'I'll pick you up at eight,' I say as I leave.

I need some historical nuggets for the introduction to my article on Beaminster Brewery. The technical portion of the piece, dealing with the production of the beer, is already written while a description of Quinnell's bar awaits its final draft. I have decided to make no mention of the fish and chip shop. Peter Williams has promised to let me have some information on the environmental impact of small-scale brewing - water consumption and the management of waste products - but what the article lacks is historical context. At the Research Centre I sign in at the front desk - *Oh for God's sake Janice smile* - and head for the common room where I order a double espresso forgetting that *to go* is not an option.

'You mean *to spill*, don't you?' the grey-haired lady behind the counter smiles but there is a *rules are rules* edge to her voice. I point out that unscrupulous dealers have been using coffee to artificially age their books for years.

'If I'm really slap dash,' I say, 'I could probably double the value of your stock.' The economics of such a strategy are called into question by the escalating price of the Centre's coffee. I examine my change before depositing the transaction's meagre pecuniary waste in an RNIB collection box next to the till. Turning to find a table, I spot Alex approaching.

'What are you doing here? We're not licensed you know.'

'This,' I say holding up my coffee, 'is my only vice.' I beam broadly hoping the fib together with my genial facial expression will undo any offence caused on the occasion of my last visit.

'How dull. Anyway, I'm glad I saw you. I managed to track down another couple of books that might be of use to you.' Alex rummages about in a pocket from which a scrap of paper is plucked. I glance at the piece of paper. The handwriting is neater than my own and the books' pseudo-scholarly titles suggest they may well be worth digging out.

'Thanks for your help, I say, 'I really appreciate it.'

'What exactly are you researching breweries for anyway?'

Hello, my name's Hugh Bradley and I'm researching an article for Dorset Scene magazine.

Spiel over, Alex seems suitably impressed. 'I'll be at the front desk if you need help locating them.'

What are the chances?

I sit down at a table next to a window with a view of the road outside. I rest my arm on the window sill but retract it when I realise a pool of water has gathered on its uneven surface. Condensation? The window's rotting frame would suggest a leak. I consider returning to the service counter to discuss the danger acid rain poses to the Centre's book collection but decide against it. I read the reference numbers for the books Alex has jotted down, finish my espresso and head for reception. 'I think I'll need your help,' I say waving the scrap of paper in the air like the white flag of surrender, 'either yours or the gang's at Bletchley Park.'

'Be with you in two ticks,' Alex replies, 'once I'm through helping Janice scare the hell out of the new arrivals.' I have never seen Janice smile before. I find myself smiling too though whether this is the humour, a caffeine rush or some other form of intoxication I cannot say.

'Let's go.' Alex is already up and leading the way. I'm led between tall canyons of books to uncharted regions of Reading Room Two. The area is inhabited by strange life forms: a pale, bespectacled old gent squinting in the dim light, a younger, androgynous creature perusing the shelves: a bearded, gnome-like man mining the scholarly seams, clutching tightly to his chest the spoils of his excavations.

'Shouldn't we be unwinding a ball of twine as we go?' I call to Alex a few paces ahead of me. Just beyond the next gap in the shelving Alex stops. By the time I catch up I'm being handed a book. I've barely had time to read the title than I receive another. I blow several inches of dust from its uppermost edge. I blink as some of the dirt, possibly the desiccated remains of the last person to read it enters my eye. I try not to make a fuss but tears stream down my cheek.

'Here,' Alex says removing a tissue from a pocket and dabbing at my cheek.

I say thanks, take the tissue and pat my eye. I'm finding it hard to see; my vision is blurred. In the half gloom Alex seems to be smiling at me.

I pick my mother up at eight. 'Where's Dad?' I ask, hopeful that some kind of reconciliation has been effected in my absence.

'At the dentist.'

I check my mother's forehead for signs of teeth marks. To my knowledge she's never head-butted anybody before.

'A check up,' she says reading my thoughts. 'They've started holding evening surgeries.'

'Does he know we're going to the cinema?'

'No.'

'You going to leave him a note?'

'Nope.'

I park the Travolta outside The Plaza where it will be handy for a quick getaway afterwards. Or during. My mother is not afraid to cut her cinematic losses. This attitude also applies to live theatre. Especially anything by Harold Pinter. This isn't to say she is hard to please. Film or theatre, anything containing a good-looking leading man, *the fella in the big picture,* will generally hold her attention.

The Plaza dates back to the 1930s although only its drab, grey exterior betrays its art deco origins. During the 1970s it succumbed to the bingo phenomenon. Its auditorium was carved in two, the stalls paradoxically being reserved for those directing their eyes downwards and the balcony for those with a preference for looking up. A smaller second screen replaced the first floor café. This, I learn at the cash desk, is where we will be viewing tonight. While I'm purchasing tickets Mum is placing a drinks order at the concession stand.

'I got you a large one,' she says also handing me a bucket of popcorn, *salt* not *sweet.* She begins the journey upstairs while I attempt to remove a couple of straws from their statically charged paper wrappers. I make a hash of jabbing the blue and white tubes into the drink containers' lids but still manage to catch up with my mother at the door to the *Century Screen.* A bored teenager admits us to the sparsely populated auditorium. The lights begin to dim. Groping our way up the aisle we take our seats in the fifth row. The upholstery is reassuringly familiar, due in part to the frequency of my visits and the fact that I have three of the red velour tip-ups at home. The genuine article, they were purchased for fifteen quid when the larger *Premier Screen* was renovated a few years back.

'This,' Mum whispers, is my favourite bit.' Images begin to flicker across the screen. I nod in agreement. Anticipation. *Nothing is so good as it seems beforehand*: the possibility that what follows could be life changing. The moment is not enhanced by the realisation that I have left my glasses in the Travolta out front. I hand the bucket of popcorn to my mother and excuse myself. The Travolta is where I left it as are my spectacles. However on my return to the *Century Screen* my mother isn't. She's gone. Vanished. There is no sign of intelligent life in the fifth row. There are no clues as to my mother's whereabouts. I stand perplexed in the aisle. It is only when a piece of popcorn bounces off my right temple that I readjust my gaze bringing it to rest on seating several rows back. A second piece of popcorn catches me in the eye. I belatedly don my glasses. Blurred edges sharpen. In the brief lull between advertisements I hear a hissed, 'Over here!' Three rows back I spot her, hand poised to send more kernels my way.

'Not a good time to play hide and seek,' I say slipping into the adjacent seat. I disarm her. 'What's going on?' I look across at our former location.

'Those two were *talkers*.' My mother points at a couple in row four. Relocation is generally a last resort. I assume plan A failed. Normally when my mother tells someone to *shut up* they do as they're told.. We sit through three or four trailers. The screen goes blank. During a wedding ceremony the congregation has the chance to *Speak now or forever hold your peace*. The appearance of the *British Board of Film Censors' certificate* is the cinematic equivalent.

So It Goes

The Regent Cinema, Lyme Regis, 1978. We've driven twelve miles to watch *Close Encounters of the Third Kind*. The Regent has just the one screen. There is no need to allude to the main feature's title when handing over your cash. 'Three for the balcony,' usually suffices. We take our seats. The Film Censors' certificate duly appears. My sister, Louisa and myself are as surprised as anyone to discover we are not after all about to watch Steven Spielberg's box office phenomenon. However, only our mother screams, 'Bloody hell! Not Peter Sellers!' as the opening credits to *Revenge of the Pink Panther* begin to roll.

Tonight there are no surprises. The main feature is as advertised. Half an hour into the film the plot is progressing nicely. The popcorn isn't faring nearly so well. Aside from pelting her son with the stuff, my mother has shown scant interest in the contents of the bucket, shaking her head every time I've jabbed the container in her direction. When my mother refuses salty snacks you know she's *really* struggling to swallow solid food - this is a person who only recently kicked a five packs-a-day *Walkers French Fries* habit. 'You should go and see Dr Ridge,' I hiss above the squeal of car tyres and the roar of gun shots.

My mother frowns.

'No way, ass hole!' On the screen the car chase has prematurely ended and some kind of macho slanging match is taking place between hoodlum and cop.

'I know about the hooker Danny.' A bullet ricochets off the car the cop is crouching behind.

'You don't know squat!' More gunshots, then the sound of scurrying feet on concrete steps.

'You can't,' I say, pausing as a volley of shots is traded, 'ignore this Mum....'

'Fucker!' The hood, the one who is in some way linked to the prostitute goes down clutching his thigh. His revolver slides across the gangway where he has fallen.

'It's not too late, Danny. We can work this out.'

'Fuck off!'

Mum doesn't so much as throw me a sideways glance.

'Don't be stupid!'

Danny is edging closer to his weapon, a trail of blood marking his progress across the floor.

'You need help, Danny. Let me help you.'

'Leave me alone!'

'Call Doctor Ridge.'

'It's not too late.'

'Tell that to Rita, asshole.' Ah, the prostitute.

'She's in intensive care Danny but she's gonna make it.'

'I will, leave me alone.'

'I don't believe you.'

'Listen to me.'

Danny's hand is almost on the revolver. Mum's crooked fingers have a hold of the popcorn carton.

'I'm scared!'

The incidental music reaches a crescendo as Danny flicks the Colt away and the popcorn is unceremoniously emptied into my lap. 'Asshole!'

At home alone during the week I rarely answer the telephone. If Beth needs to get in touch she'll text. Calls tend to be from either telesales reps or old people confused by the single digit difference between our telephone number and the doctors' surgery. If we shared a similar number to the euthanasia clinic I suspect the old buggers would dial with a bit more care. So, when I get back from St Paul's, newspaper in one hand, cup of coffee in the other, and the telephone is ringing I ignore it. The answer-phone cuts in. An unfamiliar male voice follows the beep. 'Hello there. Message for Hugh Bradley. Hi Hugh; Tom Chandler. Got your letter. Sorry it's taken me so long to get back to you...'

I don't so much place my cardboard coffee cup on the dining table as hurl it. If I'm not the first member of the family to leap over the coffee table then the kids have got some explaining to do. I yank the receiver upwards sending the push button cradle to which it is attached crashing to the floor.

'Hello!'

'Hugh?'

'That's right. Sorry, I just got in.'

'Ah.'

'Thanks for getting back to me,' I say when it becomes clear that Chandler is not going to continue. 'I hope you didn't mind me bothering you at your weekend retreat.'

'Not at all, not at all. Forgive the delay.' Chandler's speech is as clipped and economical as his prose. 'Would have got back to you sooner, only I've been abroad for a fortnight. Qui tacet consentire.'

'I've heard it's nice there,' I say.

There's a brief pause before Chandler continues. 'Happy to do the interview,' he says.

'That's great,' I reply.

'Assuming that editor of yours is interested in an old fart like me.'

'I *know* he will be.'

'Have a favour to ask in return though,' the old fart says, 'quid pro quo if you like.'

Latin. Shit. I should have realised.

'The book I'm working on is set...' *during the fall of Rome?* 'in 18th century Bridport. Currently revising the thing and I wanted to check the pub names I've used actually existed when the story's set. Been putting it off for bloody ages. Do it myself but won't be down for a month or so. Said in your letter that you use the County Research Centre a lot.'

'Yes,' I say to demonstrate I'm still listening.

'Wondered if you could check for me.'

'Of course.' At this moment in time I'd agree to anything. *Need to bed your missus old man. That okay? No problem Tom. Which way up would you like her?*

'Got a pen handy?' he asks.

I grab a pen and pad from the floor where they have lain since the conversation's frenetic beginnings. 'Okay,' I say. Chandler reels off a list of five taverns at least one of which sounds familiar. I promise to visit the Research Centre at the earliest opportunity and do some digging although I haven't the faintest idea where I might find the relevant information.

'Very kind,' says Chandler, 'di pia facta vident.' I knew dropping Latin in the Fourth form would come back to haunt me one day. What remains of our conversation is conducted in English. 'Get back to me when you can and we'll fix a date to meet,' Chandler tells me.

'I will,' I assure him. I jot down his London telephone number. 'Thanks for getting back to me.' I say. I replace the receiver and breathe deeply. Bloody hell.

Finishing the Beaminster Brewery article that afternoon proves difficult. I'm distracted. In snooker parlance I'm already mentally lining up the next shot. The body of the article is complete but I need a final paragraph. Something a little less technical than the preceding 1100 words. Online I discover a quote from *The Trumpet Major*, Hardy waxing lyrical about a local beer. Words like *piquant* and *luminous* are bandied about. Perfect. In ten minutes I'm done. I'll give the article a final read through in the morning before submitting it.

Once a month Pebble Bay Primary School decamps en masse to the local church with which it shares loose ties of affiliation. The Reverend John Carter welcomes the opportunity to speak to the youngsters of the parish - he is after all most unlikely to get the chance at Sunday service. For the staff at Pebble Bay it's one more thing to worry about. Despite Sue Warden's best efforts John Carter initially rejected the opportunity to preach at Pebble Bay and in spite of defaced prayer books and a missing candlestick or two continues to insist that his flock come to him. Shepherding it through the narrow streets that separate church and school is not a pleasant experience. I suspect the local population have the last Thursday of each month ringed in red on their calendars. The school procession is treated with the same reverence that Floridians reserve for an approaching hurricane. It is anticipated with the same relish Saxons mustered when those nice sailors from Denmark arrived in port. Human beings are a rare sight during the ten minute walk to and from the church. That just leaves passing motorists to worry about. I'd hate to think that one of them might get hurt.

We arrive at St Peter's at ten. The flock is corralled, a teacher or teaching assistant positioning themselves at the end of each pew. The atmosphere inside the church is therapeutic, present company notwithstanding. I have always drawn comfort from the Christian deity's many residences even if I've yet to be convinced of *his* credibility regarding legal title. After a welcome from the vicar the congregation sings a hymn half-heartedly and mumbles its way through some prayers. I have to remind several members of my class to stand for the next hymn. It isn't until the vicar's address is underway that the trouble starts though. Six or seven *Pokemon* cards is all it takes. I notice them being passed furtively along the row. Some sort of trade seems to be taking place. The cards end up in Jamie Goddard's hands. It is clear from the reaction of others that he is not one of the transaction's primary parties. I have already warned Sue Warden about Jamie Goddard who this morning arrived late for register with a faraway look in his eyes. Sue greeted the news with a similar mien. She clearly had other things on her mind. I catch Jamie's eye and hold out a hand indicating that I want the cards passing to me. Predictably, Jamie shakes his head. He seems to enjoy the experience and shakes it some more. I give him my best glare. This time he shouts, 'No!'

Keith Aston, sitting in the row in front turns around. He really should know better. Now he's *involved.* What's worse, he's nearer the problem than I am. Meanwhile Gregory Jackson appears willing and able to dispute ownership of the *Pokemon* cards. Only Sally Jacobs separates Jamie from the perturbed looking Gregory who lunges for the cards prompting Jamie to emit a high-pitched scream. If it comes to fisticuffs, Jamie won't stand a chance. This thought doesn't appear to have occurred to Jamie though. He holds the cards up in the air out of Gregory's reach. Keith meanwhile is making his way along the row followed by Trish Hoone, TA in Year One. It is clear that Keith intends to remove Jamie - standard procedure in these circumstances. Frankly I don't rate his chances. Distracted by the attentions of Gregory, Jamie is too late to stop Keith grabbing several of the *Pokemon* cards which he quickly passes to Trish. Having acquired leverage Keith's chances have greatly improved. Jamie is now more than happy to follow Keith along the row in pursuit of his ill-gotten gains. The slickness of the operation is only spoilt when Jamie screams, 'Give me back my cards you cow!' Once in the aisle Keith grabs Jamie's arms pinning them to his sides. Jamie lashes out with his feet and catches Trish on the hand dislodging the cards which scatter across the stone floor. With the carrot lost and Keith keen that Trish take one of Jamie's arms, the process of dragging the boy towards the door proves an arduous one.

The vicar gamely talks on. No one is listening. Sue Warden, sitting at the back of the church, has the door open and ready by the time Keith and Trish have staggered to it with their quarry. Jamie's feet are no longer in contact with the floor. He is being carried through the doorway when he summons one final act of defiance. Freeing his hands he grabs each door jamb. The whole congregation has by this time turned to face him. The vicar's mouth is still moving although no sound issues forth. Jamie Goddard's knuckles have turned white. 'You'll never take me alive!' he bellows before he loses his grip and is dragged from view. Sue Warden bolts the church door behind him.

Pebble Bay Primary School's chess club meets every Thursday at twelve noon, prompt. It counts amongst its membership, geeks, agoraphobics, pseudo-intellectuals, half-wits and egomaniacs. A broadly representative cross-section of the school population. Those members not serving detentions or queuing to imbibe their midday dose of *Ritalin* arrive punctually. Boards are collected from the large cupboard at the rear of the classroom and playing pieces are unpacked from margarine tubs, ice cream containers and shoe boxes. The sets themselves have a cosmopolitan flavour. Packing away tends to be a more disorderly process than setting up. Consequently, the colour and vital statistics of pieces in any given set can vary greatly, tiny microcosms of modern 21st century societies.

Today, eight games are up and running by ten past the appointed hour. A couple of minutes later two of the games have reached premature conclusions amidst a flurry of high fives and theatrical head scratching. At my desk I am doing a fair bit of head scratching myself. One of my pupils appears to have written his answers to the weekly spelling test in *Klingon.* Looking up, it is easy to discern victors from losers. I suggest who should now play whom. The two quick-fire winners seem more inclined to play each other's victims than locking horns themselves however.

I go back to putting a series of crosses next to Amanda Hurn's test answers but not before reminding all those present to castle *at the earliest opportunity*. Not that they should need reminding. The squares of each board are decorated with an assortment of tactical hints and nuggets of chess wisdom. An innovation dreamed up by a former club member on the receiving end of an *Are you defacing school property?* rant for a full minute before his teacher realised the phrases etched onto his board's white squares pertained to chess and not his love life. From the simple reminder regarding the correct orientation of the board *white, right* to the hauntingly poetic *get your queen out too soon and you'll look like a goon,* James Chumley had devised a whole series of tips and memory joggers that left me more perplexed than ever as to why he'd never actually won a game in the two years he'd been coming to my class of a Thursday lunch time. Within days, all the chess boards had similar inscriptions and within weeks the kids were adding their own mottoes, some with about as much to do with chess as the graffiti I'd seen on the roof tiles the other day.

Play continues in boisterous fashion for a further twenty minutes. I have learnt from experience that games lasting more than ten moves tend to go the distance. Even those of a one-sided nature. The player holding the advantage is usually reluctant to allow the fun to end. Far more enjoyable than a quick finish is the inflicting on one's opponent of a slow and painful death much like the master criminal in a spy movie who declines numerous opportunities to kill off his adversary. Each opposition piece is captured amidst a torrent of premature victory celebrations which end abruptly when the condemned is gifted a tame stalemate despite the slogan : *Quick check mate or slow stalemate* daubed all over squares H3 and A6.

Today the usual interruptions occur: The sound of swearing from the playground, two Year Six boys bursting into the room and exiting at speed via the glassed off art area that separates classes Five and Six, Don poking his head around the door and feigning surprise, 'Oh, you *are* in here Mr Bradley.'

'Apparently.'

'I'll leave the lights on for now then shall I?'

At 12.35 I leave my desk and adjudicate any unfinished games. Not all the protagonists appreciate my decisions. 'Yes, Max I know you've been in tighter spots than this, but you did lose each of those games too.' This done, chess club concludes in traditional fashion with a challenge of sorts.

'Today's challenge,' I say, 'is *The Knight's Tour.*' Working in pairs members attempt to steer a knight about the board visiting all 64 squares only once. Counters are fetched to mark the position of squares visited amidst cries of, 'This'll be easy.' Chloe and Danielle are amongst only half a dozen players who haven't given up and branded the tour 'impossible' within three minutes. A similar number remain behind to retrieve the discarded chess pieces and counters scattered about the classroom floor once the bad losers and *announce it to the world* winners have scarpered for a five minute kick about before the school bell puts an end to lunch break.

Saturday morning. It's been a tough week at school. Beth has been instrumental in returning my mind to a state bordering sanity. The bean curd was so cold last night it had needed re-heating in the oven which at least gave us time to re-set the dining table. Breakfast is running a little behind schedule this morning too. We're sipping coffee in our dressing gowns when the door bell sounds. It's my mother and father. *Seconds out, round one.* The inconvenience of their visit is ameliorated to a large extent by my delight in seeing them together, in the same room, at the same time. They refuse the offer of a hot drink having just come from a cafe up the street. Unexpected visits of this sort are not uncommon. When you live in the middle of town you get used to people just popping in.

We've lived in this central location for six years, having moved from our former abode near the town's West station for several reasons, chief amongst them school catchment areas and our former neighbour's penchant for DIY. Lean-tos were appearing with worrying rapidity on the other side of our party walls, each new addition to our neighbour, Pete's, house being preceded by several days of hammering on his side of the walls and falling crockery on ours. He seldom troubled himself with building regulations which we strongly suspected his haphazard erections contravened. Occasionally, having received an unexpected visit - for him at any rate - from the local planning department, he'd appear at our door seeking signatures to questionnaires while he moaned about having to demolish walls and dig foundations, whatever they were.

Pete couldn't understand why we moved. Nor could a lot of our friends. We could see their point. Our proposed purchase had no garden and was situated on a bustling town centre street. Reputedly the location of a school, run by Dorset dialect poet William Barnes, we fell in love with the place the moment we viewed it . We were shown in through a side door that opened onto a partially covered courtyard from which a gravelled alleyway led mysteriously past a whitewashed former outdoor toilet turned shed around the back of an adjacent house to another smaller area ideal for storing dustbins and bicycles. Downstairs, rooms had been knocked together to create an open-plan living space that afforded precious little opportunity for small children to get up to unseen mischief. Recently renovated and decorated, the house had even featured in a recent issue of *Dorset Scene* magazine. From the back bedroom you looked out across a muddle of roof tops and hidden gardens to the illuminated spire of *All Saints* church. Beautiful. There were catches though: We would not be able to park outside our house. And then there was the noise of passing traffic. A Saturday afternoon spent in the *Dolphin* convinced me the traffic would not be a problem. Beth was not so sure. Our first morning confirmed her worst fears. Seven a.m. and the first Transit vans began making their morning deliveries to the cafes and delis further up the street. At least we supposed them to be Transit vans; they might just as easily have been low-flying aircraft. Possibly de Havilland Sea Vixens. Gone already was the memory of the night before sitting out in the courtyard sipping beer and eating olives while the campanologists went at it hammer and tongs up the road at *All Saints*. After several weeks we felt shell-shocked. We talked about installing double glazing or saving ourselves some cash and moving on in a face saving twelve months' time. But we never did. The Transit drivers maintained their schedules and the drunks still staggered from the Dolphin at one in the morning with an irresistible urge to bang on windows. The laws of physics insist the noise continued to cause the membrane inside my ear to vibrate but they're a little less clear as to why my brain stopped acknowledging any of it. I'm glad it did.

'Of course we're friends!' Jim-Bob says in slightly hysterical fashion when I make tentative inquiries as to the lie of the marital land.

My mother is more subdued. 'I ran out of books to read,' is all she says regarding her husband's rehabilitation before inquiring as to the whereabouts of her grandchildren.

'It's a Saturday morning,' I say, 'three guesses.'

While Beth disappears upstairs to dress I clear the breakfast dishes from the dining table, at which my parents have already stationed themselves. I give the table a cursory wipe with a dish cloth. 'That needs binning,' my mother tells me.

'Have you been to see the doctor yet?' I retaliate, depositing breakfast crumbs *and* cloth in the bin.

'She has,' Jim-Bob says making it clear by his tone of voice that the visit had more to do with his tenacity than his wife's concern for her own well-being.

'And?'

'Dr Ridge says he's sure it's nothing to worry about. He says the achalasia is bound to fluctuate. He took a blood sample though.'

'To set your father's mind at rest,' Mum adds.

'I'm worried about you.'

'*Are you*?'

They may be talking but I get the impression the issue of how best to mark their upcoming anniversary has yet to be resolved.

'Is swallowing any easier?' I ask. My mother shakes

her head.

'How's Louisa?' Beth's re-appearance is timely. My sister is apparently well, a fact verified during a telephone call only the night before. The conversation is artfully manipulated by Beth in such a way that our visitors are given no further opportunity for conflict. The damage is done though. When they stand to leave I ask where they are headed next.

'The library,' my mother says, 'I need some more books.'

I follow up my assembly on the *Power of Positive Thinking* with one on the theme of *Doing the Right Thing*. I am truly a font of spiritual wisdom. Albert Schwietzer will play me in the movie. I kick things off by reminding the children about the concept of *As you sow, you reap*. 'This applies to how you behave as well as how you think,' I tell them. 'Suppose you do something bad to someone else.' *Close your eyes really tight and try to imagine that Robert.* 'Well eventually things will be balanced out. Something bad will happen to you!' I give my audience an example: 'Suppose David here goes up to Robert in the playground and hits him. I suspect he might get hit back. Er, Robert watch the language please.'

Order restored, I re-emphasise the point of the anecdote I have just recounted. 'As you sow, you reap,' I say. 'Now, not everything is as spontaneous as that. Sometimes things take longer to balance out.' Blank looks. 'Let's look at it another way. Suppose you find money in the playground. What should you do?'

A sea of raised hands. You want to attract the attention of school kids? Talk cold, hard, cash. It works with adults too by the way. 'So, what would you do, children?' I select pupils at random. 'No, Johnny the photocopier is out of bounds to children at break times. Yes I have heard of *finders keepers*, Oliver and yes it is sweet of you to think of splitting it with your friends Katy but….' I reel off some manufactured examples of people receiving rewards for handing in lost money and expensive objects. Confused faces are replaced by a glint of understanding once I've used the word *reward.* 'Don't ask, *Can I get* away *with this?* when you have a decision to make, ask, *How will doing this make me feel?* Do the right thing,' I conclude, 'and things will work out for the best, maybe not today, but tomorrow and for the rest of our lives ….' *Has anyone else here seen* Casablanca*?* I finish the assembly by talking about Bobby Jones, the legendary American amateur golfer who famously moved his ball by mistake while preparing to play a shot. 'Even though no one else had seen this, Jones insisted on having a penalty stroke added to his card. When praised for his honesty he replied, '*You may as well thank me for not robbing a bank'*. Jones went on to become the greatest golfer the world has ever seen.' *And yes Robert, I have heard of Tiger Woods. And for your information, he cheats.*

I don't like it when Mary goes into school crying. This morning I try everything to turn the situation around but there is no escaping the fact that we've lost her reading book. I try to reassure her that she will not get into trouble but the truth of the matter is the staff at St Paul's scare the shit out of me too. The governors have a history of appointing middle aged religious zealots when what the place badly needs is some young blood. The rest of the teaching staff look as though they drink the stuff. At Mary's insistence I talk to Mrs Ponting about the missing book. This halts the tears but I still haven't seen a smile by the time I prise Mary loose in the playground and head for home.

Love is Not a One-Way Street is still not finished. I need to re-write the ending. It's missing something. A plausible climax and resolution for starters. Before tackling the problems surrounding my story's finale I e-mail Peter Swinton at *Dorset Scene*, ask him in humble fashion if he'd be interested in publishing an article on Tom Chandler. I've made a few minor changes to *Love is…* when a text from Beth interrupts the writing process. *Who do you want me to invite to your 40th birthday party?*

The prospect of turning forty really doesn't bother me. I couldn't care less. I really don't give a shit. What's the big deal, for Christ's sake? Can we change the subject? What is it with multiples of ten anyway? To be honest I'm not a huge fan of the decimal system. Apart from the marking of dubious anniversaries has it been adapted successfully to *any* aspect of the measurement of time?

Time.

Don't get me started on that. Wasn't it Einstein who described past, present and future as *a persistent illusion*? Lately it felt more like persistent *dis*illusion. And who was it said, *Time is nature's way of keeping everything from happening at once*? Einstein clearly thought it *was* all happening at once. What if it was? Escape the idea of the linear nature of time, a straight line from cradle to grave, and all sorts of interesting things become possible. A cyclical concept of time has its appeal. There are religions, I know, based on the idea of an infinite cycle forever repeating itself until enlightenment liberates the deluded soul from *Maya's* hypnotic spell. A life already existing in its entirety. No more Déjà vu. Birth and death neither a beginning nor an end. Both part of a seamless circle. Unbroken. Our lives, less a physical journey, more a series of scenes given form by the conscious mind as it brushes over them like a laser beam decoding a DVD.

I text Beth back: *What the heck. Invite the same people you did last time.*

'Tom Chandler?' Alex says, '*the* Tom Chandler!'

I nod proudly. No, smugly. I'm still pretty pleased with myself.

'You actually *know* him?'

'I've spoken to him on the phone.' I've found honesty is generally the best policy. Initially anyway; there's always plenty of time to embellish the truth later. I explain my mission to Alex, the reason I've come to the Research Centre this morning.

When I'm finished, Alex nods, thinks for a minute and says, 'you need the Ale House Recognizances. Follow me.' Despite the fancy name the Ale House Recognizances amount to a set of black lever arch files sitting on a dusty shelf in a corner of the Small Reading Room. 'Bridport did you say? 18th Century?' Having confirmed the details I'm handed three of the files. I thank Alex profusely and make a vague promise to repay the debt one day soon.

'You know where to find me.'

'Give my regards to Janice,' I say. Sitting down at a nearby table I reach in a pocket for the scrap of paper on which I have noted the names of the pubs Tom Chandler needs tracing. I try several other pockets. An excellent start: can't even *trace* the bloody piece of paper. I realise that I have in fact left the list of ale houses at home. I emit a stream of whispered obscenities and head for the exit. 'Back in a few minutes,' I say as I pass a bemused looking Janice and Alex at reception.

My bike is right outside. Although the roads are dry the descent towards home is perilous. Riding uphill is relatively safe since the prevailing gradient invariably makes up for any deficiency on the part of my brakes. Riding homewards is a different proposition altogether. The roundabout at the top of the High Street with its adjacent zebra crossing is the first hazard that needs negotiating. Momentarily unsighted, I narrowly avoid rear- ending a white van and running down a surprised looking octogenarian. Beyond these obstacles lie three further sets of traffic lights. The laws of probability suggest I will need to stop at at least one of them. I used to be able to rely on my front brake - until recently if I squeezed its lever I could be sure *nothing* would happen. That I continue to squeeze at all is a product of habit. Hadn't my father taught me as a child to apply front and rear brakes simultaneously? Lately, however, the front brake has begun showing signs of life. Predicting when it will rouse itself from its languor is not a science however. An instinctive squeeze of said front brake today for instance has either no effect on my velocity at all or sends me damn near over the handle bars as the pads and the wheel rim unexpectedly effect a reunion of sorts. As it turns out the traffic lights at the junction with Kirk Street are the only set I need to stop at. Turning into Durnford Street I dismount nonchalantly, postman style, and open the back door. The scrap of paper I need is on the dining table. I'm pedalling back up the High Street in no time. The prospect of imminent death recedes during my relatively controlled ascent.

'You were quick,' Alex says as I breathlessly re-enter the Research Centre. The sweat cascading down my face lends Alex's quip an air of understatement. 'Durnford Street and back in what, three minutes?'
I'm seated in front of the Ale House Recognizances again before it occurs to me to wonder how Alex knows where I live. Inside half an hour I've verified the existence of three of the pubs. Of the other two I can find no trace. If Tom wants to retain them for the purposes of authenticity he'll have to risk legal action from someone intimately conversant with the Recognizances, perhaps someone with their own personal copy. I close the black file and gather my stuff together. A post-it-note on the file's cover catches my attention. I recognise Alex's neat font. Written in blue biro are the words: Finish 4. Coffee? 251094. I am certain the note was not there when the file was handed to me. By implication it was placed there while I was attempting to break my neck riding to and from home. In which case, despite the lack of a named correspondent, the note is intended for my eyes and was not left on the file accidentally. *Brilliant, Holmes*. But what did the note mean? Finish 4. Coffee? Either Alex was conducting research into a quartet of jailed Scandinavian coffee smugglers or I was being invited to meet up for a hot beverage. 251094: either the date the Finish Four began serving their sentences or a telephone number, presumably Alex's. A variety of emotions wrestle for control of my thoughts like terrorists storming the cockpit of a 747 where they encounter a pilot anticipating the arrival of that good-looking hostess he has his eye on and not four men in balaclavas reeking of stale sweat and the in-flight Chicken Kiev. Am I flattered? A bit. Surprised? Not completely: every dog has its day after all. But what else? Difficult to express, but I am aware of the need to avoid hasty manoeuvres, anything that could jeopardise the stability of the *craft*. Perhaps it would be prudent to re-assess my flight path. Yes, that's it: my *path of flight*. I put the note in my jacket pocket and instinctively glance over my shoulder. I replace the Recognizances and try to think. Need to alter planned trajectory. A fire exit? I don't think there is one. No, this aviator is going to have to go out the way he came in. I set a course for the Microfilm Room. From there it is possible to

see into reception via a glazed door. Janice appears to be alone. There is no time to waste. '*Flight one-niner-zero, you are cleared for take-off.*' I'm through the door and passing the front desk in seconds.

'Mr Bradley,' Janice says, 'I think Alex is looking for you.' *Is she in on this too?*

'Gotta run,' I call over my shoulder banking left through the main doors. Only when I'm back on my bike heading for the roundabout at the top of the High Street do I feel safe.

Hatty and Freddie are shivering outside the house when I return from St Paul's with Mary. Inside the house the kids ransack the fridge and disappear upstairs while I retrieve lunch boxes from the rucksacks jettisoned near the back door. Glancing at the clock on the wall I notice that it's almost zero hour. The incident at the Research Centre has been much on my mind. Ask the driver that came within a whisker of running me down on flashing ambers a half hour ago on my way to pick up Mary or the cashier at the supermarket who had to remind me three times to remove my card from the *chip and pin* device. Ask Mary's friend, Hayley's dad who I left to mumble obscenities to himself during the ten minute gap between the sounding of the end of school bell and the emergence of our tardy children.

'It's like standing next to the Dalai bleedin' Lama,' he'd said, mistaking my distracted silence for patient serenity when all inside was turmoil, less Dalai Lama, more Tibetan peasant, arms like windscreen wipers during the monsoon, zigzagging ahead of a Chinese tank rolling into Lhasa.

I wonder whether Alex really expected me to be outside the Research Centre at the appointed hour. 'Ow!' I'm in danger of compromising the meat-free integrity of the vegetable stew I'm preparing for dinner. I put down the knife I have been using to slice an onion, an onion I do not recall removing from the refrigerator, and run my finger or at least that portion still attached to my hand under the cold tap. I'm given to exaggeration. It's only a nick but more than enough to focus my thoughts on the carrots, leeks and potatoes that still need chopping. *Attention, attention. attention.* Reaching a spiritual nirvana would be nice, though right now I'd settle for sitting down to a hearty stew with a full set of digits.

When Beth gets in she spots the plaster on my finger and issues sympathy commensurate with the injuries sustained. Hence her refusal to kiss it better. The smell of onions may have something to do with this. My lips fare better and when I hug this woman it's like being a kid again. The world can be a big scary place.

'Hugh?' she says.

'Yes, Babe?'

'You're hurting me.'

In the morning I call Tom Chandler at his London home. I'm nervous and have to force myself not to put off the call until later. Will the man even remember who I am? *Hugh Bradley you say? Hugh? H, u, g, h? Look I'm sorry but I really think you've got a wrong number.*

I'm about to replace the handset when a female voice cuts short the twelfth ring.

'Hello?' *Well?*

I introduce myself and state my business repeating my name for the benefit of my evidently disinterested interlocutor. I hear Chandler's voice in the background.

'Who is it Darling?

'Someone about a pub, I think. Darling, are you drinking again?'

'Adversus solem ne loquitor.'

I hear the telephone changing hands and then Chandler's voice addressing me in a whisper. 'Ken, I thought I told you not to phone me at home. That was my wife!'

'This isn't Ken,' I whisper back and then wonder what the hell it is I think I'm doing. I introduce myself once again, audibly this time.

Chandler seems extraordinarily happy to hear from me or rather, extraordinarily happy not to be talking to the indelicate Ken. 'It's Hugh Bradley, Darling!' He calls to his wife cheerfully. 'Remember? That chap who delivered the note to me the morning you nearly burnt the bloody cottage down?' Chandler is sounding more sure of himself by the second. *You know, the bloke who set me up with that Phillipino hooker on my last book signing tour of the Far East.*

I tell Chandler that I have checked out the pub names for him.

'The Ale House Recognizances you say?' His voice noticeably quietens when repeating the words *ale house*. 'Very decent of you. Didn't expect you to get back to me so quickly.' He excuses himself for a moment in order to grab a pen and make a note of my findings which seem to satisfy him enormously. He promises to give me a call in a few weeks when he's next down my way. Possibly as a sign of good faith he lets me have his e-mail address which I hurriedly jot down. 'We'll do that interview soon Hugh,' he tells me before hanging up.

Extract from *Life in Dorset*, 28th June 2004.
Cousin Sharon ties the knot. Most of the Bradley family are there. My grandfather - Jim-Bob's father - will not be at the church and will attend the reception only. He does not therefore, see Sharon exchange vows with a very young looking soldier who will, after a short honeymoon, whisk his bride away to the army bases of the Rhineland. There was considerable doubt as to whether Frederick Bradley would attend even the reception. He is well into his nineties and doesn't get out much. His wife (Jim-Bob's stepmother) Laura, will accompany him. The news of their intended appearance at the reception sends Mum into a rant. Who would have thought there'd be bad blood between my mother and her husband's kith and kin? It does of course explain why Mum had heart palpitations when she found out her grandson was to be named Freddie. *We assured her we were not naming our baby boy after her nemesis. This did little to placate her. By the time Freddie was christened however she had calmed down somewhat and has rarely mentioned the issue since. She chooses today, however to let us in on a little secret. As far as Granddad is concerned his great-grandson is called* Michael*!* *'I didn't want the bastard to think you'd named my grandson*

after him!' she hisses. 'I made your father tell him Freddie was called Michael which wasn't a lie.' She has a point. Freddie's middle name is Michael, a name that does in fact derive from a relative (Beth's much mourned Uncle Mick who died of cancer shortly before Freddie was born). The situation as explained by Rose Bradley is thus relatively simple: whenever Granddad or Laura are around Freddie is to be referred to as Michael. At all other times he will be called Freddie. If a relative is encountered who might know Freddie by either his first or middle names pronouns are to be employed if at all possible. Excellent. Just excellent. Further complications emerge however, while we await the arrival of our fellow guests outside the reception venue. 'I'm not bloody speaking to Laura!' Mum informs us matter of factly while Hatty, Freddie and Mary cavort around the hotel's adventure playground. 'But you watch. Your father will be all over her, Hugh, the bitch'. Five minutes later a car pulls up and an elderly couple get out. Laura makes a bee-line for Mum who trades kisses with the bitch *and Frederick and promptly colours red when I catch her eye. Great grandchildren are summoned from the play area: 'Hatty, Mary!' My shout precedes a self-conscious mumbled attempt at gaining the attention of their brother who is eventually summoned with an unceremonious, 'Oi!' Freddie trots over. I ruffle his hair. 'Come and say hello to your great-granddad,' I say and then, as we approach the frail figure of Frederick Bradley, bend down to whisper in his ear, 'Oh, and by the way, your name's Michael.'*

The weather forecast is not good. Chesil Bank has already secreted itself beneath a cloak of fog by the time I arrive for duty at Pebble Bay Primary School Wednesday lunch-time. I find Luke alone in the classroom. The shouts and screams coming from the playground are muffled by the vapour swirling on the other side of the classroom windows. The same cannot be said for Luke's greeting. 'The bitch has gone through with it!' he says, jamming a forefinger into the opened page of what looks like the local rag spread before him on the desk.

'She's had her remaining vertebrae removed?' I ask putting down my bag.

Luke is in no mood for humour. He doesn't get up. 'Take a look at this,' he tells me. A circle of black ink surrounds a segment of text a third of the way down the page but it's the banner headline several inches higher that grabs my attention: *Situations Vacant*. The two inches of text that Luke has circumnavigated with his biro has its own sub-heading: Pebble Bay Primary School. Below this are the words, *Required for September: Year Five teacher.*

Did I mention the job-share was temporary? Come on, think about it. There had to be a catch.

Like most head teachers the term *job-share* had initially struck the fear of God into Sue. Generally speaking a head teacher views a phone call from OfSted with more enthusiasm than a request for part-time hours from one of the teaching staff. Sue's relief at being presented with a way out of the quagmire of redundancy had not completely blinded her to the potential hazards of a job-share and the extra work it might mean for her once back on firmer ground. Our request for reduced hours had been a life-line for Sue but with careful thought on her part she could have her cake and eat it. With this in mind she had us sign fixed-term contracts. That way if the job-share did not work out - if either myself or Luke turned into crazed psycho killers with all that extra free time on our hands - she'd have the situation covered. *The governors and myself have decided not to renew your contract Mr Bradley on account of the recent spate of unexplained axe murders in your classroom.* Luke and myself were fully aware of the situation but Luke in particular seemed confident that new permanent contracts would be presented to us for signing at the appropriate time. The advert in the paper cast fresh doubt on this assumption.

'She's just following protocol,' I say neglecting to read the rest of the advertisement.

'I agree. And protocol for replacing employees is to advertise for their replacements.' Luke seems genuinely concerned. The man is worked up. I suppose this shouldn't surprise me. The threat of redundancy at the school had evoked similar displays of emotion. The job-share would not have happened but for this dread of penury, a condition no doubt worsened by the break-up of his marriage. Jen had provided a safety net of sorts. Luke's new domestic arrangements weren't nearly so financially secure even if he had done well out of the sale of the former marital abode.

'We're bloody out mate.'

'It's a job advert, not a P45.'

Luke does not look convinced.

'Come on, we knew the job-share was temporary. To begin with anyway.'

'Exactly. And now we're out.'

'You know Sue. She has to do everything by the book. Human Resources at County Hall have probably told her she's got to advertise the post before she can make it permanent. Relax. What was it Sue said at the end of last year? That she was very pleased with the way the job-share was progressing?'

'Well she's obviously reconsidered.'

'So what's changed since then? Nobody died during one of our lessons, we haven't grown unsightly beards. You can still turn on the charm when you need to. Hell, you practically talked the woman into the job-share in the first place.' None of this seems to placate Luke. The man is incapable of listening to reason. It's already twelve twenty and I have a lesson to prepare for one o'clock. I give it one last shot embarking on a three minute oration in which I detail the many reasons why we are more likely to still have our jobs in September than not before finishing with the heart stirring rallying cry, 'Now calm the fuck down.'

Luke sits unmoved, emotionally and physically. 'Have you talked to Sue about it yet?' I ask him.

Luke shakes his head. 'No, Brenda only showed me the ad a few minutes before you arrived.'

'Go and talk to Sue. If you can find her in the fog. Come back and tell me what she says about all this.'

But I don't see him again until the following day. He comes into the classroom during chess club. 'Forgot you did geek club every Thursday.' Luke's smile is in stark contrast to the pained expressions that appear on the faces of the players nearest to where we are standing.

I pat Max on the shoulder. 'No, Mr Johnstone, *Greek* club is on Fridays. Remember to keep an eye on what your opponent is doing,' I tell Max and with a motion of my head lead Luke towards the desk. 'What have you found out?' I ask him.

'Sue hasn't talked to *you* then?'

'What do you think?'

Luke shrugs. 'She was busy yesterday. Thought I'd pop in unannounced today.

'And?'

'You were right. About Human Resources anyway. Before the job-share can be made permanent the post needs to be advertised. Basically, we need to re-apply for our jobs. Application forms, interviews, the works. Transparency, Sue calls it.'

The thought of jumping through a succession of hoops to arrive back at square one is a frustrating one but Luke leaves the room looking much happier with his lot. I'm in time to see Max check-mated. Today's session's finale is a beauty. I tell the members about chess grandmaster Georges Koltanowski, a Belgian-born American citizen, who once played 56 opponents simultaneously. Adhering to a time limit of ten seconds per move, Koltanowski won fifty games and lost only six. The matches lasted nine hours. *Koltanowski wore a blindfold throughout.* 'Koltanowski wore a blindfold throughout!' I repeat. Pause for gasps of amazement. I remind everyone of the Knight's Tour, the trip around the board we've been practising the last few weeks. 'Georges Koltanowski,' I tell them, 'used to perform the tour blindfolded. What is more, Koltanowski made sure his 64th move took him back to the square from which he started.' I know the feeling.

For my money, Pebble Bay's Science curriculum is far too narrow. What's more it doesn't appear to have significantly altered since the 1940s. Twenty minutes on alternate Fridays is about the only chance I'm going to get to redress the balance. There are worse ways to employ assembly time.

'Hands up,' I say, 'those of you sitting on chairs.' Jamie Goddard can barely raise his head let alone a hand but the rest of those lucky enough to have seats comply. 'In the next ten minutes I hope to convince you otherwise,' I say. I do not reprimand Gary Asquith for scoffing loudly. At least he's listening. Besides, the boy reminds me that I've got my work cut out. To begin at the beginning. 'What,' I say, 'is the world made of?'

'Rock.'

'Yes.'

'Lava,'

'Okay.'

'Water.'

'Yes.' There are more hands up. 'David Speke?' I really shouldn't have asked the boy who proceeds to subject everyone to a three minute talk on the probable composition of the Earth's core.

'You're all right but what are all these things made of?' I'd hoped for a better answer than *stuff.* Still it's a starting point. 'Let's be scientific. What's *stuff* made of?' God knows what time some of these kids got to sleep last night. They're going to need some coaxing. 'Begins with an *a*,' I prompt.

'Atoms!'

'Excellent, Ruby! Now, who's heard of atoms?' Almost every hand goes up. Ernest Rutherford would have been proud. I spend the next couple of minutes at the white board firstly trying to locate a board pen that hasn't dried up and secondly sketching an atom. I draw a red dot, label it the nucleus and write *filled with neutrons and protons* next to it. I draw several more randomly spaced dots at various other points on the board. 'Electrons,' I say. Dull bit over, I tell the children that if the *nucleus* were the size of a golf ball the closest *electron* to it would be one kilometre away. I want this to sink in so I pause and then repeat what I have said for the benefit of those who tuned out sometime around *Good morning everybody*. Just to be sure they've got the message I try another analogy. If the nucleus was the size of a full stop, *some of you are I think familiar with those,* then the closest electron would be 50m away. Less than a minute later and we've got to where I want to be: An atom is mostly made up of *empty space*. 'In fact,' I say '99.999% of an atom is empty!'

'A bit like the universe, Mr Bradley!' Bloody hell. If Thomas Clark is paying attention I'd estimate at least three-quarters of the room is listening too.

'Well done Thomas. Now,' I say, 'if everything is made of atoms, and according to scientists it is, and if atoms are mostly empty space, how come when I clap my hands they don't just pass through each other. How come when I sit on a chair I don't fall through it?'

'Because we're solid!' *Duh.*

'But we've just agreed we're made mostly of empty space, James.' *Smart arse.* There are no other suggestions. 'I'll tell you why,' I say. I pause both for effect and to try and remember what it was that long-haired Harvard professor had actually said on *You Tube* the other night. 'Our hands do not pass through each other, because they don't actually touch each other. The electrons in one hand repel the electrons in the other, the same as like-poles on a magnet, and it's this that makes our world seem solid. You are not,' I tell years Five and Six, 'sitting on those chairs. You are hovering above them! The electrons in the chair are repelling the electrons in your…' - *don't spoil everything with a badly judged reference to their posteriors for God's sake* - 'body. You are fooled into thinking that you are sitting on the chair.' The general consensus in the room seems to be that this is important information. No one, including the adult present, is quite sure what they're supposed to do with it though.

The first weekend of the half-term holiday we spend at a friend's house in the north. A hire car is obtained for the journey - the Travolta deserves a break too - but even so the journey to and from York is an arduous one. When we return late Sunday evening there is a message on the answer machine from Mum asking if we are coming round for Sunday lunch.

The trek north had necessitated compromises. Compromises vis-à-vis food and comfort which inspire me to make an effort Monday evening. Candles illuminate the dinner table, music from *Beth's* CD collection calms the assembled diners some of whom are not known for their patience whilst waiting for the food to be served. Roasted vegetables and pasta is Beth's favourite dish. Provided I whiz up the aubergine, courgettes, peppers and leeks the kids will eat the stuff too. Once Freddie accepts that we'd rather he didn't extinguish every naked flame within spitting distance – *there are more socially acceptable ways to put out candles son* - until the meal is finished proceedings flow in an unusually civilised fashion. It's good to be eating sensibly again. Food is better when it hasn't been pumped full of additives and carted about the country in air tight containers. The same can be said for human beings.

While the children don pyjamas I brew coffee and crack open a bar of dark chocolate. It's good to be home. An evening catching up on some reading is decided upon. Perhaps, I suggest, some Mahler turned down low. Spurred on by caffeine I take the stairs at a jog, supervise tooth brushing and read each of my children a chapter or two. Tonight not even filling three hot water bottles feels like a chore.

I find Beth curled up on the sofa when I return to the lamp-lit living-room. Candles flicker at strategic locations and a severely depleted glass of wine lies within easy reach of the sofa on an adjacent coffee table. Beth is reading a book; one I bought her for Christmas. Usually a novel a week reader, my wife has struggled to get into *Madame Bovary*. When Beth's book group decided to give it a go, the beautiful hardback copy I spotted in the local bookshop seemed like an excellent idea for a festive gift. Unusually though, Beth had found the text hard-going. The postponement of the book group's next meeting had suggested she wasn't alone.

'I'm going to finish this by the end of the week,' she tells me as I join her on the sofa.

'A few more sips should do it.'

'Not the wine, this bloody book. Although now you mention it.'

I return with a new bottle of red and, while wrestling with the corkscrew, remonstrate in animated fashion regarding the *bloody book's* qualities.

'Oh just pour me some more wine you pretentious bastard.'

Alcohol is only partly to blame for my wife's brusque manner. New Year's Eve had witnessed similar scenes in the Bradley household. Having listened for nearly a week to Beth's complaints about the literary merits of her Christmas present I'd grabbed my own older, grubbier copy from a shelf and quickly discovered that my wife was reading a different translation. I'd read her some passages to prove my point. 'What do you think about that?' I'd said. Beth had merely held out her empty wine glass. Having topped her up I'd reinforced my point with further extracts although my wife was clearly far more interested in examining the contents of her glass against the lamp light than in listening to me. Her only contribution to the discussion wasn't especially relevant. 'I'm beginning to understand now why Madame Bovary had an affair,' she'd said.

Tonight, I sense, may not be a good time to re-open the debate. Beth surprises me though when, full wine glass in one hand, *Madame Bovary* in the other she says, 'Hugh, you win. I admit it. Your Christmas present is shite.' I ponder my wife's magnanimous admission as she proceeds to qualify her comment. 'Your dirty, dog-eared copy is much better but my lovely hardback edition *doesn't* smell of cat's piss.' I have the sense that the discussion is over. My wife will be sticking with her copy. Short of urinating on it I can't think of any way to stop her.

About nine thirty the phone rings. It's Jim-Bob. 'Hello, Hugh.' His voice is flat, dead pan. 'Your mother and I were up at the hospital today'. Shit, I'd forgotten they were even going. 'We, er, received some bad news.'

The victims of severe trauma are said to subconsciously erect amnesic barriers in their minds, a defence mechanism that prevents them reliving horrors that could send them over the edge. An apparently well adjusted personality may be one of several that make up the mind of any one individual. Like the water-tight compartments on an ocean-going liner damage to one section need not necessarily destabilise the whole vessel. There may be some seepage between bulkheads, possibly a slight tendency to list to starboard but the ship continues to steam ahead - life goes on. Besides, the adult human being is a master in the art of deception. During its journey to maturity the average homo sapiens learns to control its displays of emotion so successfully that the façade of self-restraint is often only rarely lifted. Some call it *growing up*. Spontaneous outbursts of emotion cease in the same way that a child learns to bring the bladder and rectum under control. However, just because we've stopped soiling ourselves in public doesn't mean we aren't still shitting behind our securely fastened bathroom doors.

Half term is a time for reflection and recuperation - a period of calm. A chance to lurch from the term's white water, cling to the bank for a time, and sift through the neglected debris that has lodged there during the preceding six weeks' struggle for breath midstream. Debris like the pile of shite left on my desk from the previous Friday. The Travolta narrowly avoids a pile of the canine variety as I pull up outside Pebble Bay Primary School Tuesday morning. The car park is locked. The other vehicles on the street do not look familiar. Letting myself in the front door I notice that the alarm system has been disarmed. Someone else is about, probably Don. Sure enough, I spot his vacuum cleaner and tool box in the corridor beneath the strip light that's been flickering intermittently for three weeks. There is no sign of Don however. While I have no desire to engage the bastard in conversation, he does have a history of resetting the alarm system without warning and locking people in the building. So I risk hearing our caretaker's latest treatise on the benefits of enforced repatriation and shout his name. There's no reply. 'Don!' I call again and decide to check the staffroom. He's probably reading the paper or running his tongue around the rim of the female teachers' coffee mugs.

Or not. The staffroom is empty as a Trappist's swear box. But actually a cup of coffee is not such a bad idea. I run the cold water and fill the kettle, as much a source of noise as it is heat. I put some distance between myself and the kettle's rattling cacophony, rest my elbows on the window sill and take in the view down Chesil Beach. But the heaped pebbles hold my attention for only as long as it takes me to notice that the cover is off the school swimming pool. I hadn't realised Don started preparing the pool for swimming classes this early in the year. I leave the staffroom. Does a boiling kettle make any sound if there's no one there to hear it? *The objects of sense exist only when they are perceived.* The double doors to the playground are unlocked as is the gate into the fenced off swimming pool compound. Inside though there is no sign of Don. I'm about to leave when there's a splash in the pool. I look up and see a sea gull wheeling away. Stepping closer to the water I see pebbles littering the distorted floor of the pool and for a moment experience a degree of fellowship with my erstwhile adversaries. Those pebbles are going to be a pain for Don to pick out.

Back inside the school building I head for the main hall. The bond between caretaker and a school's gymnasium floor is an unhealthy one. The sheen Don generates on the Pebble Bay parquet is legendary. The man has developed his own polish which he hopes one day to market. The ingredients may be a secret but Don is more than happy to set aside twenty minutes of his time to talk you through the cleaning process itself, a painstaking regimen which rumour has it involves a final buffing from Don's own exposed buttocks. Turning a corner I spot Don's step ladders splayed beneath the sky light just as they were at the beginning of term. The man must have remembered his tin hat. 'Don!' I call. There's no reply and I'm not about to go up and look for him. I turn around and head back towards the staff room.

'Hugh?' a voice calls from behind me.

Turning, I see an inverted head regarding me from above the step ladders.

'You in too?' It's Luke. 'Come on up!' he tells me.

'Is it safe up there?'

'Why wouldn't it be?'

'Don't tell me even the sea gulls are frightened of you?' I hesitate a moment or two before beginning my ascent. The step ladders feel surprisingly firm beneath my feet and clambering onto the roof proves much easier than the last time I scaled their disobedient rungs. Luke gives me a hand up. I instinctively search the sky for trouble and then, seeing none, ask Luke what he's doing here.

'Come here a lot mate. Do my best thinking up here.' *Up ear.*

Behind Luke I can see a flask and mug beside which a newspaper, not usually associated with inspiring deep thought amongst its readership, is held in place by a small pile of stones. 'What have you got to think about,' I ask.

'Losing my job, the Middle East, the Rhinos being drawn away to St Helens in the Challenge cup.'

'Didn't know the Gaza Strip was keeping you awake at night,' I say.

'Okay, mostly my job and the Challenge Cup.'

'And you find this roof an aid to your meditations? Last time I was up here a sea gull nearly chewed my head off.'

Luke walks around the skylight and picks up a couple of objects. One is a tennis racket, the other a dead sea gull. 'Let's just say me and the bird life have come to an understanding,' he says.

I express my horror at this unnecessary taking of avian life by means of foul language. 'You have blood on your hands,' I conclude metaphorically before checking Luke's raised hands for the literal red stuff.

Luke follows my gaze, puts down exhibits A and B and says, 'Tippex actually.'

My confusion doesn't last long. *It ain't rocket science.* 'Nice to know that your contemplative reverie doesn't prevent you beating the bejesus out of sea birds and scrawling abusive comments on the roof slates.'

Luke shrugs. 'Very therapeutic. Here, you have a go.' Reaching into a pocket Luke tosses me a bottle of Tippex. 'It's liberating, a great way to get things off your chest.'

'And onto your fingers. Aren't you afraid Don will catch you up here?'

'He's buggered off to Exeter to get some part for the pool heater. He won't be back for a couple of hours at least.'

Reassured, I kneel down and consider my options.

'Careful down there,' Luke says, pointing to a spot near his flask, 'that bit might still be wet.'

'Don thinks this is the work of the kids you know.'

'Most of it is. Where d'you think I got the idea? First

time I came up here in the holidays I caught a couple of them in the act of describing Don as a 'fornicating twat'.

'And what did you do?'

'Corrected their spelling and told them if I caught them up here again I'd throw them off the fucking roof.'

Luke's latest addition to the roof's graffiti is in a similar vein. While he unscrews the cap on his flask and pours me a coffee – shit, the kettle in the staff room! - I inscribe the words *Don wears jack boots* onto a slate. This takes a surprisingly long time to complete. Tippex was designed to obscure not facilitate communication. When finished my message is not readily decipherable even to its scribe. Luke appears at my shoulder, hands me a steaming mug. 'Don wears joke boobs? Cutting edge mate,' he says, 'cutting edge.'

We sit down to drink although at first I'm happy just to wrap my fingers around the mug and chase the cold from them. Luke takes the opportunity to outline his plans for saving our jobs. If the roof is where the man does his best thinking he might want to consider relocating. Unless I've misunderstood, his strategy involves little more than kissing Sue's arse until it and his lips are numb. 'You got a better idea?' he asks.

Coffee drunk, my host screws his flask back together and tosses his pebble paperweights over the roof. Their cumulative splash is loud enough to be heard over the incoming surf. 'Don can pick those out later,' he says.

'You nearly hit me earlier,' I tell him.

I descend first, Luke replacing the skylight before joining me at ground level. He takes a penknife from a pocket and carefully removes a couple of screws integral, I suspect, to the ladders' structural stability. 'Don won't be needing these,' he says.

'I didn't think anyone hated the bugger as much as I do.'

'Some of us adopt a more subtle approach to life,' Luke says, pocketing the screws and his penknife, 'now, where can I sling this fucking sea gull?'

I can remember travelling to school on the number ten bus

with my mum. And the patch of waste land behind our house with its filthy, partially drained old pond. I can remember my mum warning me to stay well away from it. I can remember standing at the back door an hour later minus a shoe dripping pond slime. I can remember Mum *helping* me through the door and then coming to rest against the wall on the opposite side of the kitchen. I can remember walking home from school with Mum, past the cemetery chewing a strawberry *Opal Fruit* pretending it was bubble gum. I can remember the day my mum sorted all my muddled up jigsaw puzzles into separate paper bags. I remember searching for a missing piece the selfsame day, inadvertently combining the puzzles again. I remember my mother's reaction. Vividly. I remember returning from cubs on a Thursday night in time to watch the *Six Million Dollar Man* on our new colour television. And going on holiday to Wales where we spent the week in a caravan surrounded by hissing geese that a sunburnt Louisa feared might attack her. I remember Louisa becoming so red and itchy that week that Mum threatened to tie her hands together to if she didn't stop scratching. I remember the summer of '76 and the Silver Jubilee of '77. I remember accompanying Mum to the *Gateway* supermarket, a few doors up from the confectioner's shop my parents ran, after school every Friday where we'd buy orange juice in glass bottles before fetching fish and chips from the *Copper Kettle* across the road. I remember Mum laying out a rug on the carpet beside the fire in the living room to make a picnic of our fried food. I remember her taking us with her to the wholesalers for supplies and the cash 'n' carry with the enormous trolley on which we'd ride until Mum lost it and told us to get off. I remember Mum taking us to the Wimpy for lunch afterwards where the waitress would bring her a cheese burger and then a *Brown Derby* for dessert.

Of course all of this happened a long time ago, long before my mother was diagnosed with cancer of the oesophagus.

I've been thinking about Alex's note. I came across it again in my jacket pocket while searching for a pen at the post office.

Though clearly a request for a rendezvous was it really an attempt to instigate a more intimate relationship or was it something else? I remembered how interested Alex had appeared upon hearing of my tenuous connection to Thomas Chandler. Perhaps it was the writer and not me that Alex was interested in? *Perhaps*? Who the hell did I think I was anyway? Until I'd mentioned Chandler, Alex had treated me like any other visitor to the Centre, providing assistance when necessary and rebuking my ill-advised attempts at humour. The more I think about it the more certain I become that I have misjudged the situation. Alex had even possessed the good grace to leave a note thus sparing me the embarrassment of issuing a face-to-face refusal of further vicarious access to the great man.

Wednesday morning's post brings with it a letter from Peter Swinton. My Beaminster Brewery article will be in the April issue. If there's a feeling better than the one that accompanies news of imminent publication I've yet to experience it. For God's sake don't tell Beth though. Swinton is also anxious for an update on my pursuit of Thomas Chandler. His use of the phrase 'good luck in smoking the man out' seems a little insensitive in view of the circumstances surrounding my original request for an interview. I text Beth the good news regarding my third article then return to my ruminations about Alex.

'When will you know more?' Beth asks my mother during a visit to Zennor Road somewhere near the back-end of the week. My parents, together with Sparky, are sharing the sofa and the warmth of an unusually healthy looking fire. I'd been expecting climatic conditions similar to those inside my fridge. It's a pity my mother couldn't have found a less drastic way of getting her husband to turn up the heat. The children had stuck around long enough to claim biscuits and juice before disappearing towards the front room where the larger of the household's television sets is situated.

'Next Tuesday,' my mother replies. 'I've an appointment for next Tuesday.' On the sofa sipping tea my mother looks very well. In fact she's looking healthier than

I've seen her look in a long time. There is a cheeriness to her voice, an affectionate curiosity regarding our plans for what is left of the half-term break that makes it possible to imagine she is visiting the hospital next Tuesday for a routine check-up rather than a date with destiny. Sitting here beside the fire the scene is a cosy one. The devil is in the detail though: the refusal of a biscuit to accompany her hot drink, the guess-work employed by her husband when opening cupboards in search of tea bags. There is a presumption towards normality extant in the room. Far be it from me to dispel it. My mother is certainly keeping her end of the bargain. 'This tea is fucking awful,' she tells Jim-Bob who is, it seems, unaware until now of the existence of the water-filter jug beside the microwave.

Half-term over, I find myself alone in the house again. I set myself targets for Monday morning. Finishing 'Love is Not a One-Way Street' tops the bill. The story is as good as written but the words I throw at the computer screen conjure images of confusion only. For all the sense they make I may as well be writing the yarn in French. I brew coffee and slap a CD in the midi system. Energised by Zimmer's melodies and buoyed by caffeine I find I'm now able to type meaningless dialogue and torpid descriptive passages much, much faster than before. I can delete them pretty quickly too. I revise my targets. Saleable fiction? It ain't gonna happen. Besides, I seem to be having much more success writing about real things. You know where you are with facts. Perhaps it's time to face some.

I sign in at the Research Centre in slightly nervous fashion. Thomas Chandler may one day grant me an audience and the guarantee of another cheque from *Dorset Scene* magazine but I still have to come up with another two articles to prove my worth as an economically viable writer. Not that this has anything to do with my nervous disposition. Looking around I notice that at present there is no sign of Janice or Alex. I'm not sure if this is good news or bad. I'm not here solely to dig for ideas for a new article after all. There are other things I want to find out. Or not.

I make straight for the Small Reading Room. The previous weekend I'd discovered a book, *The Lost Railways of*

Dorset in a second-hand bookshop. This and any material gleaned today at the Centre will, I hope, lead to an article on Dorset's defunct railway stations. Having located the correct shelf I quickly realise that I'm spoilt for choice. Several books bear titles relating to my line of inquiry. Fifteen minutes perusal at a secluded table and it's clear I've more than enough information to warrant an article.1200 words is not much though. I will have to restrict myself to the branch lines of West Dorset. It is possible to have *too* much of a good thing. Besides, the stations to the west of the county are geographically closer and on the face of it more interesting. I am of course already familiar with the branch lines in question, the most recent of which closed a little over thirty years ago. Two of the books I've found are packed full of interesting anecdotes. For instance the locomotive that careened out of control during the descent towards Weymouth in the 1850s, ploughing through the buffers at the resort's terminus and coming to rest only a few feet short of the busy *Somerset Hotel*. I photocopy relevant chapters and make notes studiously before drawing up a list of stations to visit. Some of the stations will take a bit of tracking down especially, I suspect, the old terminus at Lyme Regis, now buried beneath the tarmac and concrete of a builder's yard, its station building dismantled and re-erected somewhere in Hampshire. The thought of steering the Travolta along the lanes of West Dorset searching out the remains of a vanished transport system cheers me greatly. After my earlier French cul-de-sac I feel lunch has been earned. Even if I haven't found answers to all my questions this morning. I'm about to stand up when two hands, soft and pleasantly perfumed, clamp themselves over my eyes.

'Guess who!' a familiar voice asks.

There is always a huge pile of ironing awaiting my attention following a school holiday. I decide to spend the afternoon in the company of Jane Wyman and Rock Hudson. The guilt-ridden Bob Merrick (Rock) abandons his life as selfish playboy after inadvertently causing the death of Jane's husband. In attempting to make amends he causes the accident in which Jane is blinded! Jane, her acting apparently unaffected by a failed eight year marriage to Ronald Reagan, dons dark glasses before succumbing to the charms of the penitent Rock who rebrands himself Robbie Robertson and returns to medical school several years after dropping out. An hour later Rock is handy enough with a scalpel to perform brain surgery on Jane and restore her sight! In the meantime I have licked the ironing pile into shape. The credits have barely rolled before I'm out the door en route to collect Mary.

Tuesday lunch time I phone Zennor Road. It's been a long morning. I know of people whose experience of cancer reads like the *Solomon Grundy* rhyme: feeling slightly off-colour one day, diagnosed with a life threatening disease the next, dead the day after. Then there are those that live with the illness for years. Time is a precious commodity. But still there are matters to be weighed up. *Quick and painless* against *long and drawn out* for one. Not much of a choice. An unforeseen accident might rob loved ones of the chance to say '*Goodbye*' but lingering long enough to exchange farewells may not be in the patient's best interests. All of this of course assumes my mother's condition is *incurable*. People *do* survive cancer. It's just that during the course of the morning I have struggled to think of any.

'James Bradley.' The timbre of Jim-Bob's voice at the other end of the phone invites analysis. Only two words but I know the prognosis is not as bad as I'd feared. My father's subsequent words reinforce this view. The cancer in my mother's oesophagus has not spread. Surgery is not possible but chemotherapy is to start at once. 'We need to build your mother up,' Jim-Bob continues, 'we've just been to Tesco to buy her a cream tart for her lunch.'

That weekend we visit my sister, Louisa and her husband Mute, the primordial urge to close ranks in the face of this threat to the family having put to flight concerns of a more frivolous nature. The new colour scheme in the lounge will have to wait, similarly the replacing of the Travolta's criminally neglected racing slicks with tyres possessing something called tread.

We arrive in Brighton shortly after midday. From the faded grandeur of the city centre and its cosmopolitan Saturday clientele we head for Kemptown and my sister's flat. More accurately termed a maisonette - a duplex Louisa calls it - my sister's tastefully decorated abode is situated close to the neighbourhood post office in a four storey building constructed, like its brethren, in the Regency style. Previous visits both enamoured me to and sparked an interest in, the history of the surrounding area. Its founder, Thomas Reed Kemp, apparently fled the country ahead of creditors in 1837 following a decidedly lukewarm response to his exclusive new development on the edge of town from the well-heeled inhabitants of the fashionable resort. Ironically, over the course of the next two hundred years the area became a refuge of sorts; artists, actors and homosexuals taking up residence, all taking flight from the rigours of conformity. Louisa and Mute have lived in the quarter for several years.

Parking the Travolta proves tricky and three or four circuits of the local one-way system are undertaken before a space several inches shorter than strictly required is located. I scrape a thin smear of red paint, donated by an adjacent Alfa Romeo, from the Travolta's front bumper before following my family along the pavement and up Number 23's worn front steps. Freddie beats out a tune on the door bell and seconds later Louisa's fuzzy voice greets us over the intercom. We are buzzed up.

Louisa has put on weight. This is to be expected. Her greying, shoulder-length hair is pulled back from a ruddy, smiling face that could be ten and not five years older than my own. She is thrilled to see us although her nephew, who has been crossing and uncrossing his legs since Worthing, skips the formalities and heads instead for the bathroom.

'Your uncle's in the shower,' Louisa calls after him. Head hung, Freddie re-joins the rest of us in the kitchen where an unidentified broth is steaming on the stove next to a seed encrusted loaf of un-sliced bread. Hatty and Mary respond to their aunt's amiable instructions with the alacritous vigour usually associated with square-bashers under the tutelage of a sadistic and profane Regimental Sergeant Major, gathering cutlery and crockery from familiar locations before transporting them to the adjacent bay-windowed front room. I collect condiments from a chaotically ordered cupboard and follow behind. The front room is furnished in a mish mash of styles, the majority of the pieces having been gleaned from either our Great Aunt Veronica's house the week after she was sectioned under the Mental Health Act or from more contemporary Swedish sources. That I was out of the country at the precise moment Aunt Veronica was adjudged to have gone out of her mind has always been a source of contention between myself and my older sister. Ever since, I've viewed with envy Louisa's oak book case, her folding card table and the art deco drinks trolley I fully intend to ransack later in the day. An assortment of bric-a-brac that includes an eighteen inch high *Peter Rabbit* collection box and a raffia basket (the only piece of Aunt Veronica memorabilia obtained *post* incarceration) softens the edges of even the most rectilinear of this purloined furniture.

We've just sat down to eat, spoons poised, and, in Louisa's case, out of breath, when Mute joins us having earlier been halloed somewhere down the hall by Freddie as he emerged from the bathroom with a heartfelt, *Finally*! The scent of an aftershave long since abandoned by those members of the male population without hermitic tendencies accompanies his arrival and, mingling with the indigenous aromas of soup and incense, helps to create a nostalgically heady atmosphere. 'People!' Mute says taking a seat, planting his elbows on the table and clasping one hand in the other in such a way that for a moment I think he is about to say *grace*. As his nickname suggests, Mute is a man of few words. A broad grin alone communicates his pleasure in seeing his in-laws who for their part are at least as interested in ladling spoonfuls of soup into their mouths as they are in greeting this excessively perfumed late-comer. Conversation is sparse. Empty stomachs stifle meaningful discourse. Verbal interaction can wait. At least until someone figures out where to begin.

Louisa and Mute have been together twenty years,

ten of them as a married couple. They met as post-grads at York University in the early Eighties where an interest in the esoteric facilitated their meeting around a mutual friend's crowded Ouija board. There aren't many women who can claim to have been propositioned by their suitor's illicit manipulation of a planchette across a slab of polished beech. It's not something Louisa likes to shout from the roof tops either mind you. It was after all an interest in the erotic rather than the esoteric that saw them safely through the next ten years, although for old time's sake Mute persuaded Louisa and several forewarned friends to participate in a subtly choreographed séance during which, planchette in hand, he finally popped the question a decade after their first meeting. It's fair to say married life has tested their union. A previous career in education did not make the several miscarriages suffered by my sister any easier to cope with. Nor did my own growing family. Doctors continue to assure Louisa that there is no reason why she should not one day carry a foetus to term. That's as specific as the medical advice has ever got. Nowadays all members of the family are under strict instructions not to jinx the gestation period by open reference to it. A code of practice Louisa also adheres to.

As a decidedly New Age godmother to Mary, Louisa has shown a commendable attention to her duties which began prior to confirmation of her appointment in the role. It was from a fellow practitioner of yoga that Louisa received her initiation into the realms of numerology. For someone with an inexplicably tenuous grasp of her multiplication tables my sister places great faith in the power of numbers, a science, she takes delight in reminding sceptics, that counts Pythagoras amongst its former proponents. Having plotted charts for friends and family using birthdates and the numerical values of the letters contained in their names Louisa had become highly excited at the opportunity provided by Beth's most recent pregnancy. She explained to my less than convinced wife the power a name has to influence a person's psyche and aptitudes. Beth had humoured Louisa who bombarded her sister-in-law with a variety of questions regarding the expectant mother's hopes and fears for the developing foetus. Louisa retired to consult her text books, clarified one or two points with an increasingly unco-operative Beth and returned a week later with the perfect appellation. For a newly developed chemical compound. 'Why don't we just call it H2SO4 and have done with it?' was Beth's indignant response. And so, ignoring Louisa's recommendation, we'd opted for *Mary* instead. A decision, my sister warned us, that we may yet live to regret.

While Louisa puts her faith in numbers, Mute's journey to the fringes of mysticism has been via the unlikely route of science. My brother-in-law runs an IT consultancy business from home. *Runs* implies the expending of great amounts of energy on Mute's part. If that is true the man does a good job in hiding the fact. A notoriously late riser, Mute's working day starts mid-morning following an invigorating walk around his local environs. By three in the afternoon his working day is over, the kettle has been boiled and the camomile-and-lime tea bags are steeping in readiness for his wife's return from her job as a homoeopathist at a nearby alternative therapies clinic. With a work/life balance tilted so emphatically in favour of the latter it is perhaps not surprising that Mute has had time to contemplate the deeper aspects and implications of his work. The emerging ideas contained within quantum physics in particular have strengthened rather than eroded Mute's faith in the sacredness of life and, as he puts it, the *illusory nature* of human existence. It is largely on the back of conversations with my brother-in-law that my Friday morning assemblies at Pebble Bay are written. *The objects of sense exist only when they are perceived*, may be a mantra derived from Berkeley but it came to me via Mute. The bulk of his teachings are less philosophic, more scientific. According to my brother-in-law the universe is predominantly constructed of *dark energy* and *dark matter, stuff* which cannot, as its name suggests, be seen. Its presence can be surmised, however, because of its gravitational effect on other matter. Mute assured me only last Christmas that 95% of all matter is *dark*. I'd grabbed a note book and pencil and, excusing myself from a game of charades, asked him to go on. 'Of the remaining 5% of matter, about 4.5% is non-luminous,' Mute had continued. The rest of what he said I scribbled down and checked with him later. It went something like this: the

0.5% of matter that is neither dark nor non-luminous reflects light. The electromagnetic spectrum makes up a small part of this 0.5% of luminous matter but the portion visible to the human eye is only a tiny fraction of this. 'In cosmic terms,' Mute says, 'humans are practically blind.' I am still trying to mould this information into viable assembly material, the kind of stuff that won't freak too many of the kids out. *Mum, Dad, Mr Bradley says we're all going blind!*

After lunch we stroll the short distance to the sea front. From there we head west towards the *Palace Pier.* The temperature has risen and the sun's unseasonable warmth elevates the walking experience to that of a pleasure for even the youngest amongst us. In between laboured breaths, Louisa informs me that our destination should now correctly be referred to as *Brighton* Pier, the name change having coincided with a recent fire on the long defunct *West Pier* scuppering plans once and for all of returning the rusting skeleton to its former glory. Louisa would have me believe that the two incidents are linked. It is unclear whether Mute gives this conspiracy theory any credence since he possesses his own nugget of pier trivia concerning a recently released movie set in the city during a previous decade featuring the Palace Pier erroneously under its *current* name. Anachronisms of this sort interest Mute greatly. It takes one to know one I suppose. The blue plaque on a building to our right interrupts pier prattle. Playwright, Terrence Rattigan was once a resident. *The Winslow Boy* and that bloody postal order. Ronnie Winslow's sly cigarette in the locker room: *dark matter.* Thank God for the astute Sir Robert Morton.

Freddie and his sisters are anxious to experience the pleasures of the pier as soon as we reach sea level. However, coffee at one of the bars and cafes on the beach grabs the attention of the adults who today at any rate control the decision-making process. Certain concessions have to be made though. 'Play on the beach while we have a drink and we'll go to the pier later,' I assure my offspring, some of whom are tearful. The offer of an ice cream makes my request more tempting. Throw in a flake and you've got a deal is the gist of Hatty's response. By the time these negotiations are complete Mute is approaching our table with a tray of drinks, namely an americano, two cappuccinos and an absurdly tall latte.

'Thought I was ordering a straight-forward coffee with milk,' Mute shrugs self consciously as he attempts to guide the unwieldy glass towards his lips.

'How have you been?' Beth asks Louisa having checked the children are out of earshot. This is the first time anyone has alluded to my mother's illness never mind its impact on my sister's condition.

'A mess,' Louisa replies, 'I cry without warning and at the oddest moments.'

'How is your mum taking it?' The clatter of latte beaker on saucer almost obscures Mute's inquiry.

I'm not sure what to say to this. 'Inscrutably,' is the best I can muster.

For a few minutes we exchange titbits of information garnered from conversations with Jim-Bob and my mother, both telephonic and tête-à-tête.

'Mum's a fighter,' Louisa says.

'Provided she likes the odds.'

'She won't just lie down,' Beth says, her glance of disapproval aimed more I suspect at my use of gambling-speak than the sentiment behind the words.

'She's always been terrified of dying.' Ah, yes. *Rose Bradley: A life, Chapter Two: teenage death phobias.* Once a firm believer in the concept of reincarnation, my mother's current mantra, *when you're dead, you're dead,* says as much about her views on life as it does about those on death. The prospect of returning time after time to the corporeal world ceased to inspire my mother some years ago if her oft uttered quip, '*Make it stop!*' is anything to go by. Such flippant references to ones own mortality are harder to sustain *at the sharp end* however. It's clear that at the moment none of us can say with any certainty how Mum will respond to her predicament.

'It's early days,' Mute says summing things up. His words and the arrival of an ice-cream smeared Mary at our table bring the conversation to a halt.

Back in Kemptown the children are fed pasta and a take away is ordered for the adults. Louisa insists on the consumption of alcohol with the evening meal, although *she* will be abstaining for obvious reasons. Not wishing to draw attention to my sister's condition, I make for the nearest off-licence, returning with a selection of brews and the notion that we hold our own beer festival. The idea is enthusiastically endorsed by all present. I suggest a complicated scoring system involving the awarding of points to each beer after their blind tasting which threatens to completely take the fun out of proceedings until I assure everyone that by the evening's end we will be able to name Kemptown's very own champion lager beer! A DVD playing in the guest bedroom is used to distract underage drinkers and then, taking it in turns to decant the beer into unmarked glasses the festival gets under way. Several bottles are sampled and awarded points prior to the arrival of our meal. To ensure we keep track of the points awarded to each beer a bottle top is placed face down in the order in which the beverages are sampled on the kitchen breakfast bar for later reference. This foolproof system does not survive the arrival of our Indian take away however since Mute, the only participant yet to decant is unaware of the location of the bottle tops until he has slid the box containing our meal onto the breakfast bar scattering shiny metallic discs across the kitchen floor in the process.

'You fucking idiot!' several connoisseurs shriek simultaneously when it becomes apparent what Mute has done. We may not know what we've been drinking but whatever it is we can be sure it's fairly potent. While Mute attempts to replace the bottle tops in their original order before he scattered the bastards to the four winds the rest of us, still cursing the latte drinking swine, unpack the foil trays and prise off the card lids. If the integrity of proceedings has already been undermined by Mute's heavy handedness worse is to come. The Rogan Josh, Madras and Bhuna play havoc with the participant's taste buds. Beth claims later on that it was the combination of the vegetable madras and the German Weis beer that immediately preceded the decanting of the bottle of Kingfisher that caused her to mark down her pre-festival favourite. The rest of us interrupt the totting up of points to shout her down, her husband pointing out a little too emphatically that as usual she hardly ate anything anyway! Only when it becomes apparent that his own favourite, *Cobra*, has limped in a disappointing fifth does he have any sympathy for his wife who by this time is lying prone on the sofa unaware that the title *Champion Beer* is being awarded to an obscure Indian lager called *Akash*. No, I'd never heard of it either.

Later, when everyone else is in bed Mute and I are left alone. Several espressos have taken the edge off the alcohol. 'Julian,' I say, for once addressing my brother-in-law by his real, and no doubt numerically inferior, name, 'life sucks.'

Mute does not reply immediately. For a moment I think he's fallen asleep.

'Three great kids, attractive wife, nice home. I see what you mean.'

Dying mother?

I let Mute's words sink in before replying. 'I'll admit I've gathered together some excellent raw materials.'

There's a pause.

'So you fancy my wife?'

Mute snickers. 'By *life* I assume you are referring to the three-dimensional illusion most of us mistake for reality.'

I think I can feel a headache coming on. If my brother-in-law wants to hide his ardour for my wife behind an esoteric smokescreen then so be it. The man's been pulling this kind of stunt for as long as I can remember.

'Go on,' I say, 'I'll buy it.'

In his armchair Mute's posture shifts. He has that far away look in his eyes I've seen before. Uncannily, he seems to transcend the effects of the recently ingested chemicals riding roughshod through his body.

'Hindus call it *Maya*,' he says, 'the illusion bewitching anyone under the spell of Lila, the divine play.'

I put down my coffee which seems to be lubricating the electronic links between the different regions of my brain nicely. *Incoming Information: retrieve similar data. Check.*

'*Life's but a walking shadow, a poor player that struts and frets his hour upon the stage and then is heard no more; it is a tale told by an idiot, full of sound and fury, signifying nothing.*'

In the process of reciting my schoolboy Shakespeare I have risen to my feet. This is good. I hadn't been at all sure I could still stand.

'I'm glad that expensive education of yours wasn't completely wasted.'

Abandoning plans for a moving rendition of a soliloquy from Hamlet I sit down, slightly deflated.

Mute is not without sympathy. 'Your *pertinent* interruption refers, so far as I can tell, to the same *reality* in which Eastern thought suggests our consciousness has become entrapped. What Hindus call *Maya*.'

I drain my coffee cup. When I replace it on the table my hand appears to be shaking. 'So,' I say, 'none of this is real?' I sweep my right hand across my abdomen almost dislodging a lamp on an adjacent table.

Mute picks up a porcelain figurine pilfered from Aunt Veronica. 'I hope not,' he says. Chemically dependent I may be at this point in time but I am still aware that the gist of this conversation isn't entirely new to me. I've known Mute a long time after all. I've seen *The Matrix* for Christ's sake.

'Since we're quoting from literature: '*Lift not the painted veil which those who live call Life: though unreal shapes be pictured there, and it but mimic all we would believe.'*

'Keats!'

'How much were your school fees?'

'Blake?'

'Slightly warmer. Shelley.' There is a fine line between instruction and plain showing off. Mute seems to appreciate he's in danger of crossing it. I suspect he takes the empty *After Eight* box I bounce off his head as a hint. 'Look,' he says, 'you want to feel better; I want to help make you feel better. Since you're obviously still drunk - and don't try and deny it - I'll keep it simple.'

'Gee, I'll try and follow.'

'Quantum physics says, solid matter does not exist.'

I try very hard not to look phased by this information.

'Atoms are mostly empty space held together by a mysterious force that causes them to vibrate. Change the frequency of the vibration, change the structure of the atoms.'

'Gotcha.'

'What is the mysterious force?'

For a moment I think Mute expects an answer.

'Consciousness.'

Mute pauses as though expecting me to object.

'Since everything is made of atoms, everything is basically the same stuff, *one*. Brahman according to Hinduism. We are all one consciousness experiencing itself subjectively. The separateness of things: human beings, animals, plants, minerals is an illusion. All just atoms vibrating at different frequencies. If life is an illusion then so is death. What doesn't *exist* in the first place cannot die.'

Mute casts me a smile. 'Understand?'

I do my best to sit up. I feel as though I have just been made party to information until now revealed only to the initiated. Looking extremely thoughtful I prop my chin on my hands and lean towards my brother-in-law. 'So you fancy my wife,' I say.

The role of caffeine in the creative process really shouldn't be underestimated.

Monday morning's post brings news from *Dorset Scene* magazine. The *Beaminster Brewery* feature will now appear in the *May* issue. Peter Swinton is less impressed with my idea regarding Dorset's railway stations although he says he's willing to be persuaded, whatever that means. However, the Tom Chandler piece, when it gets written, is a dead cert.

Good news this may be but it isn't until I've knocked back a double espresso mid-morning that I start to believe I can publish those six articles before my rapidly approaching fortieth birthday. Shit, I think, why not make it eight?

I decide to drive to Portland; give the Travolta a run out. It seems reluctant to join me however. Feigning a cough it splutters in the car park for several minutes before the threat of a full service inspires obedience.

It's not a great day. A dour blanket separates earth and sky. Not that the weather conditions should unduly hamper my research. According to my sources the branch line from Melcombe Regis to Portland closed to passenger traffic in 1952 although goods trains were still utilising the line as late as 1965. As expected, there is nothing left of the line's terminus at Easton save for a commemorative street name and an old bridge. I console myself that the nearby museum at Wakeham might have some relevant information or illuminating photographs. The lady manning the counter in the small room that doubles as entrance and shop looks surprised to see me. Although she doesn't actually say, '*There was a railway on Portland?*' when I ask for information about the Isle's former rail system, she may as well have done for all the help she is. I spend an hour poking around the place just the same. I'm about to leave, maybe grab a coffee en route for home when I spot an old photograph on the wall at the top of the stairs leading to the first floor. Depicted is the partially constructed Portland Bill Lighthouse. While interesting enough it is the date that catches my eye. The lighthouse will be one hundred years old in a matter of months. Topical subject matter. Gold dust. There is not a moment to lose. I put thoughts of coffee on hold, buy three souvenir pencils at the shop and jog back to the Travolta resting nearby in a makeshift car park that once formed part of an old quarry. Portland Bill Lighthouse is a five minute drive away. The Travolta offers no objections.

As I near the Bill I'm struck by the unique nature of the place. Half a mile from my destination water near enough surrounds the Travolta. So do lighthouses. Former *Trinity House* towers stand to left and right of the road. A car park looms on my right. Behind it a landscape more lunar than the one used by NASA to fake those Moon landings. And dominating the whole vista a 143 foot tall lighthouse. Land's End, John O' Groats? Eat your hearts out. The grey ribbon of road I've been following unspools before hitting auto reverse in the shade of the tower, doubling back on itself just yards from the huge smooth limestone slabs that confront the sea.

Parked, I feed a fifty pence piece into the meter and, buttoning my coat against the chill wind, walk towards the huge red and white phallus penetrating the grey afternoon sky. Inside the scrotal visitor centre I explain my mission to the girl at the reception desk. I'm directed upwards. Although the lighthouse is fully automated, Brian Granger, the former Head

Lighthouse Keeper, continues to frequent the upper reaches of the structure sharing his technical knowledge and personal reminiscences with tourists, anoraks and anyone else willing to listen.

It's a long way up. Make that *down*. Climbing the narrow, bannisterless staircase that follows the curve of the lighthouse's outer wall I am reminded of my fear of heights.

I hear Brian Granger before I see him. When visual contact is made I notice he is sharing his cramped quarters immediately below the lantern room with a party of school children. It's only when they've ascended the ladder to take a look at the structure's optics that I get the chance to introduce myself. Granger is a large, powerfully built man who seems to think crushing the fuck out of my right hand is an acceptable form of greeting. I smile at the lighthouse keeper through watering eyes and retract my pureed metacarpals. Granger speaks with a local accent, his voice deep as the perilous waters without. The man is larger than life. Thus far in our acquaintance he's done everything bar beat his chest. I console myself that a man posturing at the top of a 143ft red and white striped erection is unlikely to be genitally well endowed. Our discussion is necessarily brief. I ask Brian if I can interview him about the lighthouse's forthcoming centenary. He tells me he'd love to help but at the moment he's busy. If I want though he'll clear his schedule next Monday, give me a guided tour, answer my questions and arm wrestle me for my wife. I decline the offer of a parting handshake.

I look up *chemotherapy* in my second-hand copy of the *Penguin Medical Encyclopaedia* : *Treatment of infection with drugs that poison the infecting microbes without serious harm to the patient.* The book makes cancer sound like a chest infection. Its companion, *The Penguin Guide to Medicines* is slightly more revealing. The types of drugs used in chemotherapy are listed. As are their side effects. For a moment I yearn for the sugar coated ambiguities of the *Penguin Encyclopaedia*. I have gathered together a wide range of reference books on my bedside table. The *Chambers 20th Century Dictionary* labels chemotherapy *the treatment of a disease by means of a chemical compound.* This is a more promising start; now we're getting somewhere. But several minutes later, eyelids drooping, I'm still struggling to differentiate between an infection and a disease. *Chambers* defines disease as *a wont of health*, to infect as *to taint or corrupt something*. Beside me, Beth has long since discarded *Madame Bovary* for the night. She voices doubt as to the benefits to my mother's health of my defining *chemotherapy* and suggests that my own health might be about to suffer if I don't put down the dictionary and switch off the *bloody* bedside lamp. 'Your mum doesn't need another doctor, Hugh, she needs a son.'

The next evening I phone Jim-Bob. He fills me in on chemotherapy: Day One. It had not begun in propitious style. The Saab had steadfastly refused to start. My mother's sense of foreboding triggered, she'd grumbled, 'everything's bloody dying around here.'

'So we called a taxi,' Jim-Bob explains. 'We still got there on time.' I can picture my mother walking into *Oncology* with her punctuality obsessed husband who has just announced in upbeat fashion their arrival *on time* against all odds. '*Hoo-fucking-ray'* I can hear her say.

'Your mother's in bed now, sleeping,' Dad says when I inquire as to the wisdom of paying a visit. 'She's very tired.' I have long admired my parents' attempts to shield me from the full force of life's knocks. I have a suspicion chemotherapy's side effects are not limited merely to fatigue. I let it pass. I promise to call round the next day, ask my father to say *Hello* to Mum for me and hang up.

Extract from *Life in Dorset*, 3rd July 2000
The Bradley children are entrusted to their grandparents for the day. Rose Bradley, family matriarch and self-proclaimed Prisoner of Zennor (Road), insists on a trip out somewhere (anywhere). James Bradley, being a creature of habit decides on Pecorama, the model railway exhibition, miniature steam railway and landscaped pleasure gardens situated an hour

away in the East Devon fishing village of Beer. To suggest the stay-at-home, 'You've got a bloody garden why do you want to go out?' *sixty-one year old is a regular visitor to Pecorama is misleading - the last time he went there Margaret Thatcher had yet to win the key marginal constituency Argentinians still refer to as* Las Malvinas. *However, Pecorama is the last place James Bradley took minors on a fun, no holds barred day out if you don't count the time we visited Mum while she was in hospital having her varicose veins seen to. Hatty, Freddie and Mary are very familiar with the place and absolutely love it although their enthusiasm lasts only for as long as it takes their bickering grandparents to become hopelessly lost. As well as their elders' poor sense of direction it is the abbreviated phraseology that passes for communication employed by the less than patient Rose Bradley that adds to the party's problems. Having driven around the one-way system several times in Seaton, the seaside resort only a couple of miles from their destination, Jim-Bob, on the instructions of his wife, brings the car to a halt beside a woman he hopes is a resident. The red-faced lady sitting beside him will take things from here. Looking vaguely desperate and projecting her voice with perhaps unnecessary and ill-advised gusto, Rose Bradley barks at the pedestrian, 'We want Beer!' The woman, probably sensing danger, bends her mind to the task and within seconds has issued a series of instructions which, when followed, lead my exasperated parents to... the nearest off license!*

I'm due at the lighthouse at ten. The Travolta won't start. Even to my untrained ear it's clear that this morning my *wheels* are going nowhere. I check my wristwatch: five past nine. My destination is at least forty minutes away. On a clear run. In a car that wasn't constructed while England were FIFA World Champions. Abandoning the Travolta, I detect the whiff of panic in the air. Like fog enveloping a control tower its vaporous coils begin to compromise my ability to see straight. I return to the house, jump on my bike and make for Zennor Road. In these circumstances I know it's considered polite to call first but there are few sights more persuasive than a child hyperventilating on a parent's doorstep. Particularly if the two are related.

Jim-Bob answers the door. He expresses surprise at seeing me and indicates that I should enter. I stay put, grab hold of the door jambs - *you'll never take me alive* - and prepare to speak. By their intonation, I contrive to make the words, 'Dad, can I borrow your car?' sound as though they could be my last.

'It's at the garage, Hugh,' he says. 'It's…' This is no time for social niceties. I'm in the saddle and peddling through the front gates before my father can finish his sentence. A hundred yards down the street sanity as much as my unreliable braking system brings me to a halt. I pull out a note book from my jacket pocket and search for Brian Granger's number. There's no sign of it, probably I reason, because I wrote the fucker in my *blue* note book. I scroll down the contacts list on my mobile phone looking for the name of a friend who might be able to help. But there's no one. *Does everyone have bloody full-time jobs these days?* I put the phone away and root about in my jacket pocket some more. I pull out a crumpled piece of paper on which I see another telephone number. No. Not that desperate. I have not been near the Research Centre in weeks. Not since that impromptu game of Blind Man's Buff with Alex. But circumstances change. I realise that I *am* that desperate. It's not as if Alex attacked me with a blunt instrument after all.

Alex seems pleased to hear from me. 'I need a favour.' I say without preamble and explain the situation.

'I'll be at your house in five minutes.'

The line goes dead.

Fuck, I think, I won't. Relief fuels my ride home. I jump a few red lights, shout 'Sorry!' to an old lady who has the mistaken belief that the green man affords *her* right of way and arrive at Durnford Street somewhat out of breath. *Hand me the fucking yellow jersey someone.* Something at any rate to wipe away the streams of sweat rolling down my face. Alex has made good time too. A red Mini Cooper pulls up outside the house moments after I've rolled my bike into the back yard and checked my pockets for pen and Dictaphone. I pull open the passenger door and jump in, offering my thanks while groping for a seat belt. I'm greeted with a smile.

'Where to?' my chauffeur asks.

The drive to Portland is predictable: slow-moving traffic approaching Weymouth, a broken down bus on the esplanade and an unscheduled stop beside the quay where Alex attempts to insert three inches of tongue down my oesophagus. You know the kind of thing. I'm ashamed to say I lost it big time. I'd had enough. Those fucking buses are *always* breaking down. The thing with the tongue? Really should have seen that coming. If there's one thing worse than being mistaken about someone and making a fool of yourself, it's being right, slap bang on the fucking money. I really don't want to dwell on the subject. But to satisfy your misguided curiosity I'll indulge in a spot of regression:

Alex has already mistaken my knee for the gear stick twice and I've only just finished making it damned clear that I won't be tolerating any mistaken identity vis-à-vis the handbrake when the Mini Cooper comes to an unexpected halt beside the harbour. Before I can open my mouth - or more correctly - before I can close it, I'm jumped. Pinned beneath Alex I struggle to free myself but my left arm becomes snagged on the lever that tilts my seat forward and my right hand somehow ends up sandwiched between the handbrake and Alex's knee. It is my assailant's hands that I am more worried about though. They seem to be working their way down my chest and I have the distinct impression that they are just passing through, their ultimate destination being somewhat further *south.* In a last desperate attempt at halting their migratory path I yank my right hand upwards with all my strength releasing my hand and, as it turns out, the handbrake. The car starts to roll towards the unguarded edge of the quay. *MAN DROWNS IN HARBOUR FOLLOWING LUCKY ESCAPE FROM SEXUAL PREDATOR.* The danger of imminent molestation suddenly recedes. Back in the driver's seat, Alex manages to arrest the car's forward motion via the brake pedal with a matter of inches to spare. This close to the water's edge the Mini Cooper is attracting a lot of unwanted attention. Alex starts the engine, slams the car into reverse and then heads for the town bridge with a toneless, 'Let me know if I'm going too fast.'

It's a little late for that, I think.

At the lighthouse I'm half out the passenger door before the car has ground to a halt. 'I'll be about an hour,' I tell Alex, 'I can get the bus back.'

'I'll wait,' Alex replies, 'you can buy me a coffee.'

I'm five minutes late. Brian Granger is waiting for me inside the visitor centre. *Sorry, Brian: stuck behind a stationery bus on the esplanade , then sexually assaulted beside the harbour.* Crossing the twelve feet of floor that separates the main doors from the reception desk I steel myself for the bone crunching handshake that awaits me. Granger ignores my sacrificial fingers however, performs a nifty side step for a man so large and gives me a hearty slap on the back that both empties my lungs and very nearly embeds me in a display of souvenirs and assorted knick-knacks to the front of the ticket desk. 'Good to see you again Hugh,' he bellows, 'follow me.' I take a moment to reinflate my lungs and do as instructed.

I'd imagined the interview taking place somewhere high above the ground, perhaps the lantern room or some other wind buffeted vertiginous hideaway off limits to and beyond the physical capabilities of the general public. Instead Brian takes me through a side exit and around the back of the visitor centre to a small stone hut at the foot of the tower. 'We won't be disturbed in here,' he assures me. Once inside he motions for me to sit, expediting the process somewhat by bringing down a huge hand on one of my shoulders. I feel like a criminal about to be interrogated by a hard-boiled detective. The hut is sparsely furnished. Besides the seat into which I have been driven there is one other chair and a narrow dividing table. While I extract Dictaphone, note book and pen from my jacket pocket Brian removes three large books from a shelf and, sitting down opposite me, places them between us. 'Before the lighthouse was automated whoever was on duty had to record everything in one of these. I thought we could take a look at them later if you like.'

It seems Brian lived at the lighthouse for over twenty years several of them as Principal Lighthouse Keeper. When automation occurred in 1996 he took on a role that amounted, as far as I can tell, to caretaker and glorified tour guide. I express interest in the daily routine of a lighthouse keeper and learn that Brian's bone shattering grip was honed winding the mechanism that rotated the lighthouse's optics and in lugging five gallon paraffin containers up and down spiral staircases. 'We worked two days on and one day off,' he tells me. 'The first watch was from 4am to noon during which you'd dismantle, clean and reassemble the lens. When we burnt paraffin a lot of soot was created and the lantern used to get bloody dirty. At noon you'd have lunch and get some shut eye before the 8pm to midnight watch. Next day you'd be back on from noon to 8pm, have a four hour break, then do midnight to 4am. The day after that was a day off.'

I ask Brian if he has any anecdotes that might interest the readers of *Dorset Scene*. He takes a moment to think. 'One night,' he says, one of the keepers - no need to mention names - received several calls asking if he'd remembered to put the light on. He checked the monitoring equipment. 'Yes!' he said. Half an hour later he gets another call and checks again. When the calls keep coming he goes up to the lantern room to investigate, to set his mind at rest. Turns out he was right: the light was on. Only he'd forgotten to open the bloody protective curtains!' *Lighthouse keepers do it with the drapes open.*

The interview lasts just shy of an hour. I promise to let Brian know when publication is imminent and to return one Sunday morning at 10.30 to hear him sound the old fog horn, no longer in regular use, for the tourists. Fearing a parting bear hug or playful fireman's lift I take my leave while Brian is hoisting his log books back onto their shelf and manage to vacate the premises without further damage to my skeletal frame or respiratory system. I give the lighthouse an admiring upward glance and wonder how many souls it has guided safely around the treacherous waters off shore.

I spot Alex, hair blowing in the habitual breeze, waving at me from a large rock midway between the lighthouse and the shore-side café. Odysseus was lucky: they strapped the bastard to the ship's mast in similar circumstances.

'How'd it go?'

'Most informative,' I reply, 'let's go.'

Inside we order americanos from a startlingly albino waiter and I give Alex a quick summary of the hour I have spent with Brian.

'You didn't go up the tower then? Alex sounds disappointed.

'Nope. '

'Well I'm afraid lighthouses and lighthouse keepers don't really do it for me.'

'What about married men?' I waft my left hand before Alex's eyes hoping the glint of gold might strike a cord.

'There's married and then there's merely *ringed.*'

'I love my wife,' I say, trying to make it crystal clear to which group I belong.

Our coffee arrives. *Would you look at the crema on that.*

'You don't have to be so touchy, you know. I mis-read the signs, made a mistake. Plenty of people would be flattered.'

'I am. Thank you. But no thank you.'

Verbally, Alex gives the impression of having taken my point. Physically I'm not so sure. The polite rules of etiquette by which a married man and his companion are supposed to behave while partaking of coffee are still not being followed. Alex is leaning *way* too far across the table. Eye contact is a tad too intense. That slight smudge of crema on my upper lip? Could have taken care of that myself thank you very much.

If the wiping of froth from my face makes me feel uncomfortable things are about to get a whole lot worse. I see her for the first time as Alex grabs my hand, ostensibly to get a closer look at my wedding band. Fran is seated near a window looking straight at me. She and Beth go way back although lately, following Fran's divorce, they haven't seen so much of each other. My current predicament could be just the catalyst needed to re-establish contact. The colour leaves my face faster than an Olympic athlete pumped full of growth hormones (accidentally ingested via an innocuous herbal tea) exploding from the blocks.

'Are you alright?' Alex gives my hand a concerned squeeze. I extract it in exaggerated fashion.

'I think we should go,' I say, standing to leave, turning my back to Fran as I do so.

'I haven't finished my coffee.' *No, but you're having a lot more success with my marriage.* Alex stays put. Looks up at me. I make a strange sound, half cough, half exasperated sigh. I am about to say something, though I'm not exactly sure what, when a foreign object of some sort, an insect possibly, lodges itself in my windpipe and I start to choke. I try to contain the spluttering and wheezing routine that follows to no avail. Terrific I think as colour, I suspect purple, surges back to my facial features and Alex rises to my aid. I suspect my attempts at discretion have already been undermined somewhat. Taking a starring role in a re-enactment of the Heimlich Manoeuvre ten feet from Fran's table isn't going to help much either. As it is our albino waiter arrives at the scene first. While he slaps my back I take the opportunity to grab a glass of water from the tray he has just put down on a nearby table. I tilt my head back. The liquid burns my throat. I feel as though I'm about to spontaneously combust. *White man bring FIRE water.* Vodka and tonic unless I'm very much mistaken. Blue Label. A double at least. Excellent. Choking to death *and* pissed. This scene can't possible get any worse I remember thinking shortly before passing out.

Back in Dorchester, Alex drops me beside my car and asks for the nth time if I'm okay.

'Why wouldn't I be?' I try the Travolta again before calling the AA. An hour later I have the privilege of listening to someone describe my car as a *museum piece* before watching as it is towed away to its usual garage. I telephone ahead so that its arrival won't be completely unexpected. I replace my notebook in my desk drawer and do likewise with the Dictaphone after depressing the record button and speaking clearly into the mic: 'memo to self: instruct editor of *Dorset Scene* magazine to make cheque for article on lighthouse payable to Compton Garage'. By this time it's nearly three o'clock.

During the walk back from St Paul's with Mary I consider whether or not to mention the pantomime on Portland to Beth. I have to ask Mary to repeat much of what she says to me.

'Daddy, you *never* listen!'

'What?' I say. Mary laughs. At first I haven't a clue why.

I decide to come clean about seeing Fran. Beth hasn't spoken to the woman in months but who can resist the temptation to trash a friend's personal life? That sort of opportunity doesn't come along every day. Why did they stop talking anyway? I'll tell Beth the Travolta wouldn't start, that as luck would have it a vague acquaintance from the Research Centre spotted me pulling my hair out, took pity and gave me a lift. From there on in I'll stick to the truth. I bought coffee afterwards as a thank you and that bitch Fran, you remember her don't you sweetheart, the one that tells those awful lies about people, saw us and probably got *completely* the wrong end of the stick. *Especially when the vague acquaintance started feeling me up and together with an albino waiter carried me unconscious from the building.*

That night I make roasted vegetables and pasta for dinner. I greet my wife with an affectionate and heartfelt kiss. I remind myself, in case I'd forgotten, that I've actually done nothing wrong and sit down at the table to await my opportunity. Beth picks up her fork, looks at me and bursts into tears. Jesus, I think, Fran doesn't waste any time.

Mary says, 'I think Mummy wants her dinner whizzing up too Daddy.'

'I have had such a bad day!' Beth says when she regains control. She gives Mary's hand a squeeze, wipes her eyes and asks, 'so how was your day?'

'Fine,' I say, 'fine!'

Arriving at Zennor Road I find my mother sitting on the sofa cocooned in a rug watching a cookery show on the television. The sound is whacked right up. Beside the foot stool on which her uncovered feet are propped is a small table itself supporting a carton of something called *Vitijuice*. I ask Mum how she's feeling and she shrugs and says 'Okay,' mustering a weak accompanying smile. I join her on the sofa. She gives my hand a squeeze and for a time we watch a pair of celebrity chefs putting a group of *wannabes* through their paces. The volume discourages conversation; I assume this is deliberate. There's nothing wrong with my mother's hearing. Jim-Bob comes in and out of the room several times but confines himself to the kitchen area making only one sortie to the upholstered end of the room and this to detach the plastic straw from the *Vitijuice* and insert it into the unopened carton. 'He wants me to drink that,' my mother says granting the carton a perfunctory nod, 'as if I don't feel sick enough.'

I pick up the carton taking care not to squirt any liquid out through the straw as I do so. 'Strawberry flavoured!' I smile and recall the last time I took medicine that claimed as much. Mum's sideways grimace confirms my suspicions. Besides laying claim to a great taste the spiel on the carton also assures adherents that *Vitijuice* contains all the essential nutrients required for a healthy existence. I suspect the appearance of this elixir at my mother's elbow has more to do with her inability to swallow solid food and post-chemo nausea than any maliciousness on my father's part.

'Take it away!' Mum says, waving a hand in its direction as the celebrity chefs discard several *wannabes* with similarly disingenuous displays of regret. As I reach the kitchen sink Jim-Bob re-enters the room and by eyebrow movement alone communicates an interest in the current liquid-to-air ratio inside the carton. I shake my head and his articulate brows descend to within a half inch of his eyes before retreating to higher ground when the television is switched off at the far end of the room. I ditch the *Vitijuice* and return to the sofa having grown tired conversing with a man incapable of communicating via any means other than the supraorbital ridge. I field several questions about Hatty and Freddie and our recent visit to Louisa's. The removal of the *Vitijuice* together with tales of Freddie's potent flatulence on long haul car journeys seems to nourish my mother's spirits. Jim-Bob brings me a cup of coffee which I was not aware I'd requested - a slight twitch of my left eyebrow back in the kitchen was probably all the encouragement he'd needed.

'When do you go back to the hospital? I ask.

'We've a trip to Bournemouth Royal next week to look forward to,' my father says resorting to verbal communication and seating himself in an armchair. 'In fact,' he continues, getting up and heading for the kitchen table, 'I wanted to check with you where the Royal is and how to get there.' He returns to the sofa with a road atlas.

'It's upside down,' my mother tells him before he has had a chance to apply reading glasses. The expression on Mum's face suggests she's more worried about the chances of her husband getting her to the hospital on time/at all than she is at the prospect of another doctor sliding blunt metallic objects down her throat.

Jim-Bob has the Bournemouth street map open. 'As I understand it,' he says, 'the hospital is here.'

I study the map. 'That's Poole General,' I say, playing to my audience. 'Bournemouth Royal is over here.' I run my forefinger across the map. Poole and Bournemouth form a single conurbation. It's sometimes difficult to pinpoint exactly where one ends and the other begins. My mother expels air through slack lips in an effort to demonstrate derision. The ploy works admirably. Jim-Bob's supraorbital ridge is working overtime. It's clear my parents haven't a hope in hell of getting to Bournemouth Royal on their own.

'I'll take you,' I tell them.

'But you'll be at work,' my mother protests weakly.

'Then I'll take you this Sunday. We'll do a dummy run.'

Friday evening. Jesus Christ I'm hungry. Before heading for the Imperial Garden though I drive round to Zennor Road leaving Beth sprawled and scowling on the sofa listening to the weekly maternal monologue, wedging the odd phoneme into conversational gaps that open about as often as a mother superior's legs. *What's the matter? The price of gin gone up again? Too many apostrophes on the local Chinese restaurant's menu?* I don't seem to have much patience these days. And my language is fucking appalling.

Mum has ingested nothing all week save the odd recalcitrant sip of Vitijuice. Each face-distorting gulp of the vile concoction has been followed by a torrent of abuse. Consequently my mother is now very weak and, as of last night, delirious due to severe dehydration. She has spent the day cuffed to a steroid drip via which she has been force-fed nutrients. All this I learn from telephone conversations with Jim-Bob. When I find her in her bedroom later in the evening it is safe to say my mother's mindset is still in a state of flux. News from the outside world elicits the response, 'The sooner somebody blows up the whole bloody planet the better,' whereas by the time I stand up to leave she is on more positive form: 'I think I can get through this,' she says. Or rather whispers. Ten minutes earlier, midway through likening Vitijuice to drinking *dog piss* my mother's voice had gone. We'd both been both taken aback by this unforeseen development. The thinning hair I'd expected, but this? No. For the rest of my stay my mother communicates in hushed but no less forceful tones. Louisa, she tells me, is coming to see her tomorrow. 'A flying visit,' she says. 'She doesn't want to be away from home at the moment if she can help it. There's no point taking any chances I suppose.'

Backing the Travolta out of the driveway I nearly run down Doreen on her way in from next door. I wind the window down and begin to apologise profusely. The septuagenarian doesn't break step not even when she brushes past a wing mirror rendering it redundant so far as manoeuvring the Travolta through the front gates is concerned. *Come back you fucking bitch! G*etting out of the car to realign the mirror I have to bite my tongue. Half an hour with my gravely ill mother and *nothing*; a wonky wing mirror and I lose the plot entirely.

The next day Louisa and Mute call in. They have come from Zennor Road where, by all accounts, they found Mum slightly more cheerful than when I'd left her the day before. I offer them tea or coffee. 'We can't stop long,' my sister says, before heading for the lavatory. Upon opening the kitchen cupboard I realise that I've forgotten to buy tea bags. George

Koltanowski would understand. He used to run errands to the corner shop for his wife. He could memorise forty or fifty chess boards and beat a roomful of people blindfolded but nine times out of ten he'd forget what he'd been sent out for.

I take the opportunity, while ladling Lavazza into the cafétierre, to inquire as to Louisa's well-being.

'She's doing fine,' Mute assures me.

'What's it been now, seven months?' I ask.

Mute nods. 'There've been some scares along the way,' he says, 'but so far, so good. A day at a time, you know?'

'Did I ever mention,' I say, 'that George Koltanowski and his wife met on a blind date?' *How else would George meet his future spouse?*

Mute gives me a *What the fuck is that supposed to mean?* look. BLINDFOLD CHESS CHAMPION *MATES*.

Hey, don't shoot the bloody messenger, I think.

Beth has Tuesday morning off, ostensibly for medical reasons. The family GP, Dr Ridge is popular with his patients. In fact he's a hard man to pin down. Unless his patients are willing to give their physician's diary priority over their own a full lunar cycle is liable to have run its course before an audience is granted. Beth knows this and Nigel knows it too - he's okayed her 10.30 a.m. appointment and told her to take the whole morning off if she needs it. (Staying late to help draft the school's Self-evaluation Form has its plusses.) Putting a finger on the reason for Ridge's popularity isn't difficult. He's sympathetic, holistic in his approach and more than willing to listen. He also has a forehead lifted straight from a Tefal commercial. But that's not strictly relevant. Softly spoken and thorough, there is no one else Beth considers consulting about her increasingly malicious migraines.

By 11.15 a.m. my wife is sitting opposite me in *Taste*, the county town's premier independent coffee house and eatery. Around us Dorchester's professional classes discuss business matters alongside the idle wives of middle managers grown neurotic from inactivity. Doctor Ridge has prescribed a new breed of pill that he himself swears by. He has confirmed Beth's suspicions regarding the decreasing effectiveness of her current *over the counter* medication and has assured her that these new innocuous looking caplets won't pull any punches. She can hardly wait for her next migraine.

We're sipping refills by the time my wife is finished relating the details of her visit to the good doctor. Everything Beth's said thus far is rendered preamble though when she mentions running into Fran in the surgery waiting room. The sipping on my side of the table morphs into a rather undignified slurp. 'Ah,' I say.

'Fran told me she saw you last week at the lighthouse.

'Yes,' I pronounce the word cautiously, prolonging its delivery.

'She said she saw you with someone.'

'That's correct.' No point denying it. *I've done nothing wrong.*

'She said you looked intimate.'

'A handshake would look intimate to that emotional husk.' Did that sound a tad defensive?

'Hugh, are you gay?' *At this particular moment in time? Not especially.*

'Who is he?'

'Who is who?'

'The man Fran saw you with. The man who was touching you in the café!'

'Touching me where?'

'Hugh, this isn't funny.' Beth's eyes fill up. She takes a second, composes herself. 'Who is he?'

This is uncomfortable. It's more than likely my discomfort is being mistaken for guilt. Time to come clean. 'His name is Alex,' I say.

'Is he your lover?'

If I try really hard I can just about remember the last time I had coffee with someone and only traded small talk. 'Are you mad?' I say, 'have you not been paying attention these last twelve years?'

'You tell me.' Only a trembling hand, brushing away

a stray strand of hair betrays emotion. 'Is Alex your lover?' Loud enough this time to gain the attention of the couple at the next table. Okay, *show time.*

I take my wallet from my back pocket and slap a ten pound note on the table. 'Come with me!' I say.

Back at the house I practically drag Beth up the stairs. I kick open the bedroom door and manhandle her onto the bed. There is a fine line between exciting passion in a woman and prompting the issuance of *domestic violence* proceedings. Since Beth has already begun unbuttoning her blouse I don't dwell on the distinction for too long. Similarly the command, 'Strip' has the ring of commentary since by the time it's uttered my wife's skirt is on the floor beside my feet. My, *Who you calling gay?* machismo is being matched garment for discarded garment by my wife's, *Come on then if you think you're man enough,* bravura. In fact by the time I've joined Beth on the bed she's issuing commands of her own in addition to lying in a decidedly lascivious pose. Grasping a buttock in one hand I run my other along the length of her naked body. That's when the subtle change in the timbre of proceedings really hits me. I'd supposed that I had dragged my wife unwillingly through the streets; that I brought her here against her will whereas now she is showing the unmistakable characteristics of the willing passenger. More than that: an invigilator overseeing a test. A self-imposed test. Of manhood. The realisation creates pressure, prompts exam jitters. I try to regain the initiative, manoeuvring Beth into a position intended to reinforce my physical dominance, to emphasise her helplessness.

'Do it!' she cries, resting the initiative back once again.

No foreplay then?

Nothing else to do but comply. This is why I brought her here after all. *Thought* I'd brought her here. I feel a certain limpness between my legs. I grasp my wife's buttocks, look along the smoothly concave curve of her back, the tresses of hair decorating her exposed neck. But it's no good. Perhaps it's possible to want something too much. To *need* something too much. Our physical juxtaposition does not encourage loitering. My nerve has failed me. That much is clear. I let out an audible sigh of resignation and collapse helplessly back onto the bed.

Tuesday evening, Mute phones. Louisa is in hospital. This is all he can tell us. *Dark matter.*

Wednesday. I arrive early at Pebble Bay. Luke has the staffroom all to himself when I walk in at the beginning of morning break. 'Mr Johnstone I presume.' I'd been surprised to discover a supply teacher occupying the Year Five hot seat in Luke's stead. 'I'd given you up for lost.'

'I love unexpected non-contact time,' he replies.

'Hope you put it to good use.'

'The best possible.'

I pour myself a coffee and join him. 'I didn't know work had begun on the tunnel again,' I say.

'Me,' he says, 'I'm more worried about the people trying to get *in* than the ones trying to get out.'

The job vacancy. Of course.

'What have you found out?' I ask.

'According to Brenda there've been six applications received already.'

'Any promising candidates?'

'She couldn't say. Sue's been tight lipped about the whole thing. Brenda says she'll try and come up with some names for me.'

Our conversation is brought to an end when the staffroom door swings open and Tina, TA in Year Six totters in on shoes decidedly unsuited to the duties she is expected to perform, at least according to her official job description. If she worked in Katherine Jones's class and not Keith Aston's I suspect the issue of her footwear would have been dealt with some time ago. Keith insists he permits the wearing of high heels purely to soothe Tina's inferiorities concerning her lack of height. The rest of us aren't so sure. Mind you, her shoes pale into insignificance compared to her blouse - or at least the half she's wearing today - which at first glance appears to be cut *below* the nipples.

'Only eleven o'clock and I'm already on my knees!' Tina says.

'Sorry, Luke,' I say, wiping coffee from my chin and shirt, 'I'll get you a cloth.' By the time I get to the sink to wet and wring out a sponge for Luke's coffee stained chinos the room is filling up. Like Tina's top, the staffroom is patently too small for its combined assets. Relocation has been considered though thus far deemed impractical. By the time I've made it back to Luke I've apologised to Katherine Jones for the wet patch on her thigh and to Brenda, who seems none too displeased, for having to perform an intimate passing manoeuvre more suited to a crowded dance floor than a primary school staffroom. I do not apologise to Keith Aston for grabbing a sizeable chunk of his arse on my way past, a ritual that dates back to the days when the burgeoning number of support staff first began to turn this communal area into something akin to a swinger's convention hall.

Seats are like gold dust. Mine is long gone, commandeered by Tina who is currently, like my hot beverage, *all over* Luke. She's giving it everything she's got. The man has a reputation after all even if these days, so far as I'm aware, it's unwarranted. It's common knowledge that he and Jen are no longer together. The man looks uncomfortable. A little information can be a dangerous thing.

I stake a claim to a patch of ground between the door and the coffee machine. Beside it is a shiny new kettle. I'm about to give voice to my surprise that funds have been allocated for the purchase of new electrical equipment when I suddenly recall leaving its predecessor to boil itself to oblivion during half term. I'm still biting my tongue when Jen walks in.

'Do you come here often?' I ask her as she pours herself a coffee and tries to avoid coming into contact with any of Keith Aston's adjacent erogenous zones.

'I was groped less often on the Madrid underground,' she quips.

'Interesting analogy,' Keith says, 'but I'm thinking more night club scene from *Basic Instinct*.'

'Why am I not surprised to hear you're a Sharon Stone fan,' Jen responds.

'Blu-ray edition; director's cut. The film is a bona

fide work of art.'

'Maybe you could show excerpts in your assemblies,' I suggest, 'when you've run out of topless shots of your wife.'

The staffroom door opens again and Sue Warden enters. 'Move right down inside the carriage please,' she calls. Though several feet away and partially obscured by Tina's breasts, Luke laughs with unexpected vigour. Quips of this sort have prompted little mirth amongst the rest of the staff since Katherine Jones revealed that Pebble Bay's head has consistently poured cold water on plans to relocate the staff quarters to a more suitable location whenever the subject has arisen at governor's meetings.

'Mind the gap between the headmistress and her alienated staff,' I mutter to Jen who moments later is shunted out of sight.

'I can't seem to get near the coffee machine,' Sue informs me. Very subtle. An act of gallantry on my part would involve squeezing between Brenda and Don, a route more perilous than a jaunt through the Khyber Pass during the First Afghan War. The ever vigilant Luke is on hand to help though, materializing miraculously from between secretary and caretaker with coffee in hand. The grimace on Don's face would suggest Luke's heel has made contact with several of the man's toes en route.

'Got the bastard,' he whispers in my ear. 'Boss,' he says to Sue passing her the steaming mug, handle first.

During the remaining five minutes of morning break Luke lavishes the kind of attention on his superior that Tina would evidently have done almost anything for. The room becomes extremely claustrophobic. I notice that Don's tongue is practically in Jen's ear. When the bell signals the end of break Luke retrieves Sue's mug and tells her not to mention it.

'I hope it's worth it,' I say as he follows her out the door.

As the staffroom continues to thin I notice that Don is not as I first suspected picking something up off the floor but is in fact doubled over in pain. Jen is smiling as she walks past me. 'Got the bastard,' she says straightening her blouse and leaving the room.

At home the days pass in sombre fashion. On my days off

Beth works late. She spends considerably more time at school than at home where she gives me a healthy dose of the silent treatment. My sporadic attempts at intimacy are rebuffed out of hand. I had my chance to put Beth's mind at rest and I blew it big time. I am a victim of my own indecision. What exactly is it I'm trying to prove: my heterosexuality or my marital fidelity? Or is it both? And how am I supposed to accomplish this? Remind my wife about former girlfriends? Draw her attention to good-looking women in the street? Purchase some magazines on a relevant subject and leave them out somewhere to be discovered? The whole situation seems absurd but misunderstandings between spouses have, I know, sprung from incidents more minor than being groped by another man in a public place while one of your wife's friends looks on.

The article on Portland Lighthouse is written in fits and starts. I get the first rough draft finished late one night but struggle over the next week to apply some polish to the coarse prose. I phone Trinity House who are only too pleased to supply me with some photographs to accompany the article.

Friday afternoon at Weymouth harbour I'm a little surprised to see Beth and the children waiting for me. I've had a tough afternoon, a fight having broken out during Golden Time, that fifteen minute period at the end of the week when pupils can choose what they do. This week Dan Carpenter and Johnnie Wyatt decided to kick seven shades of shit out of each other. Sue Warden, when sent for, proved to be far more interested in her imminent weekend trip to Dartmoor than in reinforcing the code of conduct by which most human beings choose to live. Certainly she did not detain either pugilist after school and if she spoke to their parents it must have been quick because by 3.05 she was gone.

At the harbour Beth's body language suggests an unexpected thaw of sorts is in progress. While the kids eat their chips I tell her about my day. In response, Beth says more to me than she has over the course of the preceding two days during which our longest conversation had gone something like this:

BETH: (sternly) Will you please put the toilet seat down Hugh when you've finished pissing all over the floor.

HUGH: (conciliatory) Yes.

A feeling of elation gradually creeps over me at this unexpected re-establishment of diplomatic relations. The prospects for the weekend are looking up. Conversation begins to flow. Beth tells me that Nigel is having a hard time of it. The local authority has identified a worrying trend in the school's Year Six test results. On top of this the man's marriage is falling apart. *I know the feeling mate.* By the time we drop by at Harpo's to grab a coffee I've tentatively taken Beth's hand as part of the first stage in a plot aimed at earning another shot at proving my heterosexuality. Steps two and three involve Chinese food and red wine though not necessarily in that order. Harpo greets us warmly and starts to prepare our drinks. He skips the usual weekend weather forecast. 'Hey Hugh why'd you ignore me the other day?'

Uh oh.

'What are you talking about?'

'It looked like you were having a fight with that long-haired bloke. Thought that red Mini Cooper was going to end up in the harbour at one point. What was going on anyway?'

I don't need to look at Beth. My brain can conjure a pretty accurate representation of her expression without the whole lens, retina, optic nerve malarkey. Likewise, saying anything will only make matters worse. Old news it may be but it still seems to be packing a punch. Given the right provocation, so, it turns out, can my wife.

Extract from *Life in Dorset*, 25th June 2001.

Leaving Dorchester at a quarter to six I head at speed for Bournemouth. I drive with a fearless determination, a focused impatience, my concentration only occasionally broken by the reassuring voice of my elderly mother in the seat beside me: 'Hugh! You're too bloody close to the car in front!' This from a woman regularly pulled over by members of the county constabulary. A woman who once, upon unexpectedly encountering a new mini-roundabout, careered off the road and proceeded to write off her new car by attempting to steer it (unsuccessfully) between the legs of a large roadside signpost. All this outside the town police station.

In Bournemouth we head for the Indian quarter for a pre-concert meal where the amiable service and gentle sitar music, combined with the fragrant delicacies dancing on my palette, create a spiritual peace that not even my mother's frantic exhortations regarding our impending late arrival at the Bournemouth International Centre can entirely destroy. As it turns out we're bang on time. We take our seats as the lights dim and a sea of blue rinses emerge, luminous in the gloom. Seconds later there he is: a seventy-seven year old dwarf in a white suit and red shoes: Andy Williams! The old crooner rolls back the years, his voice, described by Ronald Reagan as a 'national treasure', caressing a series of never-to-be-forgotten songs and conjuring a multitude of memories, mostly of my mum vacuuming on a Sunday morning to Moon River.

As arranged, I arrive at Zennor Road at 1.30. I'm alone, Hatty's attempts at accompanying me after a rushed Sunday lunch having been thwarted by her mother who's strategy eventually boiled down to the promise of a shed load of ice cream - provided she finished her sprouts first. My mother is seated at the kitchen table about to tackle a bowlful of meringue. She is wearing a purple woolly bobble hat and greets me in the same whisper with which she said good-bye the last time I saw her. She has, Jim-Bob tells me, been off the steroid drip since early morning . This will be the third meringue consumed within the last four hours. Jim-Bob is upbeat as though whipped egg whites were recently declared an antidote to carcinogenesis. Mum is smiling too although not for long. 'Couldn't you find a bigger fucking spoon?' she rasps as her husband hurriedly returns to the cutlery drawer for a more suitable implement. It is from my mother that I have inherited a distaste for cumbersome dessert cutlery.

Mum asks me if I've heard from Mute. 'Is Louisa alright?' she asks.

I tell her that her son-in-law phoned and spoke to Beth the previous night. From what I can gather Louisa is comfortable but she'll remain in hospital for at least a month.

'This is all my fault,' my mother says.

The appointment at Bournemouth Royal later in the

week will reveal the effect chemotherapy has had on the cancer. There's no need to drive 30 miles across Dorset to assess its affect on my mother's mental well-being.

We are ready to hit the road shortly before two. I'm just finishing off a glass of water when my mother returns from the toilet sporting a wig. 'Louisa likes it,' she says. Though taken aback ever so slightly (*'Sorry Dad, I'll sweep up the shards later')* I confer my approval too and follow my parents out the door. I am surprised by how difficult my mother finds the short walk to the car. Jim-Bob times this and all phases of the subsequent journey. Once we're within the Poole/Bournemouth conurbation though he is torn between monitoring the time and trying to memorize the route. Eventually he has to choose. His wife is on hand to help. 'Look at him! Come next Wednesday he'll know exactly how long it will take to get us lost!'

Jim-Bob can see the sense in his wife's observation even if it takes some restraint on his part not to challenge the tone in which it is delivered. 'I'll add fifteen minutes to the total journey time to compensate for the rush hour,' he says.

I assure him that the route we're taking is relatively immune to the vagaries of commuter traffic. 'And the view's not bad either,' I add as the road dips towards Poole Harbour following the water's edge in the direction of the exclusive Sandbanks peninsular. The unseasonably warm weather has lured a plethora of creatures to the shore. There are windsurfers everywhere. Some are even in the water. Burly men can be seen, either discarding or donning wet-suits, behind four-by-fours and vintage camper vans. Idling vehicles in need of a place to park hover nearby like mechanised vultures. On the pavement families stroll in relaxed fashion then scatter like ninepins before the approach of proprietary roller-bladers. 'It'll be much quieter during the week,' I assure my father noticing the re-emergence of his stopwatch in the rear-view mirror. As we turn off Lake Side Road and head uphill towards Canford Cliffs, day tripper traffic gives way to largely indigenous modes of transport. Luxury cars cruise the pine flanked avenue. Bentley GT Continentals, Aston Martins and Range Rovers proliferate. Urban speed restrictions mean it's not how fast you can go that matters but how much of the road you can take up. It is the classic Mercedes 450 SL that catches my mother's eye though. Vertical headlamps, dark green livery matching the silk head scarf sported by the woman at the wheel not so much younger than herself. *'One day!'* she used to say when catching a glimpse of her favourite marque. The sight of this gleaming piece of machinery today prompts a slightly more cynical response:

'Bitch,' she says.

At precisely three o'clock we arrive at the Royal. Jim-Bob goes in alone having persuaded his wife to stay put. 'I'll get the lie of the land,' he says.

'You'll get bloody lost more like.'

My father is back unexpectedly quickly. By the time he has manoeuvred his glasses into place and checked the stopwatch it's clear he agrees. 'Look what I found,' he says proudly when I lower the passenger window. Following a brief scuffle Mum submits to the wheelchair and 54.8 seconds later is being trundled not towards the *Tourette's clinic* as passers-by might suppose but in the direction of *Oncology* wherever that might be. I am to remain in the Saab. Jim-Bob will not sanction the purchasing of a parking ticket within hospital grounds as a matter of principle. I open the book I have brought with me but I can't concentrate. I try to think of better times. After all twenty years from now am I going to remember this car park or more frivolous occasions? The gnarled Nobel prize winning author pictured on the inside flap of my book's dust jacket didn't always look like that. Okay that fisherman's sweater looks cool but Jesus Christ it's hard to tell if the photo was taken before or after he shot himself. Where are the images of the man before self-doubt, marital guilt and the bumps and bruises of a life lived to the full left him a shagged out has-been twenty years younger than he actually looked. I don't want to remember my mother as she is now. Not everyone's life ends a la Butch and Sundance, Thelma and Louise. Shit, fast forward a frame or two and that quartet might look slightly less glamorous. A life's most memorable scenes ought to be ordered by criteria more rigorous than mere chronology.

The phone rings Tuesday evening. Beth checks caller ID, shrugs and looks over at me sitting way across the other side of the room in my Siberian armchair. 'Probably one of your boyfriends,' she says.

I put down my book and cross the icy expanse of carpet dividing us. I don't recognise the number either. For all I know it could be someone from the tax office. It might be nice to hear a friendly voice. 'Hello?' I say.

'Hugh? Hugh Bradley?'

'Speaking.'

'Tom Chandler.'

Deep breaths, Hugh. 'Hi,' I say, 'Great to hear from you!'

'Listen, Hugh. I'm going to be down your way next week. Wondered if you'd like to get together?'

'I would, very much.'

Chandler says something in Latin which may or may not translate as, *better late than never.* He suggests a couple of dates for an interview either of which would suit me. 'I'm easy, Tom,' I say.

'You certainly are.'

'Sorry Tom, I missed that. My wife's talking to herself again.' I glare at Beth way down the other end of the family sofa.

Chandler opts for the following Monday at ten. 'Should be up and about by then,' he assures me. I make a note of the day and time and manage to squeeze in a *Thank you* and a *Good bye* before Chandler unceremoniously rings off.

'Who was that? Your gay writer friend?' Beth's abuse is in stark contrast to the silent treatment she's been employing post-Harpo revelation. It's as though, like a festering boil, the pus is finally bubbling to the surface.

'Oh, shut the fuck up,' I tell her. I'm pissed off. This has gone on long enough. I can feel blood rushing to my brain as well as several other organs. Shuffling along the sofa I clamp a hand over her mouth and push her forcefully back against the cushions. And this time I don't mess things up.

Later, much later, I leave a message for Peter Swinton at Dorset Scene telling him when and where I will be interviewing Thomas Chandler. The impending interview provides the boost I need to complete the lighthouse article. By the time I've e-mailed the text and accompanying images to Peter Swinton it's past one a.m.

Jim-Bob picks up the phone as the answer machine kicks in. There is little else to do but wait for my father's stuck-up answer machine alter ego to regurgitate its 'I'm sorry we can't come to the phone at present…' *because we're having tea with the fucking Queen* nonsense while 3D Jim-Bob, apparently oblivious to his other dimensional self's rant, attempts to engage his son in conversation. At length there's a protracted beep and virtual Jim-Bob falls silent. My father apologises and explains that he's upstairs in the bedroom which is why he couldn't switch off the machine in the living room.

I ask him how Mum is, knowing that she's spent the day at the County Hospital being rehydrated in part as a consequence of her continuing refusal, last Sunday's meringues aside, to take nourishment of any kind irrespective of the size of cutlery with which she is equipped. This is an increasing source of frustration for my father though, not, he claims, something the doctors seem particularly concerned about. He asks for my help. Perhaps Mum will listen to me. Next time I'm round maybe I could try and persuade her to knock back a Vitijuice or two? Neutrality has up to now been my preferred stance on this one. Who am I to dictate otherwise? Find a cure for cancer? We can't even come up with a source of nutrition that is both tasty and nutritious! *If we can put a fucking man on the Moon….* Don't start me on that one. Of course maybe this is something she needs to do whether she wants to or not. This is for her own good after all. Giving up on food could be indicative of surrender on a larger scale. Her mental faculties deteriorate noticeably whenever intravenous nutrition stops. No one thinks straight when they're hungry. Look at the shit Dustin Hoffman and Steve McQueen ate in *Papillon.* Jim-Bob tells me that until Mum is stronger chemotherapy cannot restart. I promise that next time I see Mum I'll bring it up. No pun intended. I ask my father about Mum's voice and he tells me that the tumour is apparently pressing on the vocal cords. Talk about adding insult to injury. If I had cancer I'd want to bloody well scream and shout about the injustice of it all too.

Vitijuice is not the only thing causing strife at Zennor Road. It seems Doreen has taken good neighbourliness to extremes. Her visits have become a daily event. Their duration has lengthened. Doreen's prowess as a conversationalist does not justify the increasing amount of her neighbour's time she is taking up. Her visits are now preceded by feelings of dread at number 55. The smallest minutiae of her character have been elevated to the level of gross personality defects. 'I hate the way she says Weymouth!' Mum had complained the last time I saw her. Jim-Bob has more substantial gripes, chief amongst them the inspirational tales Doreen insists on recounting. 'If I hear about any more of her friends that have survived cancer I'll throttle her,' he says. 'Every day there's another one!' What Doreen sees as good news, encouraging omens offering hope to the desperate, Jim-Bob views from an alternative perspective. It comes down to statistics. Every friend of his neighbour who pulls through makes Jim-Bob's wife's chances of survival statistically less likely. 'I want to hear about the bastards who've died!' he says.

I arrive promptly at the Old School House, West Bexington. I park the Travolta (roadworthy again after insertion of new starter motor) and approach the front door with some trepidation. Daylight and the absence of smoke billowing from the main entrance prompt me to pause and double-check I've got the right house before ringing the doorbell. There's time for a quick glance left, my eyes registering pebbles and sea, before the door opens. A man is smiling at me.

'Tom Chandler,' he says holding out a hand.

'Hugh Bradley,' I respond.

Stepping back Chandler signals for me to join him inside with the casual waft of a hand. 'Mi casa su casa,' he says. I find myself in the cottage's kitchen. 'Plonk your stuff there if you like,' he says pointing at a large pine table in the centre of the room. I deposit notebook and Dictaphone next to an assortment of breakfast dishes. A Daily Telegraph, folded in haphazard fashion, rests before one of the six chairs positioned about the table. There is a brief exchange of banal pleasantries before Chandler says, 'Show you round first if you like. Set the scene and all that. Ground floor only though; upstairs is a shit heap.'

I follow Chandler back past the front door and into a sitting room. A couple of armchairs, separated by a standard lamp carved from a dark wood of some sort, occupy one corner of the room. Opposite them, beneath a window through which I can see the Travolta, squats a leather sofa kept, I surmise for comfort rather than its decorative qualities. 'Lounge,' Chandler says. 'Very cosy in the thick of winter, if we can get the blasted fire to draw.' Chandler leads me across a Persian rug partially covering floorboards whose woodworm pocked surface is only visible at the room's extremities and past a desk cluttered with type written papers, newspaper cuttings and receipts. Beside it another door leads to the back of the house and a larger room with windows running the entire length of the wall immediately opposite our point of entry. To my left a staircase juts a foot or two into the room as though intentionally sited to guide visitors naturally upward. 'Not up there,' Chandler reminds me.

'Shit heap,' I say to prove I've been paying attention.

At one end of the room, to my right, there is a baby grand piano; at the other, to my left, a half-sized snooker table. 'This is where I like to relax. Although I usually end up frustrated: play the piano badly and snooker worse. Still, takes my mind off *other* things. Jeannie spends most of her time in there.' He points through the windows to a conservatory which I imagine would be a lovely room if some of the cane furniture were taken outside and burned. At present the room is unoccupied.

On top of the piano are several framed photographs. My host shows no sign of being irked when I examine each in turn. I notice a shot of Chandler with a famous American actor clutching an Oscar. Between them is a very beautiful woman who I do not recognise. 'Him, you'll know,' he says taking note of my interest and picking up the picture, 'beside him is my first wife.'

'Dead? I say.

'I live in hope. But alas no. The bitch.'

Scrutinising the photo further I ask, 'Has she got her hand on his…'

'Not everyone spots that. Well done old chap. Complete whore. Sleeping with the bastard she was. Last to realise. Love is blind they say.

'Why do you keep the photograph?'

'Are you joking? How many people have their photo taken with a triple Oscar winner? The man even *gave* me the gaudy thing. Said without my work on the screenplay he'd never have won it in the first place. Timeo Danaos et dona ferentes, I suppose. Like that lump of moon rock Armstrong presented to the Rijksmuseum that turned out to be petrified wood. Can't trust anyone these days.'

I'm ready to move on but my host seems to be finding it hard to leave this spot.

'Picture might come in handy one day. I'm sure his wife would find the photo of interest. Might realise what a total shit the man is. Don't quote me on that for God's sake.'

We complete our circuit of the ground floor by way of a door that leads past a toilet and back into the kitchen.

'Coffee?' Chandler asks after motioning for me to sit down.

'Please,' I say nodding my head, 'black.' By the time the coffee arrives I've tested the Dictaphone and set it in motion. Volume, I decide shouldn't be a problem. 'So how long have you owned a house in Dorset?' I ask.

'Five years and counting but we've been coming down for much longer. When she was a child Jeannie used to spend her summers at Charmouth. When we got married she started dragging me down here for long weekends. We'd stay in Bed and Breakfasts. Grew to love the place. Who wouldn't?'

I take a sip of coffee which is very strong. Chandler tells me about the book he wrote during the period he and Jeannie were looking for somewhere to spend weekends and holidays in the county. 'Had to be by the coast,' he says. 'It was while we were looking for a place to buy that I started to notice all the bloody pill boxes around here.' He spends the next twenty minutes telling me about the book he subsequently wrote in great detail, a tale of intrigue and daring-do woven into the lives of the men who manned the concrete fortresses that were erected all along the Dorset coast: the Home Guard.

'The Home Guard?' I say, surprised that a *serious* writer like Chandler had penned a book about such an affectionately maligned institution.

'The invasion may never have happened but the life of the Home Guard was not without incident. Down the coast at Eype, a Heinkel 1-11 made an emergency landing on the beach the back end of 1940. The crew were captured by the home guard manning the nearby pill box.'

I can imagine the scene: Bungling old men and wan, flat footed youths brandishing Lee-Enfield 303s stumbling onto the beach where shaken Luftwaffe aviators, assuming their position to be hopeless, immediately surrender only to kick themselves when they belatedly realise who they are actually up against.

Chandler reads my mind: 'They weren't all Captain Manwarings you know.'

I finish my coffee and accept a refill. 'Of course the book never saw the light of day.' He mentions the name of a publishing house, names one or two individuals to whom he affixes the label 'fucking idiots,' before adding hurriedly, 'Don't quote me on that for God's sake!'

Chandler's bitterness over the demise of what was clearly a pet-project lends momentum to the subject of his failed book and his subsequent retelling of the plot leads me to suspect he views *Dorset Scene* as a possible saviour. A ten part serialisation perhaps? The only thing that makes sense to me about the book is its title, a Latin one (just to kill any remaining vestige of marketability), *Dulce Bellum Inexpertis* which Chandler for once has the good grace to translate for me as, *war is sweet to those who have never fought*. When Chandler mentions that Jeannie's grandfather served with the Home Guard I take the opportunity to shift the conversation to his second wife.

'We met at a book signing in the Charing Cross Road.' he says.

You signed her copy of The Man Who Banned Christmas *and then nailed her in a Foyles stock cupboard?*

'I took her to tea at The Savoy and then we fed the ducks together in St James's Park.'

I scold myself for judging the man.

'She was married at the time but then so was I of course.'

But seeing as your wife was being rogered silly by Hollywood royalty you shagged the bejesus out of her that very night at your suite at Claridge's?

'We saw each other off and on for the next two years; when we were both free agents I popped the question at Foyles.'

And then bent her over the sale table and took her forcibly from behind?

'We kept everything very proper. Didn't consummate our relationship until our wedding night.'

I'm ashamed of myself, truly ashamed of myself.

'How often do you come down?' I ask.

'Not as often as I'd like. Jeannie is down more than I am. Likes to be by herself. I spent a good deal of time down in the autumn researching the new book.' I ask him about it. 'Tweaking it at the moment but pretty much finished. In fact,' he pauses, stands up and hurries out of the room returning seconds later with a book in his hand. 'I'd hoped to send you one of these prior to our meeting. But you know how it is.' Chandler hands me what turns out to be an uncorrected proof of his new book. Its plain cover contains a couple of quotes from the text. The book's title, *The Bridport Dagger* only appears on the spine. Chandler tells me that the book has three distinct narratives taking place at different points in history but all connected in subtle ways. The main characters: a local rope-maker, a Monmouth rebel and a railway entrepreneur are connected via their ancestry acting out their parts during the reigns of Henry VIII, James II and Queen Victoria respectively. 'Henry VIII relied heavily on Bridport rope for his navy you know,' Chandler says. 'Bridport rope was also used to make nooses, hence the book's title. They were also used on the goals at Wembley for the '66 World Cup Final. Still used at Wimbledon today as far as I know.'

At what point did we start talking about string?

'I didn't know that,' I confess.

'James II has a lot to thank Bridport for too,' Chandler continues, 'The local militia defeated Monmouth's rebels during a skirmish in the main street in 1685. The rebellion subsequently never gained momentum. Several members of the population, including Josh Lipford, one of the characters, ultimately wound up in *Bridport Daggers* when Judge Jeffries held court at Dorchester. The stories come together during the mid 1800s when the railway arrived in the town.'

Just as the steel rails connect Bridport to the outside world so the lives of its inhabitants are inextricably linked to one another via an invisible thread through time. The Bridport Dagger draws their lives relentlessly together. If they hadn't already got someone to write the blurb I'd be more than happy to give it a go.

The form Chandler's narrative takes intrigues me. Three stories playing out at different times yet sharing the same space; co-existing, contemporaneous, separated only by the reader's shifting focus. Past, present and future jostling for attention. Temporal boundaries becoming blurred, past morphing into present, itself pursued by the future. All three becoming inseparable, indistinguishable from one another. The dead resuscitated, via the act of observation. Time an illusion; death too.

'It's bloody warm in here,' Chandler announces, 'come and see the garden.'

The large, hedge-bordered expanse of green behind Chandler's house is awash with colour though dominated by the yellow of scores of daffodils. 'You're a keen gardener I see.'

'Fuck, no. Jeannie pays some old fart to come round once a fortnight.' Not exactly, *I wandered lonely as a cloud*, I think.

'What was it Hemingway said about gardening?'

I shrug, fairly sure the man did not possess green fingers, although didn't I read somewhere that his cats had an extra digit? 'Don't know,' I say.

'Me neither, must have been some other bugger.'

I ask Chandler about his most famous book. 'They're thinking of turning it into a film you know. Sold the rights years ago; nothing to do with me. Probably cast Tom Cruise as Bellingham and Ben Stiller as Spencer Percival. Set the thing on board a fucking spaceship. Get Baz Luhrman to direct, throw in a few songs, a couple of homosexuals and Bob's your uncle.' Chandler laughs, then looks serious. 'Don't quote me on that for God's sake.'

Half past nine the following morning Peter Swinton calls me. 'Hugh? How'd it go?'

I give him the low-down on the interview. I tell him that I'll spend the morning going through the tape and will try and have the article finished by the beginning of next week. 'Great,' he says. 'I'd like to include it in next month's edition. A gap has come up. If you can get it to me by next Tuesday that'd be great.' He asks me about photos. Before leaving I'd snapped a couple of shots of Chandler in his garden as well as another in his front porch. 'Don't know how useful they'll be,' I admit.

'Could you ask Chandler for some publicity shots?'

I promise to chase up the photos. I ask Swinton what he thought of my article on the lighthouse.

'That's the other thing I wanted to talk to you about,' he says. 'I received your e-mail but you neglected to attach the article.' Shit.

'What about the photos?' I ask.

'You attached those but they'll need to be *hi-res* if I'm going to use them.'

I pretend I know what he's talking about and assure him I'll get straight onto Trinity House.

'Don't do anything,' he says, 'until I've seen the article. I don't want you wasting your time.'

Very encouraging.

The lighthouse cock-up does not take long to sort out. I attach the article to a new e-mail and send it to Peter Swinton. I phone Trinity House who seem to understand my need for *hi-res* images. I receive them within the hour and get to work deciphering the Chandler tape while waiting to hear

Peter Swinton's verdict on the text.

It comes that evening. 'Basically fine,' is how the man describes my painstaking labours. He intimates that the article will be published in the autumn. Have I had any success obtaining *hi-res* images? I e-mail them to him and pen invoice number four. £150. Subtract the cost of the Travolta's new starter motor (plus labour) and I might still have a couple of quid leftover.

A few days after being rehydrated my mother is back in hospital. Ward 100 only recently reopened following conversion to office space in order to house the hospital's burgeoning administrative staff. Rapid reversion to the ward's former use suggests its new occupants quickly deduced that there were too many desks in the hospital and not enough beds. This startling insight has yet to gain any of those involved a position at NASA.

On the phone earlier Jim-Bob had brought me up to speed on the reasons for my mother's latest spell in hospital. A stent is to be inserted in her throat, a procedure designed to make swallowing easier. There is a 10% chance that the operation will perforate the patient's oesophagus. *The procedure punctures one in ten people's throats?* It's probably not as dangerous as it sounds. I've no doubt Doreen can name nine friends who've come through the operation unscathed.

Visiting hours begin at seven. I arrive about five past, finding my mother in a glazed private room. Conversion back from office space is only partially complete giving the ward a quasi-medical atmosphere and lending the place the feel of a covert facility for the treatment of sensitive cases, known only to those members of staff with a high enough security clearance. I find my mother attached to a drip which she admits is better than fending off Vitijuice cartons every ten minutes.

A doctor stopped by earlier to discuss the results from the Bournemouth Royal trip of the week before. The news, Jim-Bob assures me, is good. 'The cancer hasn't spread beyond the surrounding tissue.'

'That's great,' I say. *So the chemotherapy has had no*

effect whatsoever. My mother asks me for news of the family. 'Everyone's fine.' I tell her. How do you feel?'

'Let Hugh have a look at that thing,' Mum whispers, ignoring my question and pointing a finger at an object in her husband's hand.

'I told you I know what I'm doing.'

'Hugh, take that thing off your father.' My mother's authority is only partially undermined by her wig which moves up and down each time she speaks .The *thing* turns out to be a remote control. Watching television in hospital never used to be this complicated. Both telephone and television are now *pay-as-you-go* and accounts need to be set up before either can be utilised. Jim-Bob has had several conversations with operators in Bombay towards this end. I can see the young men and women manning the telephones on the Sub-continent shaking their heads, wondering how sahibs like my father were able to wrest control of their country for 150 years. My mother is similarly shaking her head. She is not satisfied until the remote is pointed at the TV which springs to life for long enough to prove it is functional.

'Happy?' my father asks in a less than friendly tone.

A nurse comes in and asks Mum for the completed menu, delivered earlier on for her perusal. The kitchens at any rate seem to think she'll pull through. When the nurse has gone Mum relaxes somewhat. Several clouds at present have silver linings. Besides avoiding Vitijuice her current hospitalisation has other benefits: 'Gets me away from Doreen!' she says.

'Christ, that reminds me!' Jim-Bob announces. 'I saw her in the garden this afternoon while I was digging up those old tree roots.' Mum closes her eyes. Tight. 'She wanted to know how you were.'

Mum's eyes open. 'Tell her I'm dead!' she practically spits the words. 'You should have said, *Why d'you think I'm digging this fucking great hole!*'

Jamie Goddard has barricaded himself inside the PE cupboard. Since he's neither my responsibility nor is he interfering with my Games lesson this does not unduly concern me. Not until I realise the bean bags I need for the next activity are inside the cupboard with him. 'Jamie? I need the bean bags. Can I have them?' Cue expletives. I try again. 'Why don't you go back to Mr Aston's class and let me have the bean bags Jamie?' By the time Tina arrives at the scene a few minutes later I can hear the sound of bean bags being emptied onto the cupboard floor. A few of the beans have even made it under the door. 'Looking for Jamie?' I ask. She nods. 'In there,' I tell her.

She tries the door and shrugs. 'Keith just wants to know where he is.' With this she leaves. I continue the lesson *without* the bean bags. Jamie stays put.

I've got the class lined up and ready to vacate the hall later on when Sue Warden appears in the doorway. 'Jamie?' I ask. She looks confused. It is only when she is followed into the hall by several others that I remember the memo on the staffroom notice board: 10.30, Sue showing prospective candidates around school.

There are four of them. Dave Horn is right behind Sue. I am introduced moments before a crashing sound comes from inside the cupboard. Sue may or may not have already been tipped off by Tina. Either way she knows better than to comment. Horn does not. 'Think you've locked one of them inside Mr Bradley!' he says, to the general amusement of all except the tour guide.

'If you'll follow me this way,' Sue says, giving Horn a sickening smile and a gentle prod on the shoulder, 'I'll show you the music room from where we can leave the building and walk round to the staffroom for coffee and questions. The last person to use the fire escape in the music room without a very good reason (and fire isn't one) was in the dog house for a month. The current circumstances constitute, I assume, an emergency. While I watch my class troop out of the hall I can hear Sue talking to Horn, 'Of course the hall we had at Melcombe Junior was much bigger and better equipped wasn't it Dave?' The bastard is a shoo-in.

The operation to insert a stent in my mother's oesophagus is a success. Over the phone I clarify with Jim-Bob what this means exactly. 'You mean the surgeon didn't puncture her oesophagus?' I ask.

'I mean the stent's working,' my father says delightedly. 'Your mother's eating!'

Later, at the hospital I find Mum propped up in bed minus the drip. Her wig is slightly lopsided. I ask her how she is. She smiles and gives me a faint nod and says, 'Fine.' Her powers of speech are unlikely to have been enhanced by the operation nor it seems the pressure on her vocal cords alleviated. I have brought something with me that I hope will cheer my mother up. The new Penny Vincenzi hardback is big as a breeze block and should keep her occupied for some time. 'I'll read that later,' she says, nodding towards the bedside locker on which I have placed the book. To make space I have had to remove a dinner plate on which the remains of a meal can still be seen. There is a good deal of food left including meat of some sort.

'The braised lamb was a bit tough,' Jim-Bob explains when I inquire as to the standards of cuisine. 'Still, at least your mother's eating again!'

Her husband's metaphorical cartwheels elicit only a sigh from my mother. She looks tired. The post-op painkillers and whatever else they're slipping her at the moment make conversation difficult.

'Mum's a bit up and down,' Jim-Bob says, when his wife momentarily dozes off. My mother needs to sleep. I say my farewells and tell her that I hope she's feeling better in the morning. She grasps my hand. Her pale fingers are cold.

'Every morning I wake up.' she whispers, 'and for a few seconds I think it's all been just a dream.'

I finish the article on Thomas Chandler late Friday night. By the time I've omitted the more libellous portions of our conversation I'm left with a few indecipherable Latin phrases and a smattering of hackneyed comments about the Dorset countryside. The remaining 900 words consist of a lengthy description of Chandler's living quarters as well as a summary of the detail in his new book of relevance to a Dorset readership. I'm confident Peter Swinton will approve. I put it to one side. I'll read it through Monday morning. If it still reads okay, I'll *post it* to Dorset Scene. Five down, one to go.

Saturday morning. I take Beth a cup of coffee. Propped against several pillows, she lowers her book as I enter the bedroom and greets my arrival with a feisty, 'Hello Big Boy.' On this occasion I decide against alerting my wife to her increasingly worrying tendency to exaggeration. This nit picking really must stop. Since the incident on the sofa *post* Thomas Chandler telephone conversation things have been going very well. In fact on this morning's evidence they've never been better. Nothing adds lustre to a marriage like the prospect of its imminent demise. 'You know,' Beth says, 'I might come with you this morning.'

My wife's plan is not a problem. In fact the company on the drive to Poole would be nice. 'Thought I might read the paper while the kids play on the beach and you *do your thing*.' Beth is a veritable font of innuendo. She is referring to the interview I hope to conduct with property developer, Mitch Edwards, the man at the forefront of the real estate boom that has recently earned the Poole suburb of Sandbanks international recognition as one of the most expensive pieces of residential land on the planet. The interview, together with comments gleaned from a telephone conversation I plan to have with someone *in the know* at UtopiaEstates, will form the basis of my sixth article. The derelict railways of Dorset will just have to wait. Edwards has agreed to meet with me at the offices of *Made to Measure*, his commercial alter ego, in Lilliput, Sandbanks' fashionable sister suburb and aptly named home to this colossus of the local property scene. Edwards has promised me fifteen minutes of his time on the proviso that I'm not late. I stress this aspect of my arrangements to Beth who assures me that if I take care of the kids she'll make sure she's ready on time. '*Just as soon as I've finished this chapter'*.

Beth is as good as her word. There is no need to thrash the Travolta en route to Poole and, having dropped my family beside the exclusive Sandbanks Hotel, I find I still have time for a lap of the peninsula's mansion-lined main thoroughfare prior to my meeting with Edwards.

Made to Measure is housed in shiny rectilinear premises a stone's throw from the waters of Poole Harbour. A receptionist asks me to take a seat and offers me coffee. I obey and decline respectively. I'm a few minutes early. The phone rings and the caller is informed that Mr Edwards is currently out of the office. However he is due in shortly. I bloody hope so, I think. His Maserati pulls up outside less than a minute later. An assistant appears from nowhere, opens the driver's door, and escorts Edwards towards the building. The main entrance is shunned in favour of a side door. I catch another glimpse of the man as he crosses the hallway beyond the receptionist's desk and vanishes up a flight of stairs. Another minute passes and then the receptionist tells me I can go up. 'Keep going all the way to the top,' she tells me. The kind of advice upon which empires are built.

I'm in and out in under ten minutes. I have been used to interviewing people who enjoy talking. People fond of the sound of their own voice. Authors, tour guides, sad recluses unused to an audience. Mitch Edwards on the other hand is prickly and uncommunicative. We do not shake hands. When I enter he is reclining in his chair, Italian leather cosseted feet resting on an immaculately uncluttered oak desk. I take a seat and know at some instinctive level that I'm hopelessly out of my depth. Edwards has the practised aura of a rock star and is as eager to talk as the accused at a murder trial - *shortly after exercising their right not to give evidence*. My questions sound lame and inconsequential. When Edwards asks me who I'm writing the article for and I tell him *Dorset Scene* it is clear he doesn't believe me. There are several uncomfortable pauses in the dialogue. Edwards looks bored. It is only when I ask him about his future projects that he becomes in any way animated. Rising from his seat he pulls plans from a cardboard tube and spreads them on the desk. He beckons me forward and proceeds to make sense of the confusion of intersecting lines that apparently depict a new bridge across the entrance to the harbour. The structure will replace the existing chain ferry. State of the art technology will enable it to swing open at the approach of cross Channel ferries while its vertiginous central arch will simultaneously allow the free flow of yachts and other shipping as well as the passage of road vehicles travelling to and from Sandbanks from the nearby resort of Swanage. I consider the plans. Light bulb time. Finally: a question worth asking! But I bite my tongue. *What's wrong with the fucking chain ferry for Christ's sake?'* might be the last question I get to ask. As it is the interview only has another minute to run anyway. I hear footsteps on the stairs. Turning, I see the assistant tapping his watch more, I suspect, for my benefit than Edwards'. I thank the man for his time and, like a school boy leaving the headmaster's office, having given a very unsatisfactory explanation as to how Tomkins of the lower fifth came to have his head lodged down the toilet, I slink down the stairs.

I drive back towards the Sandbanks Hotel. Gawking at the windsurfers I almost collide with an Aston Martin emerging at speed from the Bournemouth Road to my left. If his hand gestures are anything to go by the driver is none too impressed. As I drive on I catch a glimpse of red. The blare of car horns draws my attention to the rear- view mirror and I'm in time to see a red Mini execute a left turn from the right turn only lane. A thought occurs to me. No. The Mini is a couple of cars back. I can't see the driver. When I bear left at the next junction the Mini continues on towards Sandbanks. I decide I'm just a little jumpy. Still rattled by the Mitch Edwards experience. I park the Travolta on the sand dusted cul-de-sac that leads to the beach. I find Beth seated outside *Café Java*, a cappuccino untouched before her. Twenty feet away, playing in the sand, are Hatty, Freddie and Mary.

'Lover Man!' I look about me. Beth usually saves that one for more private reunions. 'How'd it go?'

'I need a double espresso.'

'Oh dear.'

I head inside to order. When I return Beth insists on a blow by blow account of the interview. When I'm finished she says, 'Tosser.' This is harsh. Edwards isn't really to blame.

'I was so far out of my depth,' I say, 'I think I've got a case of the bends. Let's change the subject.'

Beth gives me a ten minute update on Nigel's professional and marital problems. He has apparently moved out of the family home.

'A trial separation?' I ask.

'No,' Beth says, 'the marriage is *definitely* over.'

There are moans when, twenty minutes later, we

round up the gang on the beach. Beth wants a tour of Sandbanks before we head for home. The Travolta ages visibly as we drive past the yacht club and swanky cafes that herald the start of Sandbanks proper. Beautiful people sip *Illy* coffee on the pavement as the one-way system guides us to the left.

We drive past the Haven Hotel beside the mouth of the harbour. It was from this spot that Marconi sent his first radio messages. The red Mini I see in my rear-view mirror abandoning the line of cars waiting to use the adjacent chain ferry is a more basic but no less effective signal to those tuned to the correct wavelength. The Travolta swerves slightly. Beth spots my eyes' backward trajectory. 'Eyes front soldier!' she says, leaning forward and tilting her head so as to utilise the passenger door mirror. She shrugs, unable to link the inverted image with the Travolta's haphazard forward progress. *Dark matter.* I follow the one-way system taking the first available right. I know I shouldn't but I can't stop myself checking the mirror again. This time Beth looks over her shoulder. We see the red Mini simultaneously. 'Pull over,' my wife shouts, 'now!'

I do as instructed. The Mini does not slow. The smile on Alex's face as he drives past lasts only as long as it takes him to spot Beth in the passenger seat. It is clear from my wife's facial expression that she remembers Harpo's previous indiscrete harbourside revelations in detail, right down to the make and colour of Alex's car.

'I have no idea what he's doing here, Beth' I say, 'believe me.'

'Take me home,' my wife demands.

I drive on pulling back onto the one-way loop again close to the Haven Hotel. Approaching the parade of cafes and shops that mark the end of the half mile circuit Beth shouts, 'Stop!' At the moment my wife is a hell of a lot scarier than the double yellow lines on which I deposit the Travolta. Beth is out of the door in a flash. I watch as she marches along the pavement. Then I see it too. The red Mini parked three cars ahead. Beth stoops out of sight, no doubt to ascertain whether there is an occupant. Then I see her come onto the road. She stoops again. By the front wheel. She removes the dust cap and, using something metallic, she proceeds to let down the tyre. *Fucking hell.* The dust cap is tossed into the road. She approaches the rear off-side tyre and repeats the procedure.

Back in the car she barks, 'Drive!'

Sir, yes sir!

As we accelerate past the Mini we both glance left. A woman, mid-seventies I'd say, keys in hand, is inspecting the car. A man beside her is pointing at the Travolta. I step on the gas in the hope that a burst of exhaust fumes will conceal the rear number plate. Approaching the yacht club we pass more cars. In between a Porsche and a Fiat 500 we spot another red Mini.

'Popular cars,' I say. 'Want me to stop again?'

The next day. Enough said.

Monday. Janice nods in the direction of the coffee shop when I inquire as to the whereabouts of Alex. I follow protocol and sign in before striding back across the lobby and through the common room doors. The bastard is sitting alone at a table near the window. He looks up, surprised by the shadow casting a pall across the book he is reading. He looks worried. He has good reason to.

'I was on my way home,' he says before I can speak. 'I spent Friday night with a friend in Bournemouth.'

I do that supraorbital thing I learned from my father.

'There aren't many cars like yours. When I spotted your Beetle I got excited. Coincidence, you know?'

'It's a fucking Morris Minor.'

'It is?'

I nod and sit down. 'So you spot my car and decide to follow me?'

'I was curious to see where you were going.'

'I'll send you a postcard from the divorce courts.' I say.

'What?'

I explain the effect third party reports of our jaunt to Portland Bill have had on Beth. *My wife.* By the time I'm done Alex looks miserable. This is some consolation.

'I'm sorry,' he says.

'For convincing my wife that her husband is having a homosexual affair? Don't worry about it. Apology fucking accepted.' Am I swearing more today than usual?

Alex gets me a coffee. 'It's the least I can do,' he says, placing the cup and saucer before me.

'Terrific,' I say 'a fucking cappuccino.'

The cup and saucer are withdrawn.

'I've been trying to help,' Alex says, when he's replaced my beverage. 'Look, I made a mess of things, I know that now. I got you wrong. You've convinced me.

'Oh good.'

Alex runs a hand through his hair. 'I'm on a mission, see.'

I do not respond.

'To help others,' Alex continues, 'to help them avoid the mistakes I made.'

I hold up a finger. 'You're still making them.'

'I meant about acknowledging who I was.'

Oh great. A fucking *coming-out* story. We'll do this on my terms. 'Go on then. What stopped you?'

'An alcoholic father who beat me on the slightest pretext might have had something to do with it.'

The dipso moral high ground again. I could mention an inebriated skeleton or two locked away in my own family cupboard. 'Go on,' I say.

'I wasn't at all confident he'd take kindly to the humiliation of having sired a *genetic oddity*. I wish there'd been someone around to help me stand up to my father and admit to him and myself who I was, who I am.'

'And ever since you've travelled the highways and byways of the country releasing people from their sexual strait jackets? A kind of gay David Carradine?' *The path to bliss Grasshopper? Flagellation, flagellation, flagellation.*

We talk for another five minutes during which Alex apologises *ad nauseam*. 'Save your apologies for the old lady whose tyres Beth let down,' I say.

'Those were mine.'

I must look confused.

'The old lady mistook my Mini for hers. It's easily done. I came out of the newsagent's and found her waving a stick at my Michelins. She was in a right old flap until I pointed to her car further up the road.'

'Beth *will* be relieved.' I drain my coffee cup and stand to go.

'Listen,' Alex says, 'let me know what I can do to make things better.'

'Leave me alone,' I say.

The first night home after leaving Ward 100 my mother falls while attempting a trip to the toilet in the small hours. Jim-Bob has to carry her back to bed. She is badly shaken up and spends the next day in bed. When I go to see her she is wearing her purple bobble hat. Her wig lies discarded on a chest of drawers near the bedroom door. When I ask her how she is enjoying the Penny Vicenzi book I bought her she tells me that it is too heavy for her to hold. She sighs deeply. 'I wish somebody would just shoot me,' she says.

I need some photos to go with the Sandbanks piece. Charlotte at the tourist office in Poole promises to e-mail me an aerial shot used in their current brochure but I could do with more. Some old sepia snaps of the peninsular before mass colonisation would be good, maybe put together some *then* and *now* images. Be a good excuse to drive to Sandbanks again and snap the necessary companion photos.

At the Research Centre there's no sign of Alex at the front desk which is a relief. I like to think we reached an understanding yesterday. At the back of one of the photographic reference drawers in the main reading room I locate a pair of cards alluding to photographs that sound promising. I take them to the inquiries desk where I'm told there will be a ten minute wait. 'We're short-staffed today,' is the explanation I am given. I decide to grab an espresso in the common room. I order a double.

'Large or small?'

A large or small double?

'I'm sorry?' I say.

'Large or small?' the expert barista behind the serving counter has an impatient edge to her voice this time.

Okay, I think, I've got ten minutes to kill. I can do this.

'I've changed my mind,' I say, 'Make that a single espresso.'

'Large or small?' There's not the trace of a smile on her face, I swear.

'Large,' I say, 'I'd like a large *single* espresso. I pronounce the words slowly and watch her pick up a cup. She's almost at the coffee machine when I call after her, 'No, sorry, make that a small *double* espresso.'

The barista turns away from the machine, makes a guttural sound to show her annoyance and looks back at the collection of cups on the counter. *Go on pick another one, I dare you.* A few seconds pass. Barista woman is stony faced. Is that the hint of a knitted brow I can see? She turns back to the machine, presses a button and seconds later slams the brew down in front of me.

The photos are just what I'm looking for. But there are issues of copyright and cost to be considered. Previous experience has taught me that even a couple of poor quality reproductions will set me back a tenner. To use the originals in the article I'd have to pay the Research Centre a fee greater than *Dorset Scene* pays for my copy. And that before giving any consideration to tracking down the copyright holder. I order a couple of A5 copies and sign a piece of paper to the effect that I won't publish the photos without permission. Yeah, right. We're not talking state secrets here. The pictures are unlikely to make me a millionaire for Christ's sake.

On my way out I feel safe enough to ask Janice where Alex is.

'He called in sick,' she says, 'he really didn't sound himself at all.'

Excellent.

'Dave Horn….' Jen is reading from a piece of paper Brenda had handed her only moments before.

'Stop! I've heard enough,' I say clamping my hands over my ears. The first name on the shortlist for the vacancy in Year 5 has rendered those that follow insignificant. The news that Sue's former favourite has made it to within arse kissing distance of the finishing line is all I need to hear.

'What's the other piece of paper?' I ask.

Jen unclips another sheet of A4 and passes it to me as Sue Warden walks into the room. A timetable for interview day dominates the bottom half of the page. 'Lesson obs!' I shout. 'Shit, I didn't think we, *I* had to do one.'

'You won't need to Hugh,' Sue reminds me. 'I already know your strengths,' she pauses to pour herself a cup of coffee before adding, 'and weaknesses.'

'Hey, I haven't hit a kid in a long time.'

'Very funny.' She sits down. 'Jenny, how tall would you say Dave Horn is?'

Later I call Luke who has asked to be kept abreast of any developments. 'Horny Dave made the cut,' I tell him.

'That,' Luke says, 'surprises me.'

'What are you talking about? Sue was practically drooling over the bastard when she showed him round last week, the shit.'

'Yeah well I've been spreading a bit of that myself.'

'What do you mean?'

'I made sure some information about our *horny* friend's personal life reached the ears of our boss via a mutual acquaintance. Something I would not expect Sue to be particularly impressed by.'

'Well she seems to be coping with it pretty well at the moment. She was discussing his vital statistics with your ex in the staffroom at break time.'

A CT scan at the County Hospital reveals blood clots on my mother's lungs. Although re-admitted at once she waits six hours for a bed. This new development puzzles me. Are blood clots a symptom of the cancer or one of the treatment's less palatable side effects, a reminder that chemotherapy destroys indiscriminately: the cancer or the patient. Survival of the fittest. Whatever, blood clots do not sound good. Presumably the lungs function better without them.

For the first time since my mother's diagnosis I find it impossible to suppress the sense of foreboding stalking me. I have prepared for job interviews, trivial social gatherings, science lessons even, more diligently than my own mother's mortality. How many of those interviews, soirees, experiments can I now recall?

I find my mother and father on Ridgeway Ward, a big improvement on Ward 100 even if it means sharing with five other women at least one of whom is patently mad. My mother looks much better than I'd expected. Her neighbour, the mad woman, is barking orders at a visitor. She wants to watch her favourite television soap but seems to think it's being broadcast on *Radio* Three. Bedside, Jim-Bob looks a good deal worse than his wife. He has, it transpires, spent most of the night in an armchair back at Zennor Road having fallen asleep in front of the fire prior to mustering the strength to mount an attempt on the stairs. When Mum asks him what he ate for his tea it's obvious that his own nutritional intake is nothing to shout about these days either. This concern for my father's well-being is slightly unsettling, surreal even. 'He's been very good to me,' she says when Jim-Bob leaves us to chase up a promised cup of tea. *Your next stop? The Twilight Zone.*

Events are clearly taking their toll on my father. There is no respite. Small successes, like the fitting of the stent, resemble minor skirmishes in a grander war, one in which the campaign is not going nearly so well. Think Pitt the Younger rolling up those maps of continental Europe after Napoleon's devastating victories at Ulm and Austerlitz. 'They will not be needed these ten years,' Pitt said. Best not pursue the analogy further: Pitt was dead within eight weeks.

'Warfarin,' Jim-Bob says when I enquire as to the name of the latest drug prescribed for my mother. *First deadly chemicals and now rat poison, excellent.* 'It thins the blood,' my father assures me.

Conversation at the next bed is rather more animated. Mad Woman is still barking instructions to Long Suffering

Relative. 'Look it will have started by now!' she's saying. 'Give me that thing!' Long Suffering Relative hands her the remote control for the bedside TV.

'I'd have bloody thrown it at her,' Mum says, 'she's been a pain in the arse all evening.'

'It's on either Channel Three or ITV1,' Mad Woman asserts confidently although her fingers move with less certainty over the gadget in her hand which is actually pointed at her chest.

'Channel three *is* ITV1!' Mum cries but her voice won't carry. Those incurring my mother's wrath these days invariably remain unaware of the fact. I draw the curtain separating the two beds. The sideshow over, my mother asks me about my day. I supply meagre details. My bedside manner could do with brushing up a little. Jim-Bob isn't saying much either. Mum gets a reaction when she mentions Amanda, a work colleague of my father's from way back. 'You watch,' she says, 'when I'm gone Amanda will be straight down on the next train.' This light-hearted badinage fails to mask the gravity of my mother's condition.

As I leave the hospital it occurs to me my mother may not get the chance to do likewise. If the Warfarin tackles the clots and the stent continues to create the means if not the desire to swallow solid food then my mother has only the cancer to beat. Travel down a road far enough and you start to question the wisdom in attempting to turn back. Particularly when you know you'll be passing this way again sometime soon.

Outside in the cold, starry night I'm not so sure that I'm thinking straight.

Extract from *Life in Dorset,* 24th November 2001.

WHO THE BLOODY HELL IS SHEAMUS?

News from the Emerald Isle. Grandda's funeral service did not go well. It may have been a celebration of the man's peaceful, pipe smoke obscured time on planet Earth (the Irish mainland anyway - he never ventured further a field) but that's not to say there weren't moments of high drama along the way. The moment for instance that my cousins, acting as pallbearers, slid Grandda's coffin from the hearse in silence, hoisted it with great dignity onto their shoulders and only then considered the practical implications of including cousin Redwood *(seven foot two in his bedroom slippers) amongst their number. If the congregation thought they could relax with Grandda's coffin safely inside the church they were mistaken. Redwood and the seven dwarfs had barely regained their seats when the priest, commencing his sermon, announced that Grandda had left behind him three loving daughters and a brother, Sheamus. Beside me I noticed Mum nodding sombrely with the rest of the congregation. Ah yes, Uncle Sheamus, I thought. Good old Uncle Sheamus! Hang on a minute. Who the bloody hell is Uncle Sheamus? I could tell by the look on the faces of my mother and Great Grandda's two other loving daughters that the same question had just occurred to them. Silence in the church. No one spoke. No one breathed. A dummy was rammed into the mouth of that bloody baby that had up until this point been crying incessantly. If Father Tom was pausing for effect he'd achieved it. It was only when the priest called upon Sheamus to say a few words that the congregation stirred again. A figure emerged from a pew across the aisle and shuffled towards the lectern. As the man staggered up the stone steps relief was tangible all around me. 'I was baptised* Sheamus, *Father,' said Grandda's last surviving* brother, *'but everyone here calls me Fitch!'*

Paul Francis is a mine of information. As boss of *Utopia*, 'The only estate agents actually located on the Sandbanks peninsular,' he assures me I have telephoned the right man with regard to my half-finished article. The person most in the *know*. Despite this assertion, or more properly because of it, I quickly find myself running lines through previously scribed notes as my source proceeds to dispute almost all my earlier anecdotal research. 'No, Noel Gallagher *isn't* buying a house in the area,' he tells me. 'That rumour started when his brother *Liam* was spotted at the North Shore Café a few doors down from us.'

Okay, so we'll forget the Oasis angle. I mention two more famous names, a celebrity couple currently in the process of purchasing a home on the peninsular.

'Not true!' Paul remonstrates, 'although *his* equally famous father does live locally.'

Fucking hell, you'll be telling me they're not really shooting the next James Bond movie here next!

'The press aren't interested in the truth,' Francis tells me, 'that doesn't sell papers.'

Right now *the truth* is looking increasingly like a luxury I can ill afford. I'm about to thank the man for his time and e-mail Peter Swinton, see if he's interested in a *500* word article on Sandbanks when Francis finally starts to deliver. He possesses numerous anecdotes about the foibles of the area's mega rich. For instance, the writer who took out an expensive lease on a beach front property, paid in advance and didn't visit the place until the day, two years later, that she handed back the keys! Then there's the old git who wanted to sell his penthouse, the one, it turned out, he hadn't set foot in in twenty-seven years! Several other stories follow, all of them connected so far as I can tell by a common theme: Alzheimer's. *'Darling, are you sure you don't know where I left my glasses? Oh, and by the way sweetheart, any idea where that new £4 million mansion we bought last month is actually located?'* Are all the residents of Sandbanks this rich and forgetful? Is there a link between the two conditions? Is this what excessive amounts of money does to people? Someone should conduct some research. I'd be more than willing to act as a guinea pig.

I thank Paul Francis for his time, hang up and set to work incorporating the interview into my evolving article.

Some mornings at Pebble Bay really drag. I steer clear of the staff room at break time. This is for everyone's benefit. Several members of staff witnessed my reaction to publication of the Year 5 vacancy's short-list. Since that day the matter appears to have become taboo in the presence of myself and Luke. No one has uttered so much as a syllable to either of us on the subject since. The uncomfortable silences that have greeted my unexpected appearance in communal areas about the school would suggest the vacancy is still receiving an airing in my absence though. An uncomfortable atmosphere permeates the building.

At lunch time, Chess club provides an excuse for avoiding adult company although not, as it turns out, interview talk. 'Who's going to take chess club in September if you lose your job Mr Bradley?' Vanessa Waldron seems genuinely concerned. *Would someone please throw her mother off the Governing body's personnel committee.*

As well as supervising the school's 'intelligentsia', today I've also got a science lesson to prepare so when all the games are up and running and the usual warning issued regarding *Fool's Mate*, I nip across the corridor to the science cupboard for the necessary resources. Part of me would rather be going into the staff room. I cannot enter this small room without recalling previous visits. One in particular.

At first the door wouldn't budge. A second shove had done the trick however. The light was on inside. When the door closed I discovered Luke and Sheila, TA in Year One, examining something on a desk pushed against the only wall not obscured by shelving. There was nothing unusual in finding Luke inside the science cupboard. Sometimes he'd eat his lunch there treating the place as his own unofficial office accommodation. What Sheila was doing there was anybody's guess although she was doing a pretty good impression of someone fascinated by what she could see beneath an electron microscope. Sheila did not look up but Luke fired me a good natured, salutary, 'Hugh!' I grabbed half a dozen batteries and a decrepit assortment of torches. Turning back towards the door I noticed for the first time the disheveled coiffures of the other occupants of the cupboard. Luke had either just finished giving a lunch-time demonstration of the Van de Graff static electricity generator to an interested colleague or he'd recently started rogering another member of staff. The absence of a shiny metallic sphere on the desk led me to conclude it was the latter. Sheila still hadn't looked up. 'Those things work much better when they're turned on,' I told her closing the door behind me. The smile on my face, condoning as much as ridiculing the actions of the cupboard's inhabitants, died as I saw Jen coming towards me at speed.

'Hi, Hugh,' she said, 'is Luke in there?'

Chess club is really rocking. No one has succumbed to mate in four. As far as I can tell everyone has castled. In some cases *twice.* The Holy Grail appears to be a possibility. The hat-trick is definitely on. 'Let's have no stale mates today everyone,' I say after congratulating all members on their solid starts. 'When you've got your opponent on the back foot go for the kill. Finish them off. I don't want to see anything long drawn out. That's no fun for your opponent and things can blow up in your face if you're not careful.' I continue to flit from game to game. Most are evenly balanced. 'Pay attention to your opponent's moves. If you do you can avoid nasty surprises.' Apart from some strange pawn formations and the usual misplaced knights patrolling the perimeters of the boards, to the untrained eye at least, these players actually appear to know what they are doing. The club's longest losing streak could even be about to end. 'James Chumley, are you writing on your board again?'

When I phone my father for an update on Mum he tells me she suffered a panic attack in the night. 'She could hardly breathe,' he says. 'She was very scared.' Apparently a nurse had been sufficiently concerned to call for a doctor. 'Whatever you do,' she'd told Mum, 'don't fall asleep while I'm fetching help.' *Not if you want to make it through the night that is.* Mum hung in there. The ward was quiet. Through the windows she could see a full moon. The doctor never came. When my mother woke up it was morning.

The Photo shop on South Street manages to produce a couple of fairly decent 6x4 prints of the Sandbanks images I obtained from the Research Centre. I post them, together with my own photos and the finished article, to *Dorset Scene* first thing Saturday morning. My birthday is ten days away. I'm cutting it fine. If the article is rejected I don't know what I'll do. There's no sense taking things for granted but I remind myself that Peter Swinton has yet to refuse a completed piece. So far getting him interested in an article has been the tricky part. Though wary, I am confident of another *yes*. The information gleaned from Mitch Edwards and Utopia Estates lends the article an authoritative air. It is my most assured piece to date. Why do I get the feeling I'm tempting fate thinking like this?

At the breakfast table Beth had informed me coolly that she would be meeting a friend for coffee at eleven. I have until then to complete my chores which include replacing lights bulbs in the spare room and on the first floor landing and returning a book to the Research Centre that I inadvertently removed on a previous visit. Theft I think it's called.

I don't recognise the old boiler on the front desk and decide that coming clean about the book is too risky. Proving the absence of *mens rea* in my purloining of the missing volume to Alex or Janice is one thing, making a case to this stony faced crone quite another. 'No Janice or Alex today?' I ask, adjusting my posture in an attempt to disguise the book shaped bulge in my jacket pocket.

'It's Janice's Saturday off,' she replies, 'no one's heard from Alex all week.'

'I heard he was ill,' I offer.

'So did we. But Janice says his landlord claims he's just upped and left.'

When I get back to the house it's nearly ten to eleven. 'Have a nice time,' I say as Beth brushes past me.

'Did you get the light bulbs?' she asks. Now that would have been a good idea. I do not attempt to kiss my wife goodbye.

The Warfarin takes care of the clots in my mother's lungs. Doreen makes her a Pavlova to welcome her home. 'That was nice of Doreen,' I say when I call round later the same day.

'I wanted to ram the thing in her face,' Mum says.

'I take it this means you don't feel like eating again.'

I pick up the carton of Vitijuice at her elbow. It feels full. I remember the promise I made my father. I delay its implementation until the end of the cookery show she's watching. Who knows, maybe it'll give her an appetite.

'Louisa's at home,' mum tells me.

The twenty-eight days have flown by although not I

suspect for my sister.

'I'm glad for her,' Mum goes on, 'but I'd feel better if she was still in hospital at the moment.'

Right now I've had enough of the pretence, the euphemisms. *Hospital?* Why don't we call it what it is? It's a rehab clinic for Christ's sake. Louisa's been in and out of them since she lost her last baby. I know my mother blames herself for this latest relapse. 'It isn't your fault you know,' I tell her.

The phone rings. 'Shall I get that?' I ask. Mum shakes her purple bobble hatted head. 'Your father's upstairs. He'll get it in the bedroom.' The answer phone kicks in a few seconds later. Queen's English Jim-Bob invites the caller to leave a message. Then a protracted beep. It's my Aunt Sarah. Jim-Bob is clearly monitoring calls because there's a click and the man himself starts to speak. I note with alarm that the answer phone continues to record the conversation. Worse still the speaker continues to broadcast it to all in the vicinity. To turn off the machine I realise I'll need to press the flashing red record button.

'Leave it,' Mum says when I rise to this end. 'I want to hear what they have to say about me.' *Just like I heard you that time when you promised to try and get me to drink Vitijuice.* I've gone before my father comes down to tell his wife what his sister, Sarah had to say.

The post arrives late Wednesday morning. The *Wimborne* postmark on the long white envelope addressed to Hugh Bradley demands my immediate attention. Peter Swinton commences his epistle in familiar fashion: Dear Hugh, Thanks for the article on Sandbanks. Unfortunately….Whoa. Stop right there. Let me read that word again. *Unfortunately*. I read on. Swinton gets straight to the point. He won't be publishing my article. Apparently I've committed the writer's cardinal sin and produced something that could upset the magazine's advertisers. Peter Swinton feels that by focussing to such an extent on Made to Measure and Utopia Estates, the other property players in the Sandbanks area could have just reason to feel aggrieved, reason enough to re-direct their advertising revenue elsewhere. Where for Christ's sake? *Norfolk Scene, Rutland Today?*

Swinton finishes with an apology and best wishes. Whatever. I crumple the letter and miss the bin. I consider my options. A re-write? Remove the offending favouritism, restore impartiality? What choice do I have? Researching and writing another article in the next seven days is not an option. A re-write need not be too time consuming. It'll have to wait until later though. I'm due at Pebble Bay in less than an hour.

We're sitting in the Saab on a wet Sunday afternoon in Poole. A week has passed since my mother came out of hospital. She has just enquired as to the location of the nearest crematorium. Having tried and failed to park beside the quay we've ended up in a side street. Water cascades down the windscreen, celestial tears following haphazard paths across the smooth curve of toughened glass. I'm chewing on a sandwich, washing it down with a cocktail of carcinogens having mistakenly picked up the *diet* variety of my favourite carbonated soft drink. Jim-Bob is in the back forcing down a baguette he'd at first refused, then accepted on pain of death. The steering wheel may be on my side of the car but my mother still occupies the driving seat. No one says much. Radiotherapy begins tomorrow at Poole General. It is from the hospital I have just driven having familiarised my parents with the lie of the land.

The prospect of a new treatment, a possible cure for my mother's illness has been undermined somewhat by news received only two days before that the cancer has spread to my mother's liver, a region of the body we are told for which radiotherapy is not used as a treatment. A further course of chemotherapy has already been ruled out. I'm not the only one in the car wondering if the medical team responsible for the co-ordination of my mother's case is now merely going through the motions. *Co-ordination* is probably the wrong word. *Team*, likewise. Too many doctors have come and gone. Each new *specialist* spends the first fifteen minutes of a consultation trying to hide the fact that he only picked up my mother's notes for the first time five minutes before meeting her. At the playhouse you expect the actors to be familiar with the script, to have spent some time in rehearsal. The drama unfolding at the hospital appears increasingly unscripted. Improvised even. Less drama, more pantomime. Take the Warfarin. Seems you can have too much of a good thing. My mother's blood is now *dangerously* thin. *Time to ease up some on the rat poison, boys.*

The dry run to the hospital went smoothly. Jim-Bob knows exactly where he's going tomorrow. He just isn't sure why.

The final re-written draft of the Sandbanks article doesn't take me long. The several attempts at removing all direct references to Mitch Edwards and Utopia Estates that precede it take me the best part of two nights however. In my opinion the article was better in its original form. It's not, I have to remind myself, my opinion that counts though. It is too late to entrust my work to the Royal Mail. So, despite a certain wariness, I e-mail the finished piece to Peter Swinton at 2.15 a.m. taking care to ensure I have on this occasion attached an article to my salutary message. A final throw of the dice. Time will not tolerate further cock-ups. My mind is buzzing and upstairs sleep eludes me. Far across the other side of the bed, Beth inhales and exhales, inhales and exhales - the deep, unlaboured breaths of oblivion. Wide awake, I think about the future. I think about *The Deal.* In truth, up until now it had never really worried me. Not because I was sure I'd publish the required number of articles but because I know my wife. She is a reasonable person, given on occasion to self-sacrifice. Like any decent human being she enjoys seeing heroic failure rewarded. Especially when those involved are loved ones: friends or relatives who have given something their best shot but still need support and encouragement in order to achieve their goals. Or maybe just a bit more time. Alex changed all that. For *sympathetic wife* read *vindictive bitch-woman hell-bent on revenge.*

Freddie tells me that on his way home from school he saw his grandparents driving past. 'Grandma didn't look very well,' he says. *Yes, son, radiotherapy will do that to you.*

Later I go round to see my parents. Mum is in bed. Jim-Bob is in animated mood. 'Doctors,' he tells me, 'kill more people in America than guns!' He picks up a book and waves it at me before reading from a previously marked page, '*In the U.S. 120,000 people a year die because of doctors' errors! Guns account for the death of only 1,500 people.* Fancy a cup of tea?'

I nod.

My father fills the kettle from the water filter jug beside the microwave then opens a cupboard and, having poked around for a few seconds, pulls out a box containing my preferred herbal brew. When we're settled on the sofa he takes up the book again. '*Doctors are 9,000 times more likely to kill you than guns*,' he says.

And doctors *with* guns? *Police have warned residents in the Tri-State area not to approach their doctors who may be armed and very dangerous.*

It is safe to say Mum's medical treatment has altered my father's perception of health care. The book in his hands is full of stories that confirm his worst fears: drug companies making billions of pounds developing drugs that don't work, or worse, do harm; medicines ignored because they can't be patented and therefore won't make anyone any money; side effects surreptitiously turning people into placid zombies (aside from the 16,000 Americans they kill each year). 'Drug companies don't want to cure cancer,' Jim-Bob tells me, 'they can make much more money by treating its symptoms.'

My father, who has voted Tory all his life, who has supported every gung-ho! raid ordered by *well-meaning* American presidents from Vietnam to Iraq tells me about the Chilean president, Salvador Allende. 'Allende was a doctor. He was deposed, some say by the CIA, because he proposed to drastically reduce the purchase of drugs from American companies because they didn't work. The doctors on the commission that recommended this were all killed and the new regime began buying drugs again! Unbelievable.'

Assembly at Pebble Bay is not going well.

'You mean we're not to trust *anyone* Mr Bradley?'

'No James,' I say, slightly exasperated (if the desire to take the boy by the neck and shake him can be construed as such) 'that's *not* what I meant.' My attempts at inspiring my charges to develop a, *Don't let anyone or anything dissuade you from pursuing your dreams,* mentality has veered badly off course. We seem to have blundered into *stranger danger* territory and the call has just gone out to *circle the wagons*. Paranoia grips those present. 'What I'm saying is trust *yourself*. Have faith in your own beliefs and feelings.' *What else can we trust for Christ's sake?* 'Don't be distracted by what's going on around you if deep down inside you know what you're doing is right.'

Confusion. Plus fear. I can see it in their faces. I decide to go with it. 'If a stranger comes up to you and tells you to come with him, you'd say, '*No,*' wouldn't you?'

Nods. And smiles. *If we're gonna have an assembly on* stranger danger *Mr Bradley let's at least call it by its name.* 'But sometimes the stranger is clever,' I continue, 'they might make up a plausible reason why you should go with them.' I look straight at Ruby. '*Ruby, your mum is poorly and she asked me to collect you from school.* Would you go Ruby?

Ruby shakes her head.

'Good girl,' I say, 'Ruby knows deep down her mum would not do that.' Ruby doesn't look quite so sure. 'But sometimes the stranger is so clever as to invent something complicated, a reason so clever that it might make Ruby forget what she knows deep down is the right thing to do.' I pause. '*Ruby your mum has broken down and locked her car keys* and *your pet dog in the car. Your dog will suffocate unless you come with me so we can collect the spare car keys from home and drive to their rescue.* Would you go Ruby?' Bingo!

Ruby looks torn. The dilemma I have created is tearing at her heartstrings. She's having trouble thinking straight. 'Well Ruby?'

Ruby takes a deep breath and says, 'We don't have a dog Mr Bradley.'

Fuck.

'A cat, whatever. The point is the stranger is clever.' *Cleverer than you Mr Bradley.* 'They'll know what pet you have. They'll know what might make you act out of character, go against your better judgement.'

Chatter has broken out amongst the audience. The possession or otherwise of pet dogs seems to be the predominant subject. I raise my arms and call for order. I have more to say. 'Circle time later is all about pets,' I lie. This seems to placate the crowd. 'At some point in your lives you'll have to face similar dilemmas to Ruby, children.' I point at a girl in the front row. 'You're not good enough to be a dancer Chloe, and what if you get injured and end up unable to earn a living?' I swing my arm around and level it at the nearest table. 'Joe, it takes years to become a vet. Why go to college when you can earn good money now at the factory. Then you could help your mum and dad out with the rent.' *If we invade one more country citizens and bomb the fuck out of its people we can rid the world of war forever!* My time is up. Maths groups beckon. 'Inside,' I tell everyone placing my hands on my chest, 'we all know what is right and what is wrong. Don't let people confuse you with clever arguments. Be strong. Be true to yourself.'

I pop round to see Mum after work. It's clear the radiotherapy is taking its toll. Jim-Bob, perched on the bed beside his wife, tells me he has been researching alternative treatments. An appointment has been made with an acupuncturist. He has discovered a website peddling a book that trashes traditional cancer treatments and chronicles miraculous recoveries - uplifting stories of success against the odds that have inspired him to believe there may still be hope. 'It's not over yet old girl,' he says patting my mother's hand in such a way that not so long ago would have endangered his health. My mother indicates that she'd like to sit up. Jim-Bob manoeuvres pillows into place. It is only with her husband's help that she is able to reach a sitting position.

'Thanks Love,' she smiles. Beneath this immovable rock, the sedimentary accumulation of forty years' worth of bitterness and petty squabbles something yet stirs. It is as though, lured from their entrenched positions by my mother's illness, my parents have stumbled across something familiar in this middle ground, this forsaken marital *no man's land* that they'd long since given up for lost.

I have mail. Top of my inbox: peterswinton.dorsetscene@ya... subject: Sandbanks. It is not good news. Despite the fact that the article is now unlikely to lose the magazine advertising revenue there are still problems: 'the prose needs tightening up, the piece doesn't quite flow. Perhaps the original premise for the article needs rethinking.' Peter Swinton isn't to know I've run out of time. I consider my predicament. I have patently failed to keep my side of the bargain. With Beth continuing to restrict communication to a, *Need to get out of my way* basis, I can hardly hope for leniency.

The first guests arrive as the town hall clock is striking eight, the doorbell's electronic fakery obscuring peals four and five. Sitting in the courtyard nursing a preparatory beer the chimes' cacophony sounds suspiciously like my writing career's death knell. The run up to my 40th birthday party has hardly been the joyous affair I'd envisaged. Communication with Beth regarding the *Big Night* has been sparse. Fortunately, invitations were sent out long before relations between the co-hosts became somewhat strained by the *misunderstandings / flagrant bisexual promiscuity* (depending on your point of view) of recent weeks. Final preparations have been divided along traditional lines without the need for verbal communication: food and snacks, Beth; booze and music, her *good for nothing, enjoy the party, it might be your last,* husband.

Early that morning I'd received an assortment of adeptly packaged gifts from the children and a polite peck on the cheek, together with a lacklustre, '*Happy Birthday'* from my wife. I'd driven to work feeling faintly suicidal, a condition not exactly ameliorated by Sue Warden's whole school assembly. Keith, Luke and several other members of staff took me for lunch at *The Wreckers* where the expedited celebrations took the form of all present, including Bev, a former Pebble Bay TA turned waitress, slagging Sue Warden off for half an hour. When Keith stood up, raised his large glass of wine and called for quiet I'd been expecting a toast that referred at least in passing to my 40th birthday. 'The bitch must go!' though appropriate to the conversation, was something of a let down. My disappointment must have showed. 'Oh and Happy Birthday Hugh,' Keith had added sheepishly, raising an empty glass to his lips.

Party preparations had precluded the usual Friday afternoon meeting at the harbour, although for old time's sake I'd manoeuvred the Travolta along the busy quay to Harpo's where I'd stopped and wound down a window. 'My friend Judas,' I'd called to the surprised proprietor, 'Know any good gay clubs in town?'

Upon my arrival home Hatty, Freddie and Mary had interrupted their duties as members of the decorations committee to greet me excitedly. Beth had been far too busy opening a jar of olives to mark my return with anything more than a disinterested grunt. I'd dumped my things and headed straight out to the supermarket where I bought wine, beer and light bulbs thinking that belatedly restoring illumination to the landing and spare bedroom might in some way please my wife. While Beth bathed I fitted the new bulbs before turning my attention to the evening's music but even birthday *carte blanche* over the choice of CDs had failed to fill me with much enthusiasm.

'Those bulbs are too bright,' Beth had said when she'd finally joined the rest of us downstairs shortly before the appointed hour, 'I've told you before about buying 100 watt bulbs. Why don't you just buy a bloody fluorescent tube and have done with it?'

And with that the venom spitting had stopped. For with the chiming of the town hall clock (or is it the doorbell?) my wife turns back into a human being. Cinderella eat your heart out. The light that suddenly illuminates her face as she emerges from the kitchen to greet the first guests can only partly be attributed to the paper lanterns strung across the candlelit courtyard. It has more depth, a richer lustre than the superficial glow sometimes imbibed by the presence of unexpected visitors. This is not the feigned enthusiasm of the actress but a sincere transformation.

My spirits slightly buoyed, I spend the first half hour acting as sommelier to the gathering crowd of well wishers who are more than happy to exchange their cards and gifts for alcoholic beverages and directions to the nearest food, a mouth watering selection of which is spread across the kitchen surfaces and dining table.

The lounge area has been transformed into a makeshift dance floor while the prettily illuminated courtyard is intended as a refuge from the impending party mayhem within, a place to relax on the new garden furniture (picked up the weekend before at start of season prices) and a place to watch new arrivals as they come through the courtyard door from the street. A small set of speakers, sheltering a docked ipod and perched slightly worryingly on a window ledge, provides music for the garden area. Freddie has assumed control of all MP3 entertainment and several times within the first hour I have to ask him to take the volume down a notch or two. The last time we'd entertained a similar number of guests our neighbours' fists had beaten out a less than enthusiastic refrain on the other side of the lounge wall.

'What will Tim and Joan say?' I ask Beth who is beaming at me with not the least trace of facial exertion.

'Why don't you ask them?'

'What?'

'They're in the kitchen demolishing the olives.'

The revellers are drawn from all areas of my life: professional and personal; past and present; liked and suffered under duress. At nine, Tom, former flat-mate and best man shows up, slaps me on the back, dumps his holdall and heads for the punch bowl where he immediately appears to hit it off with Fran. *Who the fuck invited her?* Keith is here from Pebble Bay as are several other members of the staff including Luke and Sue Warden, my birthday party doubling as school end of term get together. Similarly, a smattering of staff from Beth's place of work are present including Nigel who thus far I have steadfastly ignored. My cool indifference will teach him to make my wife's professional life miserable.

Louisa and Mute arrive with Jim-Bob about a quarter past nine. My sister appears to be having some difficulty walking. They take up a position in the courtyard where Louisa's opening conversational gambit with the couple to whom I introduce her is, 'It is a lovely house isn't it but apparently the neighbours are dreadful. Those olives look lovely. Pass me the bowl would you.'

Enough alcohol has been consumed by nine thirty for dancing to begin. I instruct Freddie to turn off the ipod and to crank up the CD player in the lounge. Given her apparent problems with regard to forward motion I'm a little surprised to see Louisa hit the dance floor first. Tom and Fran are not far behind. Sue Warden and Katherine Jones bring the number of idiosyncratic dancers - like revellers at a silent disco - to half a dozen until a distinctly predatory Keith Aston joins the gathering throng - Nick 'Shooter' Curran tracking the elusive Catherine Tremell.

I've a feeling the neighbours may have left. There's no sign of them when I slip out for some fresh air in time to hear the town hall clock strike ten. Beth, who has been locked in a tête-à-tête with Jen beside the punch bowl for several minutes follows me, a bag of party debris in her hand. She pauses to laugh at something Nigel says inside the kitchen doorway. I know it's crowded in there but does the man have to stand that close to my wife? And Beth, is what he's saying really *that* funny?

'I wasn't expecting Nigel to actually come when we sent out the invitations,' I say when Beth catches up with me.

'Oh, he's alright.'

'I thought you hated the bloke?'

'I think Jen has had too much to drink,' Beth says, ignoring my question, 'she wants Luke back.'

'Too much to drink or she's drained the punch bowl single-handed and started in on the Scotch?'

'I think Luke has been laying it on pretty thick tonight.'

'Where is Luke anyway?' *I've hardly seen the man.*

'He's waiting for Jen in *our* spare room with a *cat that got the canary* grin on his face.'

Out of the blue Beth kisses me. *First contact*. 'Happy birthday,' she says and slips an envelope into my hand before threading her way between guests. I watch her dodging the tea lights scattered across the steps that lead to the secluded gravelled area where, tonight at any rate, the dustbin is located.

I open the envelope. Inside is a piece of white card, A5 size, a certificate of some sort. Typed in an elaborate font are the words, *This is to certify that Hugh Bradley is a professional writer and* PART-TIME *teacher having so very nearly published six articles in under a year.* I look across at Beth, see her vanishing with her little bag of garbage towards the bin. There is a lump in my throat. The evening just keeps on getting better.

The doorbell sounds. Someone, in the gloom I can't make out who, opens the door into the street. A latecomer slips through and the door closes behind them. I follow their progress through the sea of bodies, slow as swimming in syrup. At length a handsome face emerges from the undulating mass. I smile. Then I stop. Holy shit. The certificate drops from my hand. My mind races past *What the hell is* Alex *doing here?* to images of smashing crockery and later the futile taping back together of the certificate at my feet which I hasten to retrieve.

'Hi,' Alex says. 'Happy birthday.'

I take the proffered card but make no attempt to open it. I can't think of anything to say. There isn't time for a conversation. I can only think of getting Alex out of sight before Beth returns from her jaunt to the dustbin. Getting Alex off the premises would require an explanation of some sort not to mention a feat similar in scale to the parting of the Red Sea. There is nothing else for it. 'Inside,' I say, 'quickly.'

'Well you've changed your tune.' Alex follows the motion of my head and does not resist the shove by which I speed his entry to my home.

Panic severely impairs my cognitive skills. Now I have Alex inside I really don't know what to do with him. 'We need to talk,' I say, 'but not right now.'

'Point me towards the bar; I'm sure I can amuse myself until you're ready.' *Is he wearing eye-liner?*

I grab a couple of bottles of beer and hand them to Alex. 'No, upstairs,' I say, my thought processes valiantly hanging on to the coat-tails of my verbal utterances. 'Wait for me upstairs.' I'm about to suggest Alex head for the spare room then remember that Luke is currently in residence and possibly already entertaining a conciliatory and physically demonstrative Jen. The bathroom is out of the question as are the kids' rooms. 'Second room on the left,' I say and then for the sake of clarity - his *and* mine - repeat, 'The bedroom upstairs, second on the left.' My bedroom; *Beth's* bedroom. What the fuck do I think I'm doing?

Alex gone, Tom appears.

'You seen Fran?' he asks.

I shake my head. 'Try over there,' I say glancing towards the dance floor where I can see Nigel giving it everything he's got. Which isn't much. When Tom has gone I head for the bar.

'Save some for me,' I tell Jen who is not, it turns out, in any hurry to join her errant husband upstairs.

'Why do women,' Jen says, before pausing as though trying to remember where she is going with this, 'always fall for the bastards?'

It just so happens I have a theory on the subject. However, this is probably not the time to share it. At least not with Jen. But what the hell. To summarise: A man's behaviour is inversely proportional to his looks. Logic dictates that the better looking the male the worse he can behave and still get away with it. The worse the behaviour, the more obvious it is that this male will make an unsuitable mate. It is not possible to have your *beefcake* and eat it. To want what one cannot have though is human nature. 'Does that answer your question Jen?'

Apparently not.

'Look, Jen, Beth'll be back any minute. Don't do anything rash.' *Because if you do you'll in all likelihood contract one.*

'Luke,' Jen mumbles, 'need to talk to Luke.' She stumbles off towards the stairs. I watch her go thinking that maybe I should stop her. Between Jen and the stairs though is the dance floor. Its swaying occupants seem to be getting on just fine. Music as an intoxicant, it and the house liquor combining to manifest a desire to bend ones body to the complex rhythms of the hot night. I spot a clearly inebriated

Fran but it is Nigel and not Tom she is pressed against. Nearby, Keith Aston is dancing true to form - think *pissed rollerblader encounters unexpected flight of stairs*. The hand clamped to Keith's left buttock acts as an essential aid to the synchronising of his movements with the music's somewhat more predictable pulse. I'm a little surprised to spot Katherine Jones at the other end of the arm to which the buttock wielding hand is attached. The Pebble Bay Key Stage One co-ordinator seems to be having the time of her life. Her other hand is currently mussing Keith's hair in a frenzied manner. *Get a room why don't you.*

Which reminds me. I finish my drink and put down my glass. Beth arrives at the punch bowl just as I'm leaving. 'Toilet,' I tell her and push through the crowd.

Upon reaching the first floor I ignore the master bedroom and instead climb a further flight of stairs. Freddie and Mary's quarters are located on the second floor. Their curfew expired half an hour ago and unable, or unwilling, to sleep they're currently watching a DVD from the comfort of their beds.

'It's very noisy,' Mary grumbles.' *What do you expect girl? Everyone's pissed!*

'Are you *drunk*?' Freddie asks.

If only.

My parental duties take longer than planned. The fear of Alex's discovery in the master bedroom, possibly by Beth, both prompts and discourages my return to the first floor. It is a full fifteen minutes later, having promised to check on my children again before they go to sleep, that I leave Freddie and Mary and descend to the first floor landing.

Louisa - how the fuck did *she* get up the stairs? - has her ear pressed against the spare bedroom door. She puts a finger to her lips when I tap her shoulder.

'Shh,' she says, 'I think someone's fucking on your spare bed.'

I'm a little taken aback by my sister's choice of words. I'm about to admonish her when I place my own ear to the door. There is a quality of frenzied aggression to the sounds coming from within. *Fucking* if ever I heard it. 'I should have gone after her,' I say, removing my ear from the door.

'Who?'

'Jen. And now she's in there making the biggest mistake of her life.'

'Who is?' Another voice. This time behind me.

'Jen,' I reply dispiritedly, turning to face the new arrival. 'Jen!' I say again *recognising* the new arrival. 'JEN!' *Altogether now.* What is *she* doing here?!

'I think I may have broken the flush on your loo.' she says holding up a short length of metal that was indeed once attached to our toilet. I'm about to reassure her, tell Jen it doesn't matter when Tom appears at the top of the stairs.

'Where the fuck is Fran?' he says, 'She sends me for a drink twenty minutes ago then bloody disappears!' He nods his head in the direction of the spare bedroom door and says, 'She's not in there is she?'

I shrug. *How the fuck should I know? I just live here.*

'Well, if you don't mind,' Jen says matter of factly, 'I have a date with my husband.'

'No!' I shout, suddenly concerned as to the identity of the spare room's occupants. Just who has Luke got in there? Last time I saw Fran she was all over Nigel but Luke loves a challenge. He's triumphed in tighter situations than this. *What, the bastard's my hero now? Someone to be revered?* Jen certainly wouldn't see it that way. Need to keep *her* out of the spare room. Things are a getting a little crowded on the landing though. Too many bodies. Need to divert some of them. 'Try in there Tom,' I say pointing towards the master bedroom. There seems little harm in Tom meeting Alex. *Hiding suspected gay lovers* is sliding rapidly down my list of priorities.

Tom's departure coincides with renewed sounds of pleasure from within the spare bedroom. Judging by the look on her face, Jen hears them too. She tries to get past me and waves the defunct flush handle about as though she means to do serious bodily harm with it. 'I want to see Luke,' she says.

Then I hear Tom shouting in the master bedroom. 'Fran! You bitch!' The sound of scuffling follows this outburst. Then Fran's voice: 'Leave him alone, Tom.'

The unexpected fisticuffs in the master bedroom

would be of more interest if I weren't currently trying to prevent Jen discovering the identity of her estranged husband's new lover. Trouble is, I'm quite interested too. Tom and Nigel can continue to beat the shit out of each other for all I care; I want to find out who Luke's boinking on my spare bed. It's just I'd rather his wife wasn't with me when I do.

As if the landing wasn't crowded enough, Sue Warden appears at the top of the stairs. 'Loo?' she asks.

Louisa turns around, drunk enough to think Sue is using her truncated moniker. I ignore this minor sub-plot. My job-share partner is the star of the show right now. Make that *villain*. If Luke isn't rogering Jen then he must be with someone else… Whoa! A thought occurs to me. I dismiss it. Then retrieve it from my mind's recycle bin. If Tom is at present beating the shit out of Nigel watched by the fair Fran then where the fuck is Alex? Jesus Christ Luke! No. The amateur psychologist in me is up and running barging the suddenly wan looking cheerleader inside my head brusquely aside. Luke Johnstone: philandering rugby hunk for years masking a dislike of women by means of sexual conquest? It has a certain ring to it. Repressed emotions due to a rigorously policed traditional upbringing in the north of England, reinforced by impressive physical attributes and a natural sporting prowess? Jesus Christ! It makes sense. More than that. It suddenly seems so obvious.

It is while I am distracted by thoughts of a psychoanalytical nature that Jen makes her move. Before I can stop her she makes a grab for the bedroom door handle. She smiles in triumph as though she hadn't been at all sure her hand would reach its destination. The door begins to swing open. This seems to take Jen by surprise. Following the door's trajectory she pitches forward, her desperately flailing free hand gaining enough purchase on the nearby light switch to illuminate the room as she ploughs head first into the carpet. Someone screams. I'm pretty sure it's me. On the bed, frozen in the glare of the newly installed 100 watt light bulb, are two figures. Two *naked* figures. Two naked *male* figures. They seem to be attached to one another. Jen staggers to her feet. I didn't know she still had it in her. She points at Alex and his companion but seems unable to form words. I can empathise.

She runs from the room pushing past Louisa and Sue Warden whose expressions suggest they have until this moment never before witnessed the act of homosexual lovemaking. I take a step forward, nod at the spot-lit couple and, turning off the light, pull the door closed.

'Toilet's that way,' I tell Sue Warden. 'You might need this.' And so saying I hand her the broken flush handle. Sue heads off hurriedly. The route to the toilet is suddenly barred though as Tom exits the master bedroom at speed. *Backwards*. He crashes into the wall opposite the bedroom door and crumples in a heap. Another man appears in the doorway. He's also naked. 'Who the fuck was he?' Luke says, hands on hips, making no attempt at hiding his modesty. I have never been so pleased to see a naked man before in my life. *Luke is straight!* Jesus, was that out loud? Sue and Jen do not seem to share my enthusiasm at Luke's belated entrance. Particularly when a semi-clad Fran appears beside him. By the time Sue has bolted the toilet door behind her Jen has delivered the mother of all haymakers to Luke's suddenly downcast features. She has already started her descent of the stairs before Luke can find the correct verbal response. 'Shit,' he says.

Downstairs the music has stopped. All eyes seem to be on Louisa and myself as we descend in silence. Then I hear Beth's voice, 'one, two, three…'

Everyone starts singing. 'Happy birthday to you, happy birthday…..'. I'm a little concerned that my hair may have just turned white. I can feel Louisa clinging to me, struggling to stay upright, as we complete our descent of the stairs. The final notes of the song seem to last an eternity. I hand Louisa over to Mute who takes her hand gently and props her in a corner. On the dining table there is a cake with candles to be blown out and then it seems speeches to be made. *Not you Louisa.* I thank everyone for coming. I'm about to urge my guests to get back to business when Jim-Bob stands up. There is, it seems, someone still sober in the house. An adroitly delivered witticism confirms my suspicions. He stays on his feet. The man clearly has something to say.

'When my wife Rose died two years ago,' he says, 'I didn't think I wanted to go on living myself…..'

When everyone is gone I brew coffee and join Beth under the stars outside. Beer bottles and wine glasses clutter the table at which she sits. ‘One very strong espresso,’ I say. It’s been a long evening, full of incident, low on explanation. Alex for one. That he’d gone to the wrong room when I sent him upstairs I can understand. I wasn’t thinking too clearly either; he was confused. Mistakes happen. How he came to be at the party in the first place is less obvious.

‘That’s easy,’ Beth says, when I’ve finished thinking out loud. ‘I invited him.’

I’m unfazed. *Of course you did.* The evening has primed me to expect the unexpected. ‘I didn’t think you liked him.’

‘I didn’t until a few days ago when he came to see me.’

‘*He* came to see *you*?’

‘You were out, had just gone out in fact. The doorbell rang and there he was, this very good looking man asking to come inside. He told me he wanted to apologise. He said he wanted to make things right between me and you, that he’d made mistakes and that he was entirely to blame.’

‘So you knew I hadn’t…’ my voice trails off. I can still see Alex’s spot-lit dance on the spare bed.

‘Yes.’

A thought occurs to me. ‘But you weren’t talking to me. I’ve had a shitty few weeks.’

‘Me too! Anyway, I wanted you to suffer for a little bit longer. It was hard, especially this morning but I was determined to make you sweat until the party.’

The party. I admit to Beth that I’m still a tad confused as to how Nigel ended up in the spare bedroom with Alex. Beth gives me a look that suggests she knows more than she has thus far let on.

‘You know Nigel has been going through a messy divorce don’t you?’ she says.

‘Yeeess?’ *What the hell has that got to do with anything?*

‘Well let’s just say when I invited Alex to your party

I had an ulterior motive.'

This late in the evening Beth is going to have to make allowances for a certain obtuseness on her husband's part. 'What?'

'I was playing matchmaker.' *Nigel's marriage is definitely over.*

Between us we piece together the likely chain of events: Upstairs, a confused Alex encounters Luke and tells him he has been told to wait in the spare bedroom. Luke vacates, checks the master bedroom is free and waits for Jen on the landing before taking a precautionary leak in the bathroom where, in his haste, he severely weakens the toilet's flush. While I'm upstairs with Freddie and Mary the drunken whore once known as Fran drags Nigel upstairs to the spare bedroom where it becomes apparent Nigel is more interested in the indigenous male population than the disrobing trollop with whom he has arrived. Fran, somewhat disappointed, flounces half-naked from the room straight into the strong masculine arms of Luke who, if he doesn't have sex soon, *with someone*, will shrivel up and expire. By the time I'm done with Freddie and Mary and Jen has inadvertently completed Luke's act of vandalism in the toilet, both couples are going at it hammer and tongs. Enter Tom. Post love-making and trapped beneath the sheets, Luke is a little slow to assert his physical superiority over the furious Tom but eventually persuades his tormentor to leave the room and go quietly to sleep on the landing. Sue Warden holes up in the toilet, Jen runs from the building in tears and I descend the stairs with Louisa. Cue Jim-Bob. His speech. Has it really been two years since Mum died?

Inside the house again all that remains of our guests are their calling cards: Fran's coat, Keith Aston's discarded stripy tie soaking up the last of the punch, a sleeping serpent curled in its desiccated pit. And *Louisa's* handbag.

Louisa. Mum's death had hit her especially hard. Ever since, she'd alternated between bouts of heavy wine consumption and chaotic comfort eating, her weight and social skills varying unpredictably. Tonight my father's speech had made me suspect he'd turned a corner. Perhaps my sister would tag along.

I carry Tom's holdall upstairs and put it in the spare bedroom. Its owner is still at A&E undergoing emergency dental repairs as a recent text message from Nigel (who went with him in the taxi) confirmed. Having finished in the bathroom I leave Beth to brush her teeth and head for bed. I turn on the bedroom light.

'Terrific,' I exclaim. My ire does not prevent me pulling the duvet over the sleeping bodies of Keith Aston and Katherine Jones before heading back to the bathroom where I tell my wife that I'm toying with the idea of washing our bed sheets *first* thing in the morning.

I spend most of Monday morning completing my home's transformation back from all-night knocking shop to domestic dwelling. Most of the party paraphernalia has been either tossed, stored or collected over the course of the weekend. Louisa dropped by for her handbag Saturday morning. Keith Aston had stayed for a hearty brunch before heading home to his wife, his highly flammable tie trailing from his chinos' pocket. Katherine Jones had left before any of us had woken, the sole witness to her shamefaced departure being Freddie who claimed to have spied *a weeping lady* vacating the premises around seven a.m. Tom spent most of the weekend in the hospital, where he endured a sleepless Saturday night, waited five hours for the correct painkillers to be prescribed Sunday morning and made it back to Durnford Street to pick up his holdall with less than thirty minutes to spare before his train back to London. Don't know when we'll see him again.

By the time I sit down at the computer it's nearly midday. Checking my e-mails I'm surprised to find a message from Peter Swinton sent at 5.15 pm Friday afternoon.

Hugh,
Seems there's been a misunderstanding. Did you know you attached *two* versions of your Sandbanks article when you e-mailed me last week? Well, neither did I until this afternoon! I will be publishing the *second* version in the August issue. Love the photos by the way.
Best wishes,
Peter.

So It Goes

Interview day at Pebble Bay is unseasonably warm. In fine weather the school scrubs up surprisingly well as though the elements were conspiring to present the old place in its best possible light. The car park has succumbed to interviewee gridlock so I park the Travolta on the road and pause to take in Chesil Beach to my right and the tall, limestone cliffs to my left. I'm nervous. Rolling in at ten o'clock hasn't helped. A supply teacher is looking after Year Five for the morning and with my interview not scheduled until 10.30 there had seemed little point in arriving too early.

In the office Brenda tells me she hasn't seen Luke. 'I expect he'll get here,' she says.

'That'd be nice,' I reply.

'Happy birthday by the way!'

I thank Brenda for the thought and try to remember the last time I associated the words *happy* and *birthday* with one another.

Brenda brings me up to speed on the schedule for the day. Interviews began at 9.30. Dave Horn, first in, is currently being put through his paces by Sue Warden, Ted Harvey, the Chair of Governors, and a suit from the Local Authority whose name I don't recognise. Meanwhile lesson observations are being conducted in the hall where fifteen handpicked Year Five pupils are currently being taught Numeracy by a Mrs Oldman. Keith Aston and Katherine Jones presiding. I sometimes wonder if Sue Warden knows her staff at all. If Katherine has uttered a friendly word to Keith since my 40th I've not heard it. Regret can be a powerful emotion. I admit to Brenda that I'm convinced the job is Dave Horn's. She looks surprised.

'He's a crooked accountant,' she says.

Say what?

'He's just making up the numbers, Hugh.'

'What do you mean?' I approach Brenda's desk, the whiff of intrigue in my nostrils. 'Are you sure?'

Brenda nods.

'Does *he* know that?'

Brenda shakes her head.

'But I thought he and Sue had… a *thing* going.'

'They did, once. But from what I've gathered,' Brenda looks over my shoulder as though all of a sudden confidentiality mattered. 'From what I've gathered Sue came off worse.'

I feel a brief surge of adrenalin. 'And she wants revenge?' *Thank God for petty mean-spirited emotions.* 'How long ago did this happen?'

'It was when she was deputy at Melcombe Junior. Must be seven, eight years ago.' The sexual etiquette of a praying mantis and the mental recall of an elephant: Pebble Bay Primary's head teacher is a formidable woman indeed. I can hardly wait to tell Luke whose own kiss-and-tell revelations will have further dented our chief rival's prospects.

My job-share partner does not arrive until nearly twenty-five past ten however. 'Bloody inconvenient holding these interviews on one of my days off,' he says. There's being laid back and then there's this. Since ditching the metaphorical *The End of My Job is Nigh* sandwich boards in order to peddle his own brand of sexual tittle-tattle my job-share partner has become a little too confident for my liking. Recounting Brenda's news won't exactly get his feet back on *terra firma*. Anyway there isn't time. I usher Luke towards the seats outside Sue's office.

'Hold on, Hugh. Text message.' Luke removes his mobile phone from a jacket pocket. 'It's Fran,' he says, 'wishing us luck. Wants you and Beth to come round for a celebratory meal this weekend.'

'If you're going to count chickens leave me out of it,' I tell him.

'Whatever happens.' *Wharever 'appens.* 'it's our anniversary this weekend. A year since…'

I hold my hands up cutting him short. 'I'm unlikely to forget your anniversary Luke.'

Luke smiles. In the year since beating the shit out of my best man and bedding the woman who almost ended my marriage, he has become remarkably at ease with his altered circumstances. Trading unencumbered liberty for the more onerous responsibilities involved in associating oneself with a single parent and her needy offspring is no mean feat. True,

Luke hadn't gone so far as to move in with Fran - and his desire to maintain less demanding working hours didn't exactly suggest he intended making an honest woman of her just yet - but one year on he was still on the scene. And not just to satisfy his own physical nocturnal needs. Luke was just as likely to be spotted at Fran's during *daylight* hours easing the strain of the parental routine or carrying out routine household maintenance jobs neglected since Fran's *ex* had left town without warning and without leaving a forwarding address.

Luke's current cosy domestic arrangements are a little misleading though. A year ago there were some badly frayed loose ends still in need of tidying up. Jen, when she'd sobered up, had filed for divorce even before she'd finished slinging her husband's clothes and possessions into the street. Everything had gone out the same first storey window even if it had, as in the case of Luke's CD collection, originated in the living room one floor below. Luke gone, Jen had continued to do supply work at Pebble Bay on the understanding that, initially at least, she would undertake only work that fell on Luke's days off. She did not like to talk about what had happened. This arrangement suited Luke who, through shame no doubt, studiously ensured their paths did not cross. Sensing this, probably as a result of some *well-intentioned* comments of my own, Jen had begun to accept work on her former husband's half of the week and as time passed she clearly drew much satisfaction from Luke's obvious discomfort.

The interview goes well. The questions aren't going to win any awards for originality. I deal with inquiries regarding classroom practice fairly convincingly I hope while Luke describes a recent lesson in such detail that I very nearly believe he isn't making the whole thing up. Sue dwells on the difficulties inherent in a job-share, problems relating to continuity and lapses in communication for some time but her manner suggests she does not view them as insurmountable. If anything she gives the impression she has been pleasantly surprised by how smoothly the job-share has worked. Luke's personal life is not mentioned. Why should it be? The stiff from the LA would obviously rather be somewhere else. When at last we are ejected there are smiles all round.

By the end of the lunch break two of the candidates have been sent home, weeded out by the interview panel, assisted by some apparently conflicting feedback from Keith Aston and Katherine Jones. 'That man wouldn't know a good teacher if they grabbed him by the arse,' I hear Katherine confiding to Jen. She ought to know.

Dave Horn spends the midday break on a charm offensive engaging with as many members of staff as possible to whom he addresses pertinent questions, even making some suggestions as to how procedures at the school could be improved. Luke lasts barely five minutes in the same room as the man before motioning for me to join him outside. 'What a wanker,' he says when we are out of earshot, 'I can't believe he made the afternoon cut.'

Now seems as good a time as any to relate Brenda's good tidings.

'I shouldn't worry about him,' I say.

'No?' Luke says, recognising the glint in my eyes. 'What do you know?'

I spill the beans but by the time I'm finished Luke is not looking nearly as happy as I'd expected. In fact he looks unwell. I ask him what's wrong. Tell him he looks pale.

'In here,' he says, motioning to the Science cupboard outside which we have come to rest. Inside, Luke perches rather nervously on the edge of the desk. 'Listen,' he says, 'there's something I should probably tell you.'

I'm all ears.

'A year or two ago me and Sue had a bit of a thing going.'

I consider Luke's confession. 'You and Sue?' I say, 'a couple of years ago?'

Luke nods.

Not good.

Bad.

'You stupid…'

Luke, suddenly defensive, interrupts me 'How do you think we got the bloody job-share?' He says this as though every part-timer in the education system has slept their way to reduced hours.

'Tell me *she* ended the relationship and not you,' I

say. *Hell hath no fury...*

There's a pause. I expect the worst.

'She did mate.'

Thank God. Luke had been the innocent party. Then a thought occurs to me. 'Did Jen ever find out?'

'Not so far as I know,' he says, 'but then she may have been distracted.'

'By what?'

Luke seems reluctant to continue the conversation.

'By what?' I repeat.

'Sue ended things between us the day after your 40th.'

Fuck.

'Fuck,' I say.

Luke nods. 'Yeah.'

That afternoon I'm back in the class room teaching. The interview panel spend an hour observing Dave Horn and a Miss Gould teach Literacy to one half of my class, after which the remaining candidates are given license to roam the school at their leisure. In the meantime the interview panel will consider their decision.

Dave Horn spends half an hour watching my history lesson on Victorian inventions which I manage to steer artfully around to the subject of Julius Caesar. 'His most famous words of course were *et tu Brute?'* I tell the class. 'Isn't that right Mr Horn?'

The man doesn't miss a beat. 'I thought they were veni, vidi, vici Mr Bradley.'

The man has a fucking answer to everything.

At 3.30 pm precisely I join Luke and Dave Horn in the staff room, Miss Gould having failed in her bid to make the final cut. Several other members of staff are also in attendance either curious as to the panel's decision or recuperating after another tough day at the chalk face. Jen is amongst them. She has spent the afternoon in Year One. She asks me if I want a coffee.

'Thanks,' I say.

'What about a chocolate biscuit?'

'I love interview days,' I say.

Time passes slowly during which I inhabit a netherworld, fate's plaything. Whatever joy I'd derived from the apparent hopelessness of Dave Horn's situation, Luke had dashed at lunch time. At this moment in time we are equals. Which former lover does Sue resent the most? The one who dumped her or the one who betrayed her? Take your pick. Anything could happen. It's him or us. Had Sue been honest with Brenda about Horn? Even if she had what if she'd subsequently fallen for the bastard again? The man is not, apparently, without his charms. In this netherworld I see Horn clambering over the roof slates to the school bell tower, raising his arms aloft and sounding his victory peal. 'I came, I saw, I conquered!' His words ricochet off the pebbles below echoing clear across Lyme Bay.

The staff room door opens. Sue comes in with Ted Harvey. She lets the door close behind them. She looks around the room. The bitch is enjoying this, I think. Her eyes alight on Dave Horn then pass swiftly on. They come to rest on Luke, then myself. Then pass swiftly on. I expect them to return to Horn but they don't. I follow their trajectory around the room until finally their gaze alights on the woman beside the sink still clutching a packet of chocolate biscuits. She's looking at Jen. 'Mrs Johnstone,' Sue says, beaming, 'congratulations. Welcome back to Pebble Bay Primary School!'

Doctor Ridge comes to Zennor Road to see my mother. A Doctor Charleston is with him. There has been talk of inserting a tube into Mum's stomach via which nutrients might be fed. Following an examination and a short discussion Doctor Charleston advises against the procedure which he says will more than likely cause *'Complications'*.

Mum says, 'In that case I won't have it done then.' Although she is compos mentis while Doctors Ridge and Charleston are with her, both prior to and after their visit she drifts in and out of consciousness. At times she seems very muddled. When I'd first heard that morphine had been prescribed I hadn't known what to think. Before he'd left, Doctor Ridge had told Jim-Bob that his wife's failing strength was not solely due to her loss of appetite but also partly a result of the cancer's spread to the liver. He'd told my father about signs to watch for.

When I call round again early in the evening Jim-Bob is very emotional. Upstairs I find Mum, minus her purple woolly hat and wig, muttering in her sleep. More new drugs have been prescribed. They will, the nurse has told my father, keep her calm but drowsy.

Next morning Jim-Bob has an appointment at the hospital himself. I will stay with my mother while he is out. When I arrive she is asleep. 'She becomes agitated if she's woken up,' my father tells me. Downstairs I position myself next to the nursery monitor Jim-Bob has bought in order to respond quickly to any calls for help. I can hear my mother muttering in her sleep. Later I hear a whispered, 'James…James'. I go upstairs and see my mother's right leg dangling over the side of the bed. She opens her eyes when she hears my voice, asks me to lift her leg back under the duvet. This done she asks if I've got Beth an anniversary present yet. It's April. We were married in December. I tell her I've bought a present and she smiles and closes her eyes. Later she calls out and wants to know why Jim-Bob has left her alone. Isn't the doctor due any time? She becomes anxious until I tell her that the doctor is not coming today though the nurse might be. Outside it is raining heavily. In a lucid moment Mum says, 'Your dad will get soaked. Go and pick him up.' I tell her I don't have the car with me. My mother frets about her husband in the rain until she drifts off again. Some time later I go downstairs and wait beside the monitor until Jim-Bob returns.

That night we all go round to Zennor Road. Jim-Bob tells us that Dr Ridge is calling round later. We can hear Mum's coughing on the nursery monitor and my father hurries upstairs. We hear him say, 'Oh my God.' We turn off the monitor. When Dr Ridge calls round he goes straight upstairs with Jim-Bob. When he comes down he advises us all to prepare ourselves.

At home later I phone Sue Warden, tell her I may need some time off. She is very nice. We go to bed early and I know. I know.

The phone rings at ten past twelve. It's Dad.

'Hugh?' he says, 'I think Mum's just died.'

There is a photo of my mother, aged about four, standing beside her own mum, herself only three years from the grave. Her hair cut into a bob, my mother holds her mum's hand tightly staring straight at the camera. This is what I think about as I get dressed. One moment in time. A shadow painted on paper.

I'm round at Zennor Road by twenty past midnight. The date on my watch has just changed. I realise it is now my birthday. Thirty-eight today. My father is on the phone to Louisa. I go up to see Mum. Her bare head is turned to one side, tilted back slightly, her mouth open, reminiscent somehow of a baby bird. Death and new life strangely congruous. *An unbroken circle*. I move closer to the bed and rest my hand on my mother's head. Stillness. Just the sound of my father's voice far below and the ticking of the bedside clock. I think about the photo and let the memories come. I begin to cry.

Just about everyone else has gone home. Luke had been the first to go, roughly five seconds after hearing that his ex-wife had been appointed Year Five teacher in his stead from September. Dave Horn had not tarried long either. He'd gathered his things together and left with barely a word. Immobile, I'd sat quietly, recalling the day I'd stopped Jen reading out the remaining names on the shortlist. Alone with Sue later she'd admitted, strictly off the record, that not since the moment she'd seen Luke emerge naked from my bedroom a year before had she seriously considered extending the job-share. Sympathy, remorse, bitterness, a host of other emotions had influenced her decision. *'An innocent caught in the cross fire,'* I would be offered the bulk of the school's future supply work. If I so wished. At least until I'd sorted myself out with more permanent employment.

I am in no hurry to vacate the school premises. *'Honey I'm home. I lost my job!'* From my classroom I wander aimlessly towards the school hall. Don's ladders are splayed beneath the opened skylight. I climb the unstable rungs and clamber onto the bitumen. There's no sign of the caretaker. Birdlife too is conspicuous by its absence. I walk across the roof, find myself a vantage point and look down at the beach below. A trail of flotsam and jetsam commemorates the morning's unusually high tide. Borne from embarkation points as mysterious as the invisible currents that have transported it to this place at this time, the collection of lost and abandoned detritus is pecked at by maturing herring gulls their plumage a dreary grey in the late afternoon sunlight. As helpless now as it was against the irresistible urgings of the vast liquid mass it has traversed, it is the passive nature of its journey that imbues each object's voyage with meaning - a higher purpose denied the ocean's animate inhabitants by their own desperate and clumsy attempts at self-propulsion. Oceanographers, I know, can plot an object's course across the planet's vast open waters with impressive accuracy. Add free will and a pair of flippers and predictions are likely to go awry. The senses, prone to distractions, have a penchant for misinformation: fears, illusory dangers and half-truths that can lead to deviation from the *plotted course*, the path of least resistance; panic-driven detours via more circuitous routes. Frantic paddling that leaves the traveller too disorientated to head with any confidence in the right direction. The five senses have their uses but we ignore our instincts at our peril.

I don't think I will take Sue Warden up on her offer of supply work. I've done several days' cover at a school much closer to home already and there is the promise of much more if necessary. Permanent part-time positions are hard to come by and teaching in a full-time capacity would, I believe, constitute paddling of a most frantic type. Besides, *Dorset Scene* recently published *Lights, Camera, Action*, a 1200 word piece on Dorset's many movie locations - my fifteenth article for the magazine - and there is talk of a regular column entitled *Five Go Forth in Dorset* in which I hope to chronicle the Bradley family's numerous excursions about the county. And then of course there is fiction. *Love is Not a One Way Street* recently underwent a fourth re-write following its most recent rejection. I've started tentative work on a semi-autobiographical novel. Write about what you know the sages say. Now there's a thing.

Up here on the roof I can see for miles. To my front, the white tipped waves, the grand sweep of pebbles, the hullabaloo of the gulls. Behind me, lichen covered rooftops and the steeply rising hills concealing the *Verne* prison. Above, the *don't you believe it* blue of a clear sky. Write about what you know. *Write about what you know.* I close my eyes, blot out the pretty painted pictures and take a deep breath.

THE END

Made in the USA
Charleston, SC
18 June 2012